Red H

Roger A. Price

To
Surjit
With thanks

[signature] Oct 23

NOTE FROM THE AUTHOR

The main premise of this story was first created in 2018 as an idea for a TV drama.

When I created the DS Draker series of novels concept in 2021, I decided to take this premise and adapt it to give Martin Draker, Cath Moore and Colin Carstairs of the North West Regional and Organised Crime Unit something to keep them busy.

Whilst writing this novelisation, Russia has invaded the sovereign state of Ukraine and the horrors taking place there unfortunately continue as I write this note.

Please bear in mind that real events which have yet to take place may impact my tale.

This remains a work of fiction and any resemblance to living persons is coincidental.

In loving memory of my mum.

RED HERRING

Chapter One

North of England, 2022.

The man knew that his bulk could make him look obvious, and wearing a loose fitting jacket didn't help much. He was also wearing a Manchester United baseball cap pulled down low, which he was itching to discard as soon as operationally possible. He recalled with much pleasure how the Ultras had kicked the crap out of United fans when they beat one of the Moscow football teams years ago. He couldn't remember which one it was; could have been Spartak, or CSKA Moscow; it didn't really matter. But he just wished that Old Trafford had been the target, not that it really mattered where the locale was. His superiors had told him that security would be far more lax in Preston, and they were right about that.

Preston was a small city thirty miles north of Manchester, he'd not been there before and he wouldn't be coming back in a hurry. He walked down a hill away from the city centre, and noticed that the headquarters of the English Football League was here as he passed the building. That would have been a good target, though it would have proved tricky to get inside by the look of it. But unfortunately, his hatred of British football clubs was not part of the operation. He pressed on down the hill and would do so until he reached a major junction which preceded a major river; the River Ribble, according to the map he had earlier studied. He would then turn right and head north which would lead him to the Dockland area a couple of miles away.

At the western end of the docks was a marina where a waiting pleasure cruiser would take him safely out of the city area towards the Irish Sea. He would be dropped off before then at a seaside resort named St. Annes on Sea, from where he would be driven back to West Lancashire; back to his job on the farm. He looked at his watch; 8.15 a.m.; in two hours he should be there.

As he neared the bottom of the hill he saw a skip close to the road junction, and was glad to be able to throw his cap into it. He was well away from any city centre CCTV now, and it was good

1

practice to keep changing one's profile when one could. He walked past a motor garage and crossed over the road again as he headed towards the docks. An earlier study of the map had identified a road which went around the back of the area, and was less in the public eye than the main route which followed west around the dock basin. The back road eventually passed over a swing bridge close to the marina. Ideal.

As soon as he was on the back lane he slowed and started to relax. Then he noticed a British Gas van pass him and park up a hundred metres ahead. He'd seen the same van parked near the English Football League HQ, he was sure. He switched back onto full alert, even though it probably meant nothing. He was just about to glance behind, when a dark blue saloon car pulled past and stopped by the kerb about fifteen metres ahead. Its engine running, with what looked like four men inside. He was about to cross over the road to get a side-on view of the motor, when he heard car engines behind him. Not revving or anything, but just there. He turned to look and saw a second dark coloured saloon pull alongside him, while a further one pulled in behind him.

There was grass banking to his left, but as he considered his options it all went noisy.

The four men in the forward vehicle burst out and ran at him with automatic weapons raised. Three from the car next to him joined the party in similar vein, and he guessed that others from behind him were also in-bound.

He was quickly put under an armed challenge from two flanks. All of the idiots were shouting at him, almost incoherently as they talked over each other. But what was clear, was that all of the men were wearing overalls and they were also wearing baseball caps. Except theirs didn't say 'United 'till I Die', but did say 'Police'.

He wasn't armed and would have been massively outgunned had he been, so he had no option but to be compliant; for now. He was told to put his hands - with fingers interlocked - onto his head and to slowly get onto his knees and then to lie flat, face down, which he did. He was quickly searched, though he knew his pockets were empty of anything, and then his hands were plasti-cuffed behind his back before he was allowed to get back to his feet. All pretty standard stuff.

Then a livered police van pulled up and he was bundled into the back as one of the men read him his rights and said that he was being detained on suspicion of committing terrorism offences. In a couple of hours he will have committed a further one; a much bigger one. He smiled at them.

Within ten minutes he was marched into a custody suite at Preston Central police station. He refused to answer any questions and was duly stripped and given a paper suit to put on. He was then taken to a small room where the clowns attempted to take his fingerprints with a scan-type device. They shouldn't have taken his plastic cuffs off. He head-butted the first cop, kicked the second in the bollocks, and manged to deck four more - with injuries - before the seventh floored him with a Taser.

He was then dragged to a room and plonked onto a metal chair as his motor functions started to return. A man in a white coat examined him and told the army of cops now stood around him, that he was fit to be detained and interviewed. He knew he had to play the long game now, so put both his hands in the air to suggest that there would be no more trouble. He then slumped in his chair to further show that he was compliant.

They backed off and the tension in the air lifted.

He made himself as comfortable as he could on his chair and avoided eye contact with the cops. He then cracked his neck to ease the muscles, and picked out a stained tile on the hard floor's surface, and commenced to stare at it.

'What's he doing?' he heard one cop ask. He didn't look up.

'God knows,' said another.

'Hey, what are you staring at?' said the first voice.

He didn't answer and didn't look up; no amount of provocation would work on him now. All he was interested in was the mark on the floor tile.

After a couple of minutes, the second one muttered some abuse at him before they all trooped out of the room. He heard a key turn in the lock once the door was closed. He still didn't look up;

he'd seen all he needed to when he'd been dragged in. The room was about seven metres square, very bright with white painted walls, and had a steel desk screwed to the floor in the centre. He was sat at one side of it facing the door. At the other side was a further steel chair. To his right was a mirror on the wall which had an unnaturally dark reflective surface to it; obviously a two-way one.

A clock on the opposite wall showed the time as 9.10 a.m. He smiled, not long to wait.

Chapter Two

DS Martin Draker and Field Intelligence Analyst Cath Moore arrived at Preston nick together. They often did as they were now an item, which could be tricky when you worked together, but so far they had managed it both in and out of work. They both had flats in Manchester, but Martin knew that Cath was looking to move nearer her work. They both worked for the North West's Regional Organised Crime Unit, and were stationed at a satellite office in Preston. Martin had stayed at Cath's last night, which was why they had shared a car. As soon as they pulled up in the station's vast rear yard, Martin could tell something serious was happening. Loads of police were running to their vehicles and then screeching out of the yard like their backsides were on fire.

'Looks serious,' Cath commented, as they got out of their vehicle.

'And some,' Martin replied. He could tell when something was uber serious as opposed to just serious; there was an added level to the speed with which cops reacted. This was definitely uber. As they approached the rear access to the building, its door flung open and several more officers came piling out at speed; some still struggling to pull their coats and equipment belts on whilst doing so. Uber, uber.

As they were nothing to do with Lancashire Constabulary - and therefore not involved in day-to-day policing activities in Preston - Martin knew that irrespective of how serious things looked, it would have no bearing on them. He couldn't have been more wrong.

Colin Carstairs, their DCI was already in their shared office and looked flustered. The red patch on his receding hairline had reached an unprecedented shade of puce. Matched only by the colour of his chin which had clearly been the recipient of some serious rubbing.

'Thank God you are here, was about to call you,' Colin started with.

'What's going on?' Martin asked.

'A serious terrorist incident. And the Lancashire Chief, Don Rogers has asked us to take the lead.'

'Where's the North West Counter Terrorism Unit?' Martin asked.

'The whole hub is in London on a joint operation.'

'So why us?' Martin pushed.

'If you recall, I did a two year stint with them on secondment before I joined NWROCU,' Colin said.

Martin had forgotten that. 'So we are it?'

'Pretty much. Some of them are racing back as we speak, but they won't make it in time. And I still have my access codes, so at least Box will speak to me,' Colin added.

Martin knew that Box - or The Security Service - were very particular who they would speak to or deal with inside the police. The fact that Colin still had access was major. 'So what have we got?'

'A coded call with voice distortion to a direct number inside MI5, saying that a bomb has been planted somewhere in Preston.'

'Sweet Jesus,' Cath spat. 'Any idea where?'

'No, but I'm trying to coordinate searches of likely targets such as transport hubs, public buildings, places of national note et cetera, et cetera.'

'What can we do to help?' Cath asked.

Colin turned to face her and said, 'I'll use my access codes to set you up with an intel officer at Box and you can coordinate and develop any intelligence we or they have.'

Cath nodded and quickly jumped onto her chair and brought her computer terminal to life. Colin turned to face Martin, 'You can interview the prisoner.'

'Prisoner. We have a prisoner?' Martin said, shocked.

'I don't know where the info came from, yet, but we received a description of a potential suspect in the area. Armed Response Vehicles deployed to the Docks and arrested a man who is now in the cells. But he's not saying a word.'

'Who is he?' Martin asked.

'The "who" doesn't matter right now, but the information suggests that he is *the*, or one of, *the* bombers.'

'So he knows where it is.'

'And you have the unenviable task of trying to get him to tell you where.'

'No pressure there, then.'

'You're good in interviews; you have that way about you, a natural communicator. If anyone can open him up, you can.'

'I bet you say that to all the Martins.'

'MARTIN,' Cath shouted.

'We haven't time for levity,' Colin added.

'Sorry, just my way of coping. Okay, how long have we got?'

Colin looked at his watch, and Martin instinctively did the same, it wasn't long after nine.

'If the bastard who called it in was telling the truth, then we have little over an hour.'

'Shit,' Martin said.

'Then it goes boom. Come on, follow me,' Colin said, and then rushed out of the office. Martin followed closely as Colin led him the short distance down the corridor from their ground floor office to the interview rooms; each one had an anteroom attached. Martin followed Colin into the annex to the first interview room. Inside was a small desk and a two-way mirror looking into the main room. Both men came to a halt, and stood shoulder to shoulder as they looked through the mirror.

Martin could see the prisoner in a white paper suit sat on the chair facing the door. He was a brute of a man and the paper suit looked to be at least two sizes too small, which just accentuated his stocky physique. The man was staring at the floor. 'How long has he been doing that?'

'For all of the ten minutes or so that he's been in there. He hasn't moved.'

'And we have no idea who he is?'

'He's not spoken a word, and it took seven cops to get his fingerprints.'

Martin turned to face Colin in surprise.

'But only two have gone to hospital,' Colin added.

'Bloody hell,' Martin said, as he turned to face the mirror again. Then said, 'But that means his fingerprints have a story to tell, one he doesn't want us to know.'

Colin nodded, and said, 'True, but don't forget that his identity is secondary; for now.'

'Yes, but it could provide levers.'

'Good point, I'll get Cath on it to drive the searches through as quickly as is possible.'

'In the days before the Police and Criminal Evidence Act, we could have applied some real pressure to him.'

'That is why they brought PACE in.'

'But by the look of him he's not one to be bothered easily.'

Colin nodded.

'Undue pressure would probably only annoy him.'

'You sure you'll be okay in there on your own?' Colin asked.

Martin knew that Colin had too much to do organising the police on the street, areas to be searched, putting Cath to work with MI5, and chasing the fingerprints and a ton of other stuff. But he was actually relieved. It wasn't often one could do an interview on one's own nowadays, and he suspected it would work better for him in these circumstances. He told Colin that he'd be fine. Plus, he'd noticed the size of the two uniforms who were stood guard on the outside of the interview room door.

And as if reading his mind, Colin said, 'At the first sign of trouble, call the boys in blue in.'

'I will,' he answered.

'They are both armed with Tasers and are itching for a chance to use them in payback for what he did to their mates; one of whom has a broken nose.'

Martin nodded and they both left the anteroom. But before they headed in separate directions, Martin said, 'I know time is short, but I'll try my best.'

'I know you will. It's all anyone can do.'

'I just hope my best is good enough.'

Colin answered with a half-smile and then turned and hurried away. Martin took a deep breath and turned the other way.

RED HERRING

Chapter Three

Martin paused by the two burly uniform officers stood guard outside the door to the interview room, and introduced himself. They both nodded and one unlocked the door. Martin could feel his heartrate start to quicken. Still facing them both, he said, 'If I holler, don't hang about gents.'

The cop to the left hand side, who was the bigger of the two, just, answered, 'Don't worry, sarge, we'll be in there quicker than my mate can pick up a dropped pound coin.'

'Good, because I am about to wind him up; and then some.'

The other said, 'Hey, I'm not that tight.'

'Yes you are,' the bigger one said, as he nodded at Martin to acknowledge his last comment.

Martin left them to their banter and opened the door to walk into the room with as much confidence as he could display. The prisoner was in the same position, and still staring at the floor. He showed no reaction to Martin's presence who instinctively glanced to see exactly what the prisoner was looking at. It was just some sort of stain, a scuff mark, perhaps, nothing more. He then slammed shut the door using the underside of his right foot so he could keep facing forward. No reaction, so he took the vacant chair opposite the prisoner, who looked even more of a handful from this distance.

Martin slowed his breathing and tried to relax himself a little, and then after a short pause he introduced himself. The prisoner didn't reply, but he did glance up at Martin before returning his gaze to the floor. That was a start at least, Martin knew. A slight break in the prisoner's routine. He quickly turned on the recording machine screwed to the table top, and then introduced himself and asked for the prisoner to name himself. He didn't reply, so Martin recited the legal caution to him and then sat back in his chair. There was still no response from the brute in the white paper suit. Martin was only too aware of the ticking clock and knew he would have to move quicker than he would

9

otherwise have liked, so he jumped straight in. 'Teach you that in the army, did they?'

No response.

'What's your name?'

No response.

'Your prints will tell us. They clearly convey a story; or is it that you just don't like holding hands?'

Still no response.

'Even if you have no form, we can still check against military records. Because you are military, aren't you?'

Nothing. Martin was only too aware how tiring it was holding a one-sided conversation. But he also knew that it could be equally hard not to say anything in reply. Especially if the questioning became tasty. 'This is a counter terrorism investigation, and we can do many things under that remit,' he added to further silence.

Martin allowed a longer pause before continuing, 'All I need are the target details.'

Silence.

'That way we get to save many lives, and you get to see the outside world again.'

Nothing.

'I don't even need your name, just where the attack will take place.'

The prisoner moved his weight from one buttock to the other, but still didn't answer. At least he was starting to feel uncomfortable on the chair.

'Look; time is short - as you well know - so here's the deal; lives for a life sentence.'

Again, no reply. Martin glanced at the door to reassure himself of its proximity before he carried on. 'As you have no name I'm going to call you Mr Weakling, because that's what you are: weak.'

Bingo. The prisoner looked up at Martin and stared at him. Martin could see his hate-filled expression for the first time. His black eyes matching his dark heart. But he saw something else; rage. Hidden, supressed anger. He could work on that.

10

The prisoner returned his attention to the floor, but pushed his chair against the hard surface as he did so which made the metal legs scrape. Martin involuntarily jumped at the noise, and the prisoner returned his gaze to Martin. Then smiled.

Martin keen to regain his cool quickly added, 'Don't misread me weakling. Just tell me where the device is. It's over.'

The prisoner then jumped to his feet which surprised Martin who fought to keep the look of shock from his face. In the split-second that followed, Martin assessed that the prisoner wasn't moving towards him. He was sorely tempted to call in the Taser squad, but knew that would undo everything. He held his counsel as the prisoner stood still, clearly considering his next step.

Then the prisoner walked over to the mirror and stood with his back to Martin whilst staring a fixed look into the glass.

'Teach you that in the army, too?' Martin asked.

No reply.

'Which regiment? The pansy flower picking one? Pansies picking pansies,' he said. He hated having to use gender or sexual orientation slurs - but he knew that with steroid-induced macho narcissists like this guy - any attack on his masculinity might prove to be his weakness. Mr Weakling must have a flaw somewhere. He glanced over his shoulder at the steel door and prepared himself in case he needed to move sharpish.

The prisoner kept looking through the mirror, but spoke in a heavy accentuated Eastern European accent, 'I could snap you like a pencil.'

'Hurrah! The weakling speaks,' Martin said, as he shifted his legs further away from the table.

The prisoner turned to face Martin but remained stood by the wall, and said, 'And have done so for far less insult.'

'Sorry if you find me irritating, but you are about to kill many innocents.'

The prisoner walked towards the table and then retook his seat, much to Martin's relief, but he scrapped his chair on the floor again as he did so. Martin flinched again, but less than the first time. He was annoyed with himself at being caught off guard. The prisoner smiled at him as he settled in his seat.

'Innocent by whose definition?' the prisoner asked.

Having fully regained his composure, Martin leaned back and said, 'I'm asking the questions; or are you thick as well as weak.'

The prisoner ignored the remark but glanced at the wall clock, Martin followed his gaze; the numerals read 9:30. Martin instinctively looked at his own wristwatch; its digits showed 9.10. He quickly pulled his shirt cuff down to cover it up. He looked up at the prisoner who was back to staring at him, 'So weakie, what's it to be? There has to be a trade we can do?'

'Teach you that in girl detective school?'

Martin nearly smiled at the insult. It meant his earlier slur had worked; this guy was a weapons-grade macho man and hater of all not in his own image. More buttons for Martin to press. He ignored the comment and instead said, 'Look, it's like I said, as this is a counter terrorism investigation, it opens lots of doors. We can do many things, offer many things—'

'Save it,' the prisoner interrupted with, before retuning his attention to his favourite floor scuff mark.

Shit. It felt like they had gone full circle, back to where they started. Martin's phone buzzed an incoming message from Colin - he needed a word, urgently. Maybe a quick break wasn't a bad thing. He turned the recoding machine off and quickly left the room. He let out a long breath as walked to the anteroom.

Chapter Four

Martin was glad of the short reprieve as he entered the anteroom. Colin turned away from the two-way mirror to face him, 'You're doing great.'

'Thanks, but you are being too kind, could be doing a lot better.'

'No, you have made a great start, believe in yourself; I couldn't do what I've watched you do.'

'You been in here the whole time?'

'On and off; nearly messed myself when he came up to the mirror. God only knows what it's like in there?'

'Must admit, I'm glad of a short break.'

'Has he noticed the clock?

'He looked at it once, I'm pretty sure he accepts it. A shame we couldn't put it even more forward.'

Colin grimaced, 'I think twenty minutes was pushing our luck; anymore and he would surely have noticed.'

'If he brags as the appointed time passes, it won't give us long to react.'

'I know; it's just a failsafe punt. Hopefully you'll get under his skin before then.'

Martin looked at his watch; it was now 9:30 for real. 'I better get back in; we have less than an hour. Anything from Cath?'

'That's why I've pulled you out; I've linked her up with Five and they have ID-ed him from facial recognition.'

'Wow, that's brilliant.'

'Igor something or other; ex-Spetsnaz commando. Russian national.'

'How did they ping him so fast?'

'Been on a watch list.'

'What?'

'I know it sounds bad, but they have to be intel led, like us. He came in on a bent Ukrainian passport a month ago. He was considered low key. He's been working on a strawberry farm in

13

West Lancashire. Five ran surveillance on him for a day - just to have a look - but with no intel he wasn't considered high risk.'

Martin thought about what Colin had just said; it must be a nightmare for the security services having to be so selective. And with limited resources it must be a constant battle where to use them to most effect.

'It's good that you have got him talking, but we could do with opening him up a bit more,' Colin said.

Initially, Martin wondered if Colin was having a go, but before he could defend himself, Colin continued.

'This is why I dragged you out. I may have a can opener for you.'

'Go on.'

'When Five ran out on him, they photographed him in a compromising position with another fruit picker.'

'Yeah?'

'And according to Five he has a wife back in Moscow,' Colin said, before handing Martin a manila folder he'd been holding to his chest. 'The photos are in here with his full details.'

'Well, this should be fun.'

'Do you want me to join you in there?'

Martin considered it for a moment but politely declined. He'd be better off carrying on as he'd started. It would change the dynamics bringing someone else and not in a good way. He explained this to Colin who looked relieved.

'Well, if you're sure. And I do have to ring the Home Secretary as soon as I can. Don Rogers has told me that she wants direct updates from silver commander - as in me.'

Martin thought he'd rather face the prisoner again than do Colin's job. He was just about to rush off when it occurred to him that most Russians have affairs, and would the photo threats be enough. He voiced his thoughts.

'He's not an oligarch, so it may still help, but I wasn't thinking of you threatening to send them to just his wife,' Colin said and started grinning.

'What?'

'You need to threaten to send them somewhere else.'

14

'Where?'

'To his wife's uncle.'

'And who would that be?'

'One Nikolia Volkov no less. And before you ask, yes, the President of Russia.'

But before Martin could voice his surprise, Colin's mobile rang and after he answered with a 'Yes Ma'am', he mouthed the words 'Home Secretary' at Martin. He nodded and turned to leave, and as he left the anteroom he heard Colin say, 'Yes, my best interviewer is heading back in there now, and he has the intel update from Five.'

The pressure was on.

Two minutes later he was back in the room. Igor, as Martin now knew was his name didn't look up to acknowledge his re-emergence. Martin quickly sat down and slapped the folder on the desk for dramatic effect. He restarted the recording machine. He then quickly ran through the introductions, giving Igor an opportunity to say his name before reciting the caution again. He failed to respond. He then turned to face Igor squarely and said, 'Any change of heart?'

No reply.

'We know who you are.'

This dragged Igor's attention away from the floor, but only as far as a snarl aimed at Martin. 'Sneer all you like... Igor.'

Igor's expression turned to one of genuine surprise; shock even. Martin knew he had to capitalise quickly before the astonishment wore off. 'And we know that you've been a naughty Igor.'

A long pause followed which felt excruciating given the time pressure weighing down, but Martin held his silence and eventually Igor responded.

'What are you talking about?'

'You and the girl.'

'What girl?'

Martin opened the folder; read the details written on the inside of the cover, and then flicked through several large re-printed photos showing Igor naked and entwined with a woman. He

15

selected one, closed the file and then placed the photo on the desk image upwards. He slowly turned it around to face Igor from the correct side.

Igor stared at the photo and shouted, 'SUKA.'

Assuming suka was an insult, Martin added, 'It's not her fault. You'd been watched.'

'Well, you know what the target is then, so why all this?' Igor was visibly rattled.

'We don't, and you know we don't.'

'So what is this? I tell you where, or you tell wife, is that it? Is that all you got?'

Martin could see him shifting more and more restlessly on his chair, but before he could say what was next on his lips, Igor beat him to it.

'Just do it. What do I care, I know I'm not going home anytime soon. I don't see the wife waiting twenty years. So do it.'

Martin took a deep breath, here goes; 'It wasn't your wife I was intending to show it to. Well, not just you wife.'

'I don't understand, you English talk in riddles.'

'You will understand…in about ten minutes when Uncle Nik checks his inbox,' Martin said as he instinctively freed his legs from under the table.

Igor spun around to face Martin full on and stared at him for what seemed like an eternity; with an even more hateful glare than he would have thought possible. The seconds passed.

'In any other circumstances I would kill you with my bare hands.'

Martin could see the colour in Igor's face was now a shade Colin would be proud of, but he had to press on, and asked. 'Why, don't you like Uncle Nik?'

'Volkov is insane. You have no idea what the lunatic would do to my family.'

'Why, doesn't he have plenty of mistresses?'

'Oh, but it's different for the mighty Volkov. He has a big ego but a small dick; both true.'

'That's not a very nice way to speak about your boss.'

Igor looked even angrier than just before and spat, 'Anyway, you call me Igor; there are lots of Igors in my country.'

Martin glanced at the inside cover of the folder and then said, 'Igor Jakinsky; not too many of those Igors, I'm guessing.'

Igor opened his mouth but then closed it.

'Igor Jakinsky ex-Spetsnaz and currently a GRU operative.'

'Okay, you know who I am; you know I work for GRU, so you know that my country is my boss, not Volkov.'

'Interesting, I thought all your lot were pathologically loyal to Volkov, like a bunch of love-struck half-wits,' Martin said making sure that his legs were fully free from the table. 'You do know what pathological means don't you?'

Igor looked almost fully-cooked as he spat his next answer out, 'Of course I know what it means. I speak your stupid language well, as I do several other ones; unlike you Brits who arrogantly only learn English.'

Martin ignored the insult and carried on following his mental script, 'Anyway, forget about your family for the moment, I'm sure at some stage you will find yourself banged up in a cell with a fellow Rusky for company...one who actually likes Volkov...and one who is also massively better endowed.'

Igor didn't answer but just stared again; Martin wasn't sure how much further he could goad him without it all going tits up. But he had to push on and said, 'I guess I should thank you.'

'For what?' Igor spat as Martin glanced at the mirror and nodded, making sure Igor could see him do it. He then lent forward and turned the recording machine off, before retrieving the small CD disc from it and putting it in his top pocket.

Martin stood up - pointed to the pocket - and said, 'Uncle Nik is going to love listening to this while he reads his emails.'

Igor jumped to his feet knocking his chair over as he did so. Martin quickly said, 'Relax, it's only a prop. The recording is elsewhere.'

This caused Igor to pause. Martin shouted, 'GENTS,' and within three seconds, both uniform cops were in the room with their Tasers drawn. Martin put his arm up to halt then behind him, as he and Igor stared at each other.

Seconds later Igor broke the impasse and said, 'You absolute bastard.'

Martin replied, 'You started it.'

Igor slowly righted his chair and returned to it, he looked slightly less volatile. Martin knew that if anything was going to come from Igor it would be less humiliating if the other officers were not present. He took a risk and asked them to stand down. Both officers nodded and slowly holstered their Tasers and backed out the room.

Martin stayed stood and watched Igor as he saw the man calm some more. A resigned look appeared on his face. He looked up at Martin and nodded a sort of thank you for clearing the room, or that was how it seemed to Martin.

A further short standoff followed before Igor looked down and then muttered, 'Preston Railway Station - platform six, in a rubbish bin.'

'When?'

Igor glanced up at the clock and said, 'One hour.'

Martin knew this must be a lie if the original coded call was true, it meant that they had thirty minutes. But he didn't have time to argue now that they knew the location. As the clock on the wall was twenty minutes fast, Igor's 'one hour' was reduced to forty minutes. Choosing between the coded call information and Igor's claim - correct time adjusted - it meant that the actual detonation time could be anything between thirty and eighty minutes hence. He'd take thirty, they could still stop this. He turned to the mirror and shouted, 'Did you receive the location?' A moment later his phone buzzed a text from Colin saying 'Got it, on it.'

He then turned to Igor and said, 'Thank you.'

'Can I trust you?'

'Depends if anyone dies.'

'What happens next?'

'Like I said, it depends if anyone dies.'

'If no one dies?'

'You might get to choose.'

'Between what?'

'Two lives: one choice a good life, the other a bad life. Oh, and Uncle Nik gets no emails or audio. Nor does your wife.'

Igor slumped back onto the table and looked exhausted, beaten and saddened. As the choices Martin had alluded to appeared to have struck home.

Martin turned to leave but quickly added, 'You know how the game is played; now if you'll excuse me, I have a bomb to stop.'

Chapter Five

Simon Devlin had recently celebrated his sixty-fifth birthday, and wasn't too sure what he would do with himself in a year's time when his retirement was due. He'd worked for the railways in its many guises since it had been state owned, and had loved every minute of it. He always took pride in his work, and it annoyed him when he took over from someone else on the maintenance team who was less serious about the job than he was. He hated to see an unkempt platform and the sight of an overflowing bin would send him into a rant. Some of his workmates reckoned he had OCD, but he knew he just took pride in his job. His wife Julie often said that she wished he 'showed the same level of attention when it came to the housework'. He knew that was a fair cop. He was still fit for his age as the job was active and kept him under twelve stone, pretty normal for his height.

Today was no different to any other weekday, it was moderately busy and he had done most of his work. He just had the bins to empty on platform six and plenty of time to do it. He glanced at his watch, 10.00 a.m. His four hour shift would end in thirty minutes. He was on a split shift today so would have to book back on at two this afternoon. This was the one thing he wouldn't miss in twelve months' time; the dreaded split shits. They were a con as well; two four hour shifts didn't allow for a paid meal break. This was why he plonked himself down on a platform bench for ten minutes to have a coffee. Small victories add up.

Preston station was old but had recently had a full update and refurbishment, and Simon took pride in it. It was situated on the West Coast main line, mid-distance between London in the south and Glasgow in Scotland to the north. As he slurped his brew and gazed across the railway lines to platform six, he saw a young woman struggling with a babe in arms who was crying. The woman looked flustered as she attempted to push a changed nappy into the side entrance of one of the bins. It tumbled out onto the floor. Damn bin must be full to the brim. He shouted across at the woman, who was trying to bend down to pick it up whilst holding on to her child. 'Leave it, love, I'll come across and get it. I need to empty that bin, anyway.'

The woman looked across at him, and he waved his hand. 'Thank you,' she said. 'I have to feed this little one next.'

Simon smiled, she reminded him of his own child and grandkid. He pointed behind her to the toilet block and she followed his pointer and nodded. He poured his coffee back into his flask and stood up; brew time would have to wait. He pulled his cart and headed towards the walkway which would take him over the east set of lines to platforms six and seven.

As he neared the walkway, which was near the main entrance hall, he saw several uniformed police officers run into the station. He immediately realised that they were not the normal British Transport Police, but from the local constabulary. One stopped by him - a sergeant - and asked, 'Do you work here?'

Simon glanced at his Network Rail uniform and yellow luminous over-vest before he answered, 'Yes, why, what's going on?'

'We need to close the station and get everyone out, ASAP,' the sergeant replied, and then he rushed off without further comment.

Simon looked across at the bins on platforms six and seven, there were six in total. He'd worked here long enough to have to endure many evacuations, all false, mostly hoaxes. He also knew that he'd end up stood outside in the rain for an hour or more while the station was searched, only to have come back in to finish his work before he could sign off. He could leave the bins full for the next shift to sort out, but that wasn't Simon's way. Plus, once he'd quickly emptied those last few bins, he could finish his shift and head straight home. No waiting in the rain.

He pulled his trolley up the stairs and started to trundle it up over the pathway. He glanced across in the direction he was headed, and saw the young woman with the babe in arms rushing into the toilet block. He crossed the bridge and was halfway down the steps to the platforms, when the station public address system kicked into life: *"Would all persons please make their way to the exits in an orderly fashion. The station is now closed due to a police incident."*

Simon was nearly at platform six; it would only take a few minutes.

***

Igor was back in his cell feeling pretty low; that clever-arsed detective had done him. How the hell did they find out who he was so fast, and more importantly who his hated uncle-in-law was. And how had they picked him up so quickly in the first place. The mission was going to rat shit. If Volkov was getting in a tiz over NATO, the failure of this mission, if indeed it was a failure, wouldn't help his blood pressure any. His brief had been simple, blow something up and false intel would blame IS - or whoever they chose - in order to direct the West's attention elsewhere. But he still had one play to make, and if that worked out, the bomb would go off and his handlers would be none the wiser. He should be able to convince the lame girl detective that it must have just gone off early. After all, he had given them the correct location. It might buy him some grace when he was eventually handed over to the security services, which he knew would be soon.

Then the hatch in his cell flung open and a tray appeared with a blue plastic plate of something resembling food on it, together with a blue plastic mug of tea or coffee. The head of the custody sergeant who had booked him in, appeared behind the tray, and said, 'Hurry up, I haven't got all day even if you have.'

Igor slowly got off his wooden bunk and started towards the cell door, and said, 'You used to be on stage, no?'

Then the tray flipped in and landed on the floor, the food and drink flew everywhere.

'Oops,' the Sergeant said, 'Is that funny enough for you?' before the cell flap slammed shut.

Igor looked at the mess on the floor and sighed before returning to his bunk and sitting at one end with his back to the wall. 'I'll have the last laugh,' he said, quietly, before he looked at the wall clock and smiled.

Chapter Six

Ten minutes later Martin was driving like an idiot throwing Colin all about the passenger side of the car. Fortunately, the railway station was only a mile or so from the nick. 'I really didn't think Igor would have opened up quite so quickly,' he said.

'Shows how shit scared they are of Volkov,' Colin replied.

'But why the Russians; the Cold War has been over for decades?'

'No idea. I quickly filled in the Home Sec. as you were bringing the motor out the yard.'

'What does she say?'

'There is a COBRA meeting later today, that's all she said.'

Martin nodded and concentrated on his driving.

'Do you believe the timescales?'

'Not sure who to believe the most. The call makes the deadline in fifteen minutes,' Martin said, while automatically looking at the dashboard clock: 10.15 a.m. 'Whereas Igor's time is much later.'

'At least we are here before the earliest one,' Colin said, as Martin pulled over at the side of railway station bringing their brief conversation to an end.

As soon as they were out of their vehicle they were met by a uniformed superintendent who introduced himself as Tom Wheatfield. Introductions quickly done, Tom briefed them that the main entrance was being kept clear for the public to leave the station and for the Army's bomb disposal mob to set up. They had just arrived in town when the location became known. In the background Martin could hear the public address system on a loop saying every few seconds, *'Would all persons please make their way to the main exits in an orderly fashion. The station is now closed due to a police incident.'*

This only added to the sense of drama. A police cordon had now cut off the one-way street which passed the front of the station, and several constables were struggling to protect the great British public from getting too close.

23

Tom was interrupted by a uniform sergeant who approached almost dragging an ashen faced man in his 40s wearing a scruffy suit. 'Sir, this is Graham, the station manager.'

Tom, Martin, and Colin turned to face Graham as the sergeant delivering him rushed off.

'Are all the public out?' Tom asked.

'Yes, all the last stragglers came out a few moments ago, as did your search team, but we'll keep the tannoy message running.'

'What about your staff?'

'Yes, pretty sure.'

'What do you mean, "pretty sure"?'

'I need to recheck the assembly point around the front,' Graham said, and then hurried away. Tom, Colin, and Martin followed the short distance to the front of the station, which had a long driveway to it its main entrance normally used for taxis and cars picking up and dropping off. As they neared, Martin could see a group of civilians stood on the left hand side, and two bomb disposal vehicles parked on the right. Two army staff were busy kitting up, and the sergeant from a moment earlier approached. 'Sir,' he said to Tom, 'The Army wants the station staff removing ASAP to the outer cordon on the street.

Graham shot off to speak to them, and a moment later they all set off running down the driveway towards the main road, away from the station. Graham then returned and slew to a halt by Tom, Colin, and Martin. Breathlessly, he spat, 'We are one missing; a station cleaner hasn't come out.'

'Shit,' Tom said.

'I'll try ringing him,' Graham said, as he pulled his phone out of his pocket.

'NO,' Martin and Colin said together, stopping Graham in his tracks.

Then a young woman carrying a baby came running out of the station. Martin jumped in her way, 'Excuse me, is there anyone else in there?'

She slowed as she replied, 'No, just the maintenance guy, he came and got me, I was feeding my baby, hadn't noticed what the tannoy was saying. Thank God he did, or I'd still be in there.'

'So where is he now?'

'He shouldn't be far behind me,' she said, and everyone instinctively looked to the main doors. There was no one there. Martin thanked her and directed her to carry on to the outer cordon.

'We'll have to go and find him,' Martin said to Colin as he looked at his watch. It read 10.26. 'Platform six is thirty seconds from the entrance hall,' he added.

Colin glanced at his watch and said, 'Okay, two minutes in; max. And we leave on my shout.'

Martin nodded and set off running the short distance to the entrance with Colin close on his heels.

***

Simon watched as the young woman with the baby hurried off the platform and he dragged his trolley to the base of the steps. He could leave it there; the next shift could sort it out. He looked at the last bin, the nearest to the steps, it was the overflowing one. He'd left it until the last on purpose as it would be the heaviest, no point dragging unnecessary weight around the length of a platform when you didn't need to. Thirty years of experience had taught him how to prioritise such things. It was the bin the woman had struggled with the nappy with. He'd pushed it back in on his way to the toilet block to tell her to leave. She'd not heard the tannoy, apparently.

It went against his nature to leave a bin unemptied but he knew he was the last person in the station; he'd have to get out before he ended up with Graham on his case. He parked the trolley near to it and as he passed the bin, the damn nappy fell out, again. Sod it; it would only take a few seconds to empty it. He glanced at the station clock above his head. It read 10.27 a.m.

***

Martin was just entering through the open front door of the station when a huge explosion ripped through the air. A tsunami of dirty air smacked into him, halting him in his tracks, before it picked him up and flung him backwards through the air. He couldn't see anything; it was as if he was in a cloud of debris dust thrown up when a sixties high-rise is brought down. He couldn't hear anything except the painful ringing sound piercing his head.

His next sensation was that of being thrown onto the concrete floor, back first.

He lay motionless, stunned, deaf and blinded, but alive. It took a few seconds to start to regain his senses. He sat up slowly and began to take in his surroundings as the debris cloud thinned. Colin was face down a few metres to his left. 'Colin?' he shouted, through the eerie silence which existed.

'I'm okay, I think,' Colin shouted back, and Martin could see that he was starting to stir.

Martin picked himself up, and the moment he did, the becalming silence that had prevailed in the few seconds after the blast came to an end. It was broken by an ear-splitting cacophony of screams which rang out from the direction of the main road.

Chapter Seven

Martin and Colin were given the all clear – physically - by the attending paramedics, but they both knew that the emotional and mental damage would take a while longer. As would the annoying ringing in Martin's ears. It was quieter than before, but still distracting. But all in all they had been very lucky. Thirty or forty seconds later, they would have been in the eye of the debris storm from the blast; and not just the air pressure wave which found its way out through the main doors as the area of least resistance. The majority of the debris from the blast had blown across the platforms, whereas the pressure blast had vectored through the entrance hall which had constricted it, adding to its ferocity as it had accelerated through the main doors.

Once they started functioning properly, Martin checked that no one else was hurt, which was a blessing, and Colin tasked a local DI to organise the forensic searches as soon as the Expo Officers from the MOD cleared the scene safe to enter. According to the lead Expo, a Sergeant Scanlon, it shouldn't take too long.

They had initially tried to re-enter the station as soon as their heads had cleared, but Sergeant Scanlon stopped them. He assured them that there would be nothing left of the missing maintenance guy, and they had to check for any secondary devices. They had to cede to his experience. Graham approached them looking as if he was in a trance. 'What was his name?' Martin asked.

'Simon Devlin, sixty-five years old, due to retire next year.'

'Jesus,' Martin said.

'Family?' Colin asked.

'A daughter and a new grandchild.'

'Jesus,' Colin said. 'Do you want us to talk to his next of kin?'

'Thanks, but that's my job. I know his wife, Julie, it will better coming from me,' Graham said.

'I'll accompany you if you wish,' Martin offered. He knew how utterly dehumanising the giving of such bad news was.

'Thanks, but I've got this.'

'I don't mean to rush you but...' Colin said.

'I know, before she hears it on the news. I'm on my way,' Graham said, and then he turned and walked away.

'Good luck,' Martin shouted after him.

'Come on, let's get back to the nick and get cleaned up. We have work to do,' Colin said, and Martin followed him back to where their car was parked.

Five minutes later they parked in the police station yard and Cath was waiting for them. As soon as Martin was out the driver's seat she flung her arms around him. 'Thank God, you are both alright,' she said, with tears in her eyes.

It felt wonderful to feel Cath's warm arms around his neck, and to take in the sweet smell of her fragrance as she buried her face in his collar. But he also felt wracked with guilt. Colin told them both to head to the canteen, as he had to ring the Lancashire Chief, Don Rogers and the Home Sec. Cath said she'd bring him a bacon butty and coffee back. Once inside the building, Martin told Cath that he'd meet her in the canteen and headed to the gents to straighten up. He could feel grime on his face and in his teeth, and hoped it was just dust.

Thirty minutes later, he was starting to feel slightly better; cleaned up as best as he was able, and with the disabling effect of the initial shock starting to ebb. It was being replaced with anger, rage so tangible he could almost chew it. He'd make sure that the bastard in the cells would pay a heavy cost for his atrocious slaying of an innocent and decent man. And he'd not rest until all his comrades were caught, too. There was no way that this was a one-person job.

Before they could order a bacon butty to go, for Colin, he joined then at their table.

'I've just come off the phone from the chief - Don Rogers - and the Home Sec., who has already had a chat with Don and Counter Terror Command. Both CT and the Home Sec. are pleased with what we have managed thus far,' Colin said.

'Except—' Martin started to say.

Interrupting him, Colin said, 'I know what you are going to say, but they have to move fast and there are already suggestions

28

on the table directing how we proceed, and before you ask, I'm going to let the chief explain. It'll be better coming from him.'

Martin wasn't sure what Colin was saying, but didn't like the sound of it. 'Isn't CT taking over?'

'Not as such; there is something going on in the Capital which may or may not be related, and may or may not come to anything, but it is taking everyone they have. Their regional commander, an assistant chief constable called Susan Jennings, will oversee what we do, and is of course in continual contact with CT National Command in London.'

'So we are stuck dealing with that bastard in the cells?'

'Afraid so, for now at least. We are expected in the chief's office ASAP.'

Martin rose to his feet as did the other two, but before they made a move Colin put his hand on Martin's shoulder.

'Don't forget I did two years on secondment with CT.'

'Yes,' Martin answered.

'So I know how they think.'

'Yep.'

'They have to look at the bigger picture,'

'Granted.'

'And that is sometimes at odds with the way we would naturally think.'

Martin knew he was right to suspect that this was sounding bad, and said, 'Go on.'

'What you'll hear in the chief's office might burn, and if it does, try to keep a lid on it.'

'What do you mean?'

'Lid on it; and that's an order. You can both blow off steam once we are back here.'

Martin and Cath both nodded and Colin removed his hand and they all trooped out of the canteen.

Chapter Eight

Colin led the way into Don Rogers' spacious office on the top floor of Lancashire Police's headquarters at Hutton which was effectively a small suburb of Preston. They had been ushered in by the chief's staff officer, who sat at a small conference table which jutted out from the chief's large mahogany desk. The staff officer took out a notepad and pen; he was clearly there to take notes.

'Come in, please grab a coffee and take a seat,' Rogers said, from behind his desk.

Martin had met him a few times and liked the man. In his 50s, he still looked the ex-guardsman that he was, a large six-footer who had rigidity about him. Whether stood or seated; it matched the gravitas of his rank.

They all took a seat at the conference table and grabbed a coffee. The set up always reminded Martin of a wedding top table, with Rogers being the bride and groom. But there was a large laptop open at the far end opposite Rogers, which Martin hadn't noticed the last time they had been there.

'Can I start off by saying what an excellent job you have all done so far, and at such short notice, too. The Home Sec. is very pleased,' Rogers started.

Martin's mind wandered to think of the maintenance guy, Simon Devlin; he wondered how Graham the railway station manager was getting on with the death warning message. He'd give him a call later to find out.

'And I know one poor soul has lost his life, but for you three, it would have been much worse. Including, you two, but for the grace of God,' Rogers said, looking at Martin and Colin over his reading glasses.

Both men nodded.

'And due to a mixture of operational commitments and how this has started, the Home Sec. Miranda Daniels wants you three to carry on with the investigation, on behalf of CT for the time being.'

Martin opened his mouth but Rogers continued. 'Colin here is ideal to act as SIO having worked with CT, Cath is now linked into MI5 intel, and you, Martin, have started brilliantly with our guest.'

The thought of having to further interview, and build a greater rapport with Igor turned his stomach.

'But before we continue, there is someone I'd like you to hear from,' Rogers said, before nodding at his staff officer.

The staff officer, who hadn't been introduced, but whose name badge said Chief Inspector Roberts turned to the laptop which then sprang into life. It showed a middle-aged woman in a smart blue business suit, sat behind an even more impressive desk than Rogers', with a backdrop of a window which consisted of several small panes set in an old-looking sandstone housing. Martin recognised her immediately; it was the Home Secretary no less.

'Good morning to you all, I have been listening to Chief Constable Rogers and concur with his comments. The nation has much to thank you for thus far, and I am so glad that DCI Carstairs and DS Draker are unharmed.'

'Thank you, Ma'am,' Colin answered for them both.

'And I want you to carry on with Jakinsky as you have made such a good start, and time is of the essence; we need to know why, and with whom else. Plus, where any further munitions might be. DS Draker, how do you see him responding now?'

'He gave up what he had to in order to protect himself, and might not be inclined to help further unless we can find additional stimuli. He obviously responds to valid inducements. But now the bomb has gone off before we could stop it, and that one person has lost their life, he might think he is destined to serve a lengthy prison sentence so will clam up, ma'am.'

'As tragic as the loss of one life is, we can perhaps use this to our advantage.'

Martin had no idea what she meant and glanced at Colin, who looked guilty; he knew, or at least suspected. Martin asked the obvious question but was not expecting the reply.

'If the Russians think the operation is a success, then Jakinsky is still in play. We can offer to keep him away from charges if he turns, and gives everything we need. I'm advised by Jeremy at Six, that their normal protocol after a successful mission is for a deeply placed asset to go dark for 12 months. We can use that with him; it gives him a way out if he plays along. It gives you an inducement to offer, DS Draker. And remember, national security is at stake here and takes precedence. We can always reverse our decision later if we see fit.'

Martin looked at Colin who simply raised an eyebrow. Now was not the time to argue. But the thought of Igor becoming a political pawn, and thereby evading justice was an intolerable one.

Colin jumped in, probably to ensure Martin did not, 'Ma'am, if this is how you want to play this—'

'It is.'

'Then we can say to the media that the maintenance guy, whose name is Simon Devlin, found the device and bravely helped the evacuation. That he remained to the end to ensure that the young woman and child were clear before attempting to leave himself. Putting his own safety last, and paying the ultimate price for his bravery.'

Martin glared at Colin but held his counsel.

'Jeremy at Six has suggested the same, excellent, chief inspector. We can make Simon a national hero, which of course he is, and ensure that his family are catered for financially. It will allow the Russians to believe that their operation was - in-part - a success. But more importantly, they will not know that we have Jakinsky. It will give us all breathing space while we work out what is really going on here. Thank you, but I have to rush; I'm expected in The House of Commons ten minutes ago.'

And with that she was gone and the screen went black. The next ten minutes were spent setting tasks and agreeing responsibilities. Martin was quiet and was trying to get his head around it all. He sort of got the bigger picture thing, but the thought of Igor potentially escaping justice burned deep within his soul. It made him feel nauseous.

Colin mentioned that everyone involved at the scene would need rounding up and putting on a need-to-know document, with the threat of spending time in the Tower of London if they transgressed. Chief Inspector Roberts said he could arrange that ASAP, for which Colin thanked him. The chief told him to add his name behind the order to reinforce the seriousness. Roberts picked up his pen and paper and rushed out the room, this would need doing before any press release could go out as per the script.

As soon as the door closed, Colin turned to Martin and said, 'Told you that you would hear stuff that went against the grain.'

'You knew what was coming?' he asked.

'No, but had an idea. Having worked with them all - CT, Box, Six, et cetera - sort of prepared me.'

'That is why they are happy for you to lead on this, Colin,' Rogers threw in.

'It's just the thought of that murdering scumbag evading justice,' Martin said, before he stopped himself from going further.

'It's a trade-off, detective sergeant; if it saves lives, then it's a price we have to pay,' Rogers added.

Martin let the chief's last remark sink in, and knew that it was true. He could stomach it, just, if it saved lives. 'I know, boss,' he answered. He would just have to tell his face that when he next sat down in front of Igor.

They all bade the chief goodbye and trooped out of his office and headed back to Preston. The five mile journey seemed a lot longer than it had on the way in, and there was mostly silence in the car. Then Cath broke it by saying, 'You got Igor to tell you where the bomb was, Martin. You: not CT, not MI5 or MI6. And you and Colin saved a lot of lives today. You should be very proud of yourselves.'

Martin looked in the driver's mirror and smiled at Cath in the back seat; she was an artisan of saying the right thing at the right time. He knew her words were true and it lifted his spirit. He added, 'And you helped ID him and his links to Volkov, which gave me the levers to use.'

Cath smiled a reply at him.

'We are a team, and we stay strong and do whatever we have to do; agree?' Colin asked.

'Agreed,' Martin and Cath replied.

'One thing I'm certain of though is that this is far from over, which means there is a greater threat to stop,' Colin added.

'Agreed,' Martin and Cath repeated.

RED HERRING

Chapter Nine

Colonel Pavel Popov was a career soldier in his 50s who had spent the last ten years in the GRU; he loved intelligence work and all the grey areas which existed within it. The creative thinking needed was far in excess of some of his peers serving in other jobs within the Russian Federation military. Indeed, many of comparable rank were little more than desk-jockeys playing war games in some imaginary conventional war with NATO and the west.

Notwithstanding how much Volkov was in a constant tiz about NATO pushing ever east, and his dreams to recreate the old Soviet Union; Popov knew that Volkov would not want a war with NATO. He'd been advised not to invade Ukraine but hadn't listened; at great cost. Had Ukraine been in NATO he would not have invaded. It's a pity they weren't. Popov had advised that the blunt instrument approach was the wrong way to go. He'd been reprimanded for suggesting such.

However, Popov still considered himself at the sharp end of what could be achieved in the here and now. He knew many of his contemporaries watched from the shadows wishing him to make a mistake so they could plead for a chance at his job. But Popov didn't make mistakes; he took risks, but they all paid off because he always had a plan B, or a C et cetera, et cetera.

He was sat at his large desk in his huge office in a government building in Moscow not too far from the Kremlin; but far enough. The room was gloomy though, even with the curtains drawn fully open, as the décor was becoming dated. He looked around as he awaited news; he might treat himself to a refurb or a better office if everything panned out the way it should.

A knock at the door broke his reverie. He shouted a command to enter as he glanced at his watch: 4.10 p.m. (MSK time), 2.10 p.m. (UK time). The door opened and in walked one of his staff, Sergeant Boris Ivanov, 'Well, son of Ivan?' he asked. He often ribbed Ivanov this way, as he knew that the sergeant's father was actually called Ivan - who had a worse name - poor man. Ivan

35

Ivanov. Ivan the son of Ivan. He wondered if the sergeant's grandfather was called Ivan, too. He could see a slight contortion on the man's face. 'What it is sergeant, don't you like my jokes?'

'Of course, sir.'

'I am only playing with you, now down to business.'

'It is confirmed, Colonel, but there appears to be only one casualty.'

'How so?'

'According to a press release by the Brits, a maintenance worker discovered the device.'

'Igor should have been more careful,' Popov said, and then smiled.

'Indeed, sir.'

'But of course, it doesn't really matter as we know this was only ever supposed to be the start of it.'

'Indeed, sir,' Sergeant Ivanov repeated.

'And have we heard from Igor?'

'No, sir. He appears to have gone dark.'

'Excellent.'

Sergeant Ivanov nodded an acknowledgement at the Colonel.

'You may go now, but keep me informed.'

'Sir,' Sergeant Ivanov said, and then turned on his heels and left. As soon as the door was closed, Popov picked up his secure desk phone and dialled a number from memory.

***

Martin and Colin went home to shower and change and grab some lunch, and both arrived back in their office within five minutes of each other. It was 2.30 p.m. and the break had done Martin good. He was now more mentally in tune with what he had to do next. 'To get Igor to give us more, we will need additional to prod him with,' he said, as Colin sat at his desk.

'While you've been away, I've been liaising with MI5 and they are desperately searching their databases for anything that may help,' Cath jumped in with.

'Thanks, Cath. And noted, Martin,' Colin said.

'In fact, to get him to open up further, might essentially be a step towards fully turning him,' Martin said.

'That's exactly what counter terror command wants us to do. And I know it is asking a lot, but their brief having discussed it with Five, is for us to carry on as we have built up a bond of sorts, which can be added to rather than them starting from scratch with fresh faces.'

This surprised Martin, he would have normally expected that the security services would have whisked him away sharpish by now. 'I guess they are paying us a huge compliment.'

'They don't do anything without a reason; they want you to do whatever you have to from hereon in. Then, as and when Igor turns, they can start afresh with him, with no prior baggage,' Colin said.

'So we get to be the bad cops, and they are the good cops?'

'Yes, or to be more accurate, you are the bad cop. Here's a list of things you can offer with their blessing. Read it and shred it,' Colin said, and handed over a piece of paper to Martin. As he was reading it Colin added, 'You have to understand, it works better for them this way, as our relationship with Igor is only ever going to be short lived, whereas theirs, hopefully, will last for a lot longer.'

Martin nodded as he finished reading the brief which was amazing in its breadth, and he duly put it through the crosshead shredder as Cath looked on.

'Sorry Cath, that bit has to remain for our eyes only, no offence,' Colin said.

'None taken, but my imagination is going mental,' she replied.

'Don't worry, there are no thumbscrews listed,' Martin said, grinning at her. Then he turned to face Colin, looking more serious and said, 'Joking apart, there is enough in there to give PACE a heart attack.'

'These will not be PACE conversations; nothing said will be used in evidence. They will be classed as intelligence interviews. The only person in a courtroom who could ever be privy to them would be a trial judge, so she can issue a Public-Interest Immunity order to keep the contents secret. That's if it ever got that far,' Colin said.

'But what if he admits further offences?' Martin asked.

'Meaningless, until he is interviewed under caution in a PACE interview and repeats the remarks. But don't forget our priority at the moment is national security, not building a prosecution,' Colin added.

This was always the bit that troubled Martin the most, his natural cop instinct to obtain justice on behalf of Simon Devlin's family was an ingrained concept. 'So the murdering scumbag will evade justice?'

Colin didn't answer, he just made an apologetic face and said, 'Maybe, maybe not.'

Martin knew Colin couldn't really know, and he would have to put it to the back of his own mind if he was to focus on the task at hand. After a short pause, he said, 'How do we know he won't bubble us as soon as he is able to contact Moscow?'

'We have the earlier recording don't forget, but could do with some more icing on that particular cake, if possible.' Colin said.

'He could still blow us out, and we'd never know.'

'True; but we have to try. And don't forget that we still have the threat of a murder charge to hang over him.'

'Oh I won't. But if it doesn't work.'

'Then we try something else,' Cath threw in.

Martin smiled at her, always the positive one, and it eased the tension a little.

'He has to turn if he thinks there is any chance of being set free,' she added.

Martin nodded.

'He just has to believe it,' Colin said.

'Okay, let's go,' Martin said.

'Do you want me to join you this time?' Colin asked.

'Thanks, but no thanks. It might spoil the vibe, for now, but I'll holler if I need you.'

'Fair enough, I think the Home Sec. is chairing a COBRA meeting and might want a three-way chat at some stage between me, somebody from Five and Jeremy from Six.'

'I'm glad you told me that, it makes my task feel a lot simpler now.'

All three laughed which eased the strain further, but Colin's next words soon flipped that back.

'One last thing.'

'Yep,' Martin replied.

'The worry at Five is that there may be a second device. It's another reason why we are keeping primacy.'

'Dear God,' Martin said.

'I've not had that from my intel contact at Five,' Cath added.

'That's because there is no intel; it's apparently no more at this stage than a known MO. We just have to rule it out, and quickly. Then we can move it on after that.'

Martin nodded his understanding as he got to his feet. He felt the pressure of the country's safety on his shoulders, and it felt heavier than anything he had had to carry hitherto. He just hoped and prayed that he was up to the task. He took a deep breath and headed out the office.

Chapter Ten

Martin made his way to the interview room and nodded at the same two cops stood guard. He paused and said, 'Thanks for earlier, you were in like a shot and it worked.'

One nodded and the slightly taller of the two said, 'No problem; just holler again if you need us back in; for effect, or to *self-defend* the shit out of that toss pot. Either is good for us.'

'Cheers lads, I will,' Martin said, and then took a deep breath and opened the door.

Inside, Igor was sat on the same chair, but had swopped his paper suit for some ill-fitting tracksuit bottoms and a t-shirt that was too small, which Martin knew came from the unclaimed lost and found bin. It was almost comical and somehow made Igor look less threatening. He looked up as Martin entered and actually looked pleased to see him. Martin took his seat.

'I was true to my word, no?' Igor said.

'Ish.'

'Ish? Ah, this means you will not be true to yours.'

'Unfortunately, one poor soul lost his life.'

'You surprise me, I thought more would die.'

Martin had to swallow and dig deep not to show an overreaction; he was supposed to be getting under Igor's skin, not the other way around. But did say, 'You better not be disappointed.'

Igor looked ambivalent and said, 'Not disappointed, just surprised. You obviously didn't get there in time. Not my fault.'

Martin swallowed again, and said, 'We did, but it went off early.'

Igor shrugged and said, 'Maybe it was disturbed, or maybe it just blew early, it happens sometimes.'

'"Disturbed", you never mentioned any anti-handling traps.'

'You never asked.'

Martin swallowed once more, but knew he had to try and advance the situation, so asked, 'Okay, let's try and move things on; what do you expect to happen now?'

'I need new identity and passport.'

'Don't you want to go back to Moscow?'

'I can never go back.'

'Why?'

'Only one dead, they will know operation is blown.'

'That's not exactly true.'

Igor looked intently at Martin and asked, 'What do you mean?'

'That's what I've come to talk to you about.'

'I don't understand.'

Martin reached into his pocket and pulled out a remote control and pointed it at the two-way mirror on the wall; the kit had many functions and after he had pressed a couple of buttons the mirror burst into life as a TV screen. It was showing BBC News. 'This is being broadcast on a loop by many channels.' He then unmuted the sound.

***

Colin locked the office door and put his finger to his mouth to let Cath know that she wasn't supposed to be there, so she needed to keep quiet. He pressed a few keys on his laptop and then his monitor burst into life. On screen was the Home Secretary Miranda Daniels, at her desk as before, but looking into the screen from a side-on position. At forty-five degrees to her was a middle-aged skinny man in a dark suit, he looked like a banker or an IT consultant, but with a glow of Old Etonian about him.

'Detective chief inspector, this is Jeremy from Six, whom I mentioned to you earlier.'

Both men swapped salutations and Colin recognised him, he wouldn't have recalled the name, but he was sure that he had met him during his time on secondment to counter terrorism.

'But first, let's all listen to the news as of half an hour ago,' she said, and then pressed a couple of buttons on her keyboard and Colin's monitor turned fully into a TV screen. It was showing a BBC news broadcast, the reporter was stood outside Preston railway station. In the background Colin could see that the MOD vehicles were still in situ, and the reporter was facing Superintendent Tom Wheatfield.

'So, Superintendent, the reason you were able to evacuate all the public, was down to the sole actions of the cleaner who discovered the device.'

'Yes, totally, and the poor man lost his life in the process, leaving behind a widow, a daughter and a grandson.'

'Having first discovered the bomb in the bin, could he have not fled with everyone else?'

'Details are still scant, but we believe that he hung back to ensure that a young woman and her baby were safely away first.'

'That is so sad.'

'Indeed. In saving lives he gave his own.'

'Thank you for your time superintendent, I'll let you get on, you must be very busy.'

Tom nodded, turned and walked out of shot. Whereas the reporter turned to the camera full-face and said, *'Police are unable to name the dead hero yet, but already; the local MP is calling for him to receive the George Medal. And a UKFundHeroes page has been set up for his widow, titled "Preston Bomb Hero", and it has already reached an astonishing half a million with one anonymous donor pledging four hundred and fifty thousand.'*

The transmission then ended and the screen returned to the Home Secretary's office as before.

'It appears that the press have certainly bought the disinformation,' Daniels said.

'Everyone loves a hero, let's just hope our Russian friends buy it, too,' Jeremy said. 'And I can't wait to play with our new friend once Colin and his lot have done.'

Daniels gave Jeremy a withering look and said, 'Don't forget that a man has lost his life.'

'Quite, Home Secretary,' Jeremy said, stiffly.

'"Done" as in broken him and turned him,' she said, qualifying his remark.

'Looks like you'll get to have all the fun, chief inspector,' Jeremy added.

'It's Colin, but you can call me *detective* chief inspector; and I hope you aren't expecting us to start pulling his fingernails out,'

42

Colin said, realising that he was starting to sound like Martin. He must be rubbing off on him, though he was just glad he wasn't here listening to this sanctimonious man. He glanced at Cath who would be able to hear - if not see the exchanges - and she just raised her eyebrows in support.

'It's an idea,' Jeremy said.

'Now, now you two, it's about building relationships and working together. Am I sensing some history between you?'

Then Colin remembered where he knew him from. He'd been at a briefing once led by him but his name had not been Jeremy, which was what had thrown him. He was a condescending git then, as he now recalled.

'Our paths may have crossed when the chief inspector was on CT, but I barely remember the details,' Jeremy said, dismissively.

'Well, I think you and your team are doing a fine job, Colin,' she said, and glared momentarily at Jeremy again.

He cleared his throat and added, 'A fair point Home Secretary, they did get the location in the nick of time, even if one poor soul did succumb.'

'Can you give us any intel as to why, I thought the Cold War was long over?' Colin asked.

'The Cold War was never over, and it just became colder,' Jeremy said.

'You can elaborate, Colin has clearance,' Daniels said.

'Volkov not only hates NATO's stretch eastwards, but he hypocritically wishes to encroach more Westerly. It's why he got into bed with the Syrians so he could park some of his boats in the Med. It's also why he tried to do the same in Cyprus.'

'Until we had a little Greek chat with the Cypriots,' Daniels added. 'Not forgetting his atrocious invasion of Ukraine and all the pain and suffering there.'

'But why bomb us?' Colin asked. 'Won't that risk triggering article 5 of NATO, and bring on a world war?'

'We don't know,' Daniels said. 'It does seem like one hell of a risk, but do not forget we are not dealing with a rational mind.

43

And he has attacked us before, albeit in a deniable way; which again this also is.'

'They could be hoping to blame IS, the Taliban or God knows who in order to redirect NATO's attention elsewhere, probably back to the Middle East,' Jeremy said.

Then a ringing telephone on the Home Secretary's desk interrupted the conversation. She picked up the handset with one hand and Colin could see that it was not a normal looking handset. She raised her other hand to silence Jeremy and Colin.

'ID Code: Alpha Sierra Blue; go ahead,' she said, and then appeared to listen intently. After a minute, she thanked the caller and hung up.

'Our little brothers and sisters from across the river at Thames House?' Jeremy asked.

'Cut the cheap banter, Jeremy; but that was MI5, they have received a message from a validated source. IS have claimed responsibility and are about to go viral with it.'

'Excellent, the fame-hungry bastards probably think it the work of some lone jihadi,' Jeremy said.

'This is why Igor's detention must now remain Top Secret. And you need to ensure that there is no second device and obtain the location of Igor's munitions hide, Colin?'

'Totally understood, Home Secretary,' Colin said.

'Then it's our turn,' Jeremy had to throw in.

'We all done, now,' Daniels said, but more as a statement than a question, and Colin's screen went blank.

RED HERRING

Chapter Eleven

Martin closed down the TV screen returning the device on the wall back to a two-way mirror. He then turned to face Igor and asked, 'So what do you think?'

'I still don't understand?'

'The bomb was a success; as in it went off as instructed.'

Igor didn't respond, but kept his gaze on Martin, which was intense. 'Look, this isn't some trick, I'm sure we can find the same news on your state-run channel if you want proof.'

'So the press believes, I accept this. But it doesn't mean Volkov does.'

Before Martin could respond he felt his mobile buzzing in his pocket and took it out to check it: a text from Colin. He read it and then said, 'Not just the press. But IS believe it, they have just claimed responsibility.'

'So you let me go now, no?' Igor said, and then laughed.

It was forced and made Igor sound less sane. Not that someone who wants to bomb civilians, just because their boss tells them to can be in full control of their normal human faculties. 'Your boss, Volkov was probably hoping that IS or similar would jump on the glory bandwagon.'

'I keep telling you, Volkov is not my boss,' Igor spat.

'Okay, but he is a much loved family member isn't he?' Martin was tempted to tell Igor what he really thought, but decided to keep up the pretence; for now. 'I bet you are all over him at private gatherings.'

'I am polite and professional, that is all. Not like those others who run around him begging for his approval,' Igor said, as he shifted aggressively in his chair.

It squeaked on the floor again, but this time Martin didn't flinch, and pushed on, 'You say that, but I bet you are the first in line to stick your tongue up his arse?'

Igor glowed red and his face contorted as he spoke, 'I hate that maniac nearly as much as I'm growing to hate you.' He then paused, and said, calmer, 'It's okay, girl detective, I know what you are trying to do, and it won't work.'

'Okay, look I'm only testing your earlier remarks.'

'Why?'

'To see if you really do not like Volkov, or is it all part of your scripted patter should you be arrested.'

'Patter?'

'Never mind. Just testing your true feelings.'

'I love my country but not the man in charge; he cares only for himself, and not the motherland. But why do you test?'

'Because it means we can work together, it means we can trade.'

'I already told you where the bomb was; now it's your turn to keep your promise.'

'And I will, but I need to know that there is no second bomb,' Martin said, hoping that Igor would see the need to clarify this; it made no sense to his own cause not to.

'Okay, there was to be no second bomb if the first one was a success,' Igor said.

'Excellent, we are getting somewhere now.'

'But if they consider that the bomb is not a success…' Igor said.

'As I said, IS have already jumped on the glory wagon, so we can get the Foreign Office to make noises about dire consequences to IS et cetera, et cetera,' Martin said, as he received a second text from Colin. He read it and turned back to Igor smiling, 'Your firm already have accepted it, and guess what they have said?'

'Just say.'

'Your lot have responded straight away via your state-strangled media channel saying that the UK and NATO should concentrate on the real threat against them and leave Russia and her interests alone. I can find a copy of the broadcast if you need proof.'

Igor chewed over Martin's comment and said, 'Okay, so Volkov believes my operation was a success. This IS claim must be the outcome they wanted. But I was never told this beforehand, I just follow orders.'

'So no second bomb?' Martin said.

'No second bomb.'

'So your handlers won't be trying to contact you to order one?'

Igor shook his head, and Martin was starting to believe him. 'But?' he said.

'But?'

'But we will need to make your ordinance safe, surely you can understand that?'

Igor didn't answer.

'We wouldn't want some child finding it and suffering as a result, would we? Apart from the obvious, it would kill any deal with us.'

'You think me an amateur? You can relax, the ordinance is safe. No child will find it.'

'Forgive me if I can't take your word for that.'

'So I tell you where stash is, and then I get a new passport?'

'But of course; what were you expecting, a radioactive cup of tea?'

'That wasn't us.'

'Of course it was. But let's move on for a sec., won't your handlers be expecting to contact you, regardless of their acceptance that your mission was a success?'

Igor fell silent again.

'Look, I'm not prying for secrets here, just trying to protect you.'

'How?'

'Well, the last thing we all want is for them to find out that you've been nicked, correct?'

'Volkov would murder my family, but why is that a concern for you?'

'It concerns both out interests, albeit, that yours are highly personal. But what if Russia accepts that the mission is a success - as it seems - but that it has led to you being compromised. We could release your description as a person wanted having been seen near the railway station blah, blah, blah or whatever.'

'Why?'

'Because there are evasion protocols designed to keep you here, and safe, if you feel that your ID has been compromised.'

Igor stiffened in his chair and looked at Martin with genuine surprise on his face. 'How do you know this?'

'Because withdrawal of an asset such as you must be seen as a last resort.'

'I don't know what you mean. You have been reading too many comics.'

'No I haven't, and yes you do. You should go to your stash and grab a new set of ID documents and then go to ground.'

Igor looked at the floor again, but Martin could still see the expression of incredulity on his face. The information he'd been given on that shredded brief had been pretty accurate. 'After first letting your handlers know, yes?' he pushed.

Igor looked up, 'If you know all this, why ask me?'

'Because I don't know how long.' Martin said. But he did, according to the brief it was for a period of twelve months. But this was now a test of trust, he needed to hear it from Igor.

'How long what?' he asked, his voice now much quieter, almost as if he was worried that his handlers could hear him. A non-voluntary sign; and a good one.

'How long are you expected to stay off-grid? We can't help protect you unless we know.'

Igor failed to reply once more and returned his gaze to the floor. Training kicking in whilst he wrestled with his situation.

'I do know how long a life sentence for murder is, though,' Martin said, desperate to keep the mental pressure applied.

Igor glanced up at him.

'Which you richly deserve for killing that innocent bin man.'

Still nothing.

'Probably thirty years in your case.'

Igor returned his attention to the ground.

Martin could feel his temper starting to rise as he thought about Simon Devlin and his poor family, while this monster in front of him was playing hardball. 'I'm tired of offering you something which I pathologically don't want to,' Martin spat, unintentionally.

But it affected the situation as Igor looked up again, but this time he looked far less arrogant. Martin could feel the whole aura in the room shift.

'One year,' he answered, before slumping back in his chair as if he just given up Russia's biggest secret. He looked up again and added, 'How do I know that I can really trust you?'

Martin felt much calmer and answered, 'Why do you doubt me?'

'You said before "it depends if anyone dies". And someone did die.'

'I did, but things change.'

'What things?'

'Your value, apparently.'

'What does that mean?'

'I've been authorised to tell you that we will look after you for your protocol dark period, pay you while you act as our consultant, our advisor, so to speak.'

'Then what?'

'You can either go back to Moscow claiming a full compromise, or you can still have your new passport and money and leg it. We will arrange for your wife to join you, it will be entirely your choice.'

Igor then sat up straight as the reality of Martin's words hit him.

'You want me to betray my country?'

'You already have, we just want to extend things a bit.'

'A bit?' Igor said, his voice rising.

'Well, a year to be precise.'

'Take me to my cell, I'll do my time for murder, this conversation is over,' Igor said, all his confidence back.

'Don't be too hasty,' Martin said, as he could feel the room atmosphere start to shift once more.

'You probably never intend to let me off murder anyway.'

'You can have it in writing,' Martin said, desperate to regain control.

'I don't believe you, and you can tell Volkov about the woman, I don't care.'

'Aren't you forgetting the CD, not to mention today's comments,' Martin said, frantic to claw things back.

'Compared to what you ask now, it is nothing; I'd rather stick a thousand oca up my arse.'

ROGER A. PRICE

Chapter Twelve

Martin was nursing a mug of coffee back in the office, having quickly brought Colin and Cath up-to-speed. His emotions were all over the place, elated one moment and dashed the next. This was the ying and yang of interviewing, which was far more of an art form than people realised. It was also very tiring, it took a huge emotional toll on the interviewer as well as the interviewee; especially, when the stakes were as high as they currently were. He leaned back in his chair and felt a crack in his neck which eased some of the stiffness he was feeling. He'd come so far with Igor, got so close and then lost his grip. 'I should have left the "you come and work for us" speech until after he'd given up the location of the stash; in hindsight,' he said.

'Look, Martin, you achieved an amazing amount in such a short space of time, so don't berate yourself,' Colin said. 'And as for hindsight, forget it.'

'Yeah, but the "should have" squad will be quick to quote it.'

'You leave CT command, Rogers, and all the others in London to me; I'm your buffer from them, you just get your breath back and then we can chat through our next approach.'

Martin smiled at his boss; he really appreciated his support and could only image what some would say to him.

'And if any tosser uses the word hindsight, I'll remind them that hindsight is only quoted by those blinded by their own inadequacies, as they can't do what you are doing in the first place,' Colin said.

'Cheers, Colin. I guess when he gave up the timescale on the evasion protocol, I thought I had him, thought he had broken and turned. Suppose I got a bit giddy and pushed on in the moment.'

'And why wouldn't you? Makes sense to me.'

'Anyway, what is an "oca"?' Cath asked.

'I had to look it up,' Martin said. 'It's the Russian version of a wasp.'

Cath burst out laughing and Colin joined in forcing a smile from Martin. It felt therapeutic.

When the mirth died down, Colin suggested that they head to the canteen while he rang the chief and Home Secretary to keep them up-to-date, he'd join them presently.

Both nodded and Martin followed Cath out the door. Ten minutes later, they were both settled at a table in the corner of the canteen and starting to dig into the day's special - a chicken curry. Between mouthfuls of food, Cath briefed Martin on her overheard conversation Colin had had with London.

'That Jeremy sounds a charmer,' he said.

'Honestly, I'm sure he couldn't live up to a stereotypical image of an Oxbridge educated MI6 officer more, if he tried.'

'I've met a handful from Five, or the Security Service to give them their proper name, but I've never interacted with Six, or the Secret Intelligence Service, before,' Martin said.

'I've never engaged with either, it's all very exciting.'

'How are you getting on with Five's intel liaison?'

'A lass called Gill, or at least that's what she calls herself, but she's really lovely, it's just like dealing with any other analyst to be honest.'

'That's good.'

'Anyway, where did MI5 get the nickname Box? I was going to ask Gill but bottled it.'

'Oh that's just an old one, probably defunct now. They used to have a Post Office box back in the non-digital days, which was known as Box 500. The nickname came from that.'

'Oh, I was wondering about Pandora's box,' Cath said.

They both laughed and Martin said, 'Probably more appropriate.' He then went on to ask Cath if she had obtained any worthwhile intel from Gill.

'Not really, but the unknown may be interesting.'

'What do you mean?'

'Well, Gill gave me access to the MI5 surveillance logs from the day they spent following Igor around when they first became aware he was in the country.'

'That's good.'

'Yeah, and I've cross-referenced all the data with our intel systems but drawn a blank.'

Martin finished his last mouthful of rice and said, 'I get it that they had absolutely no intel on Igor, which is why he was considered low-risk, but were any follow up actions done?'

'It appears not, and that is where the unknown might be interesting.'

Martin let Cath finish her last forkful and waited for her to continue.

'It's the woman he was photographed with, she has not been identified and no further enquires have been made. I told Gill that as we are local, we'd have a look at that.'

'Good idea, but it must be difficult, these farms must have dozens of unregistered casual labour coming and going no questions asked.'

'But if we can trace her, she might know something about Igor which can help.'

'I can't see him being the one to spill any pillow talk, but you're right, it's a lose end which needs tying up, regardless.'

'Are you planning to go back in with Igor?'

'To be honest, now that we know that there is no second bomb ticking away, it lifts the time pressure a little, so I thought I'd give him a break from me,' Martin said, knowing that even though this was true, he too, needed a mental break from the rigors of interviewing Igor. But added, 'Not that we don't need to know where his hide is fairly quickly, but a short break might help.'

'Do you think the hide is safe?'

'Igor is ex-Spetsnaz - special forces - I'm sure the stuff is safely hidden, probably been there for decades, but we obviously still need to neutralise it.'

'I can see if Gill can help, they must have intel on old Soviet arms stashes; if that's where it's from.'

'Good idea, it's as good a guess as any. Colin has obviously become delayed, let's go and see what he wants us to do, and then send him to the canteen before that lovely curry sells out.'

Five minutes later, Martin and Cath walked back into the office as Colin was coming off the phone.

'How'd it go with the Home Sec. and Rogers?' Martin asked, gesturing towards Colin's phone handset.

'Fine, everyone is relieved to know that there is no second device, but they are obviously keen to learn about any stash Igor has,' Colin said.

'As we all are,' Martin replied.

'But that wasn't them,' Colin said, nodding at his desk phone. 'It was the custody suite, Igor has just head-butted the custody sergeant, claiming that he had spat in his food. Christ, we don't need this.'

'Is he okay?' Martin asked.

'Fortunately it's only superficial.'

'What about a change of staff; it was the sergeant's team that were attacked when he was first brought in and they tried to fingerprint him. Obviously, tensions are high. A fresh team might break the aggro, and make my job a bit easier.'

'Normally, I would agree, but due to the sensitivities involved, the whole custody suite has been emptied of other prisoners, and is sealed off and closed to new arrivals. Replacing the whole custody staff would mean adding several more names to the need-to-know list. I'll go and have a word, see if I can't bring about some order even though it's understandable that tempers are frayed.'

'How are those officers?' Cath asked. 'The initial ones?'

'Two off sick, still; one with a broken nose, the other with concussion, and the others are back to work carrying a few bruises and an intense desire to get their own back. Leave it to me, I'll lay the law down with them, we don't have time for any distractions.'

Martin and Cath briefed Colin as per their discussions over lunch, and he said, 'Excellent work, Cath; we've been so focused on Igor and the immediate threat, that we have failed to stand back.'

'And look at the wider picture?' Martin threw in.

'My God, we may make an officer out of you yet, sergeant.'

Martin laughed and said, 'That would be nice. Detective Inspector Draker has a good ring to it.'

Cath rolled her eyes and said, 'God, your head is big enough as it is, thank you very much!'

Colin added, 'Right, to business, I'll sort out the shit in cells, you can follow up Cath's lead. And I agree that giving Igor a short break is a good idea. Plus, the woman, if you can trace her, might give you a bit more to use in your next interview, Martin.'

Both Cath and Martin nodded, and as he grabbed his coat, Cath said, 'And don't forget to eat, sir,' and smiled.

'Yes, ma'am,' Colin said.

'Now, that does have a ring to it,' she quipped.

'Oh, that reminds me, Rogers has agreed to you being sworn in as a special constable, it'll give you better access and police powers such as search and seizure. We can discuss the fineries to it all and sort you out with a warrant card, later on. But for now, if you can nip down to the Magistrate's Court, I'll ring the clerk while you are en route. It'll only take a second to swear you in, and then it's all official.'

'Colin, I could kiss, you,' Cath said, with utter glee in her voice.

'Never mind that, now get out we have work to do.'

Martin was well chuffed, too. It was something he and Colin had discussed in secret previously. Now that Cath was a *field* intel analyst, she was interacting with criminals, and they both knew that she would need some protection and enhanced training. Not just for things like search and seizure as Colin had used as a quick example. But in the fullness of time they could get her some personal protection training. And being a special - or volunteer constable, as they were termed nowadays - it would allow her to carry handcuffs, a baton and even pepper spray once fully trained.

Martin realised that due to the seriousness of the current situation, Colin must have decided to hit the chief Don Rogers with it blind. 'Come on, Constable-elect, let's get you sworn in, and then we can get to that farm in West Lancashire.'

Chapter Thirteen

Preston Magistrates Court was only a five minute walk from their office so Martin and Cath decided to stretch their legs, plus there was nowhere realistically to park. The structure itself was covered in white tiles which always looked grubby. The building was around fifty years old and looked it. Having spoken to one of the clerks, Cath was whisked away whilst one of the magistrates' courts was in recess as the justices considered their verdict on a minor shoplifting case.

Martin sat on a hard wooden bench and watched the interaction of a family who appeared to be awaiting their case to start. A young male with bare arms covered in tattoos was pacing up and down and swearing as his solicitor had yet to show. Who Martin assumed was his partner, was sat down with a young child in a pram. She too had bare arms covered in tattoos; and he couldn't help noticing that her tattoos were of a better quality, in that they had several colours involved. As opposed to the prancing male, whose markings were all the same drab blue colour. Or maybe the woman's were just newer. Her arms looked like rolled- up comics, but that was still a nicer look than the man's. He wondered if the kid had tattoos. Probably a bit young. Martin had nothing against personal body inking, per se, but the couple did fit in with the stereotypical view of a family of jobless thieves from a rough part of town. He could only hope that the child broke the chain and didn't become a product of his or her environment.

The male youth came over to Martin and asked, 'Are you from Fisher and Fishers?'

Martin guessed that was a firm of local briefs, and as he was wearing a two-piece suit and a collar and tie, unusual for him, the youth had assumed he was a solicitor. He was almost offended that he didn't appear to the youth as a detective. That said, he usually wore casual clothes but had dressed up for a change, hoping it might add to his gravitas whilst conducting interviews with Igor.

'Your brief not arrived?' Martin said, not answering his question.

'No and we are on next. The beaks are considering their last case and then it's me, for fucks sake.'

Still not answering the youth's initial question, but allowing his presumption to continue, Martin said, 'What are you charged with?'

'Shoplifting.'

'How are you pleading?'

'Not guilty.'

'Did you do it?'

'Yeah, but I never plead guilty.'

'What's the evidence like?'

'The bastards have me on CCTV.'

'So why not plead to it and then you can give mitigation?'

'I was actually thinking about doing that, and it would be a first, but my brief talked me out of it.'

Hearing this made Martin's blood boil; small town briefs making guilty clients run a summary trial just so that they could milk the legal aid. A plea of guilty would be in their client's best interests. 'I'm guessing you've got a bit of form?'

'Yeah, mainly thieving cause of the smack, but since me kid came along I've stopped the gear. Got myself clean so have stopped thieving, too. Got responsibilities, like.'

Martin actually felt some sympathy for the man now, if this was true. 'You on a bender?' he asked, knowing that if he was on a suspended sentence then jail time was likely regardless of his plea.

'Was, but not now.'

'Look, it's not my business, but why don't you sack your brief, he's just after a bigger payday.'

'That's what me bird reckons.'

'Plead guilty and tell the magistrates what you just told me, and have your family at the back of the court as you do so. It'll go much better for you than running a trial and being found guilty, they won't listen to mitigation, and they'll punish you for wasting time and money.'

'Why can't I have mitigation if I'm found guilty?'

'You can't have an excuse for something you said you didn't do.'

'Thanks, mister, I'm going to do that. Which firm are you from? Not that I'll need another brief, like, I'm going straight, but just in case.'

'I'm just passing through; but good luck, stay clean, and get a job and look after your family.'

'Thanks; by the way, what's your name?'

'Martin Draker,' he answered, instinctively, not really sure why he gave him his real name.

The youth nodded and then shook Martin's hand and he felt guilty about his earlier stereotypical meanderings over the tattoos. He watched the man walk back to his family, just as a man in a crumpled suit rushed up to them. Martin heard him say, 'Now, Mr Arnold, I am fully prepared to run this trial, but I don't think it wise for you to give evidence in your own defence.'

'I don't think anything you say is wise, I'm going to represent myself; you're sacked.'

'But, but you don't stand a chance defending yourself.'

'I won't be; I'm pleading guilty.'

Then a grinning Cath reappeared and walked over to Martin, just as the court clerk came through the court main doors and shouted, 'Regina versus Denis Arnold: Denis Arnold to the dock please.'

'Here,' the youth said, and started to walk towards the clerk. 'Cheers mate,' he said to Martin as he walked past.

'What was all that about?' Cath asked.

'Tell you later, but first, tell me how you got on?'

***

Ormskirk is a medium-sized market town which dates back centuries. It sits on the flatlands of rural West Lancashire. A large area of arable land between Preston to the north and Liverpool to the south, with the Victorian resort of Southport to its west. They were looking for a place named Gosling's Farm which is lodged somewhere between Ormskirk and Southport, near a hamlet called Scarsbrick. It was about an hour's drive from Preston and it took most of the journey for Cath to calm down. She'd clearly loved the whole experience, and said she hoped to continue to break new ground in her developing role. Martin was in no doubt that she would; she was effectively re-writing the analyst's manual; not that one existed.

'I can't wait to get my warrant card,' she added.

'Don't forget that with it comes responsibility.'

'Yeah, but think of all the nightclubs I can get into free.'

Martin laughed and said, 'Not sure that still happens.'

'Anyway, what where you going to "tell me later"?'

Martin told her and she burst out laughing, 'I love it.'

'The brief shouldn't have been so greedy. It's probably why the lad had never held his hands up before now.'

'I hope he avoids jail,' she said.

'Must admit, so do I, now. Wouldn't have said that before talking to him,' Martin said, as the sat nav directed them off a normal road onto a narrow lane. It then ran onto an untarmacked section which Martin guessed was a private road. On both sides of the track he could see vast polytunnels which seemed to run for miles. 'This looks like the place.'

'Yep, how do you want to play this, partner?'

Martin smiled and then answered, 'Direct and off the cuff.'

They then drove past a rotten wooden sign with faded writing on it which read 'Gosling's Farm' with the words, 'No Cold Callers' underneath. Ahead Martin could see a number of brick built outbuildings with a large detached farmhouse in the centre with a large gravel-covered area at its frontage. 'Game on, Constable,' Martin said, as they drove onto the centre concourse and pulled over in front of the house.

RED HERRING

Chapter Fourteen

Martin and Cath got out of their car and were about to approach the large wooden front door of the farmhouse when a voice called from behind them. They both turned around to see a man in his 40s, stocky, wearing a tatty wax jacket and Wellington boots appear from one of the outbuildings. He walked slowly towards them with a slight stoop and in a bow-legged way. Most farmers Martin had met had that similar gait, as if they were all doing a John Wayne impression. This must be the farmer.

'If you're selling, I'm not buying, and if you're lost, buy a sat nav,' the farmer said, as he neared.

Martin exchanged a glance with Cath before he replied, 'I'm not lost and I have a sat nav, but thanks for the advice.'

'Look smartarse, I'm a busy man and you are on my land,' the farmer said, as he came to halt a few feet from them.

'Are you always this welcoming to visitors?' Cath asked.

'More so to the pretty ones; you can stay,' the farmer said, and then laughed at his attempt at humour.

'I don't think your wife would be impressed,' Cath countered with.

'I don't have a wife.'

'That doesn't surprise me,' Martin muttered.

'What did you say?' the farmer said, who was starting to look irritated.

'Okay, enough,' Martin said, and threw his hands in the air. 'We are not here to wind you up, but we are from the police and just need a moment of your time.'

The farmer tensed and took on a very hostile look as Martin got his warrant card out and showed him before whipping it away, adding, 'I'm DS Martin Draker and this is my colleague Cath Moore.' Before the farmer could respond, Martin took one of the compromising photos of Igor and the woman from his pocket and showed it to the man. He let the farmer study the picture for a second and then added, 'We think you might know this woman.'

59

'Looks like the lucky bugger is enjoying himself,' the farmer said with a leer.

Martin looked at Cath and raised an eyebrow acknowledging the passive misogamist overtones in his comment. As if it only mattered to him that the man was enjoying himself.

'Just answer the question,' Cath said sternly.

'I hope you aren't suggesting I know her the same way, are you?' the farmer said.

'You wish,' Cath muttered.

'Eh?' he asked.

'We wish to trace her,' she added.

'Can't help you, ain't never seen her. So if that's it?'

'We are reliably informed that she, in fact both of them worked here. We are hoping she still does,' Martin said.

'The man may not have been in for a day or two and won't be coming back,' Cath added.

'Who told you that?'

Martin dearly wanted to say '*An MI5 surveillance team*' and then watch the colour drain from his arrogant face. But instead said, 'A reliable source.'

'Well, your source is wrong, never seen either of them before, now get off my land.'

Martin couldn't believe the last bit, talk about stereotypes, 'Shouldn't that be "gert orf my land"?'

'Now you listen here—' the farmer started to say, before Martin cut across him.

'No, you listen to me, and listen well. I'm uninterested in how many unregistered illegal fruit pickers you employ here.'

'Hey, I pay all my staff the living wage.'

'In cash?' Cath asked.

The farmer didn't answer.

'So no national insurance paid by them or you?' she pushed.

The farmer again failed to reply but his gaze was darting between Martin and Cath, weighing them up. 'As I said, we are not interested in your casual workers or your creative accounting, but we do need to know who the woman is, and where we can find her?'

'Now,' Cath added.

'I've got nothing to hide,' the farmer said, suddenly looking more emboldened.

'I'm sick of this. Just tell us and we are gone. But if don't, then Cath here will put a call into the friendly Tax Inspectors based just down the road in Bootle. And forget your employer creative accounting; they will rip apart your own tax liabilities for shit paper.'

'Probably seize your farm to pay off years of unpaid tax,' Cath added.

'You wouldn't?' the farmer asked.

'Cath, if you would, please?'

'Certainly,' she answered, and pulled her iPhone out of her handbag and started to scroll down the screen. 'Ah, here it is,' she added.

'Mention possible modern-day slavery, too; that'll get them running,' Martin said.

'Will do,' Cath answered, as she put the handset to her ear.

'Hey, there's no need for that, all my workers are here freely.'

'I'm sure they are, but just illegally. And we need to ensure the tax office turn out.'

'If they say they have a work permit, then who am I to—'

'Check?' Cath said, and then turned her attention to her phone and spoke into it. 'Oh hi, my name is Cath Moore from Lancashire police, can you put me through to your on-call inspector please?'

'Just the woman's details,' Martin said.

'Okay, Okay, I remember her now. Please stop,' the farmer said.

Cath cut the call. 'Go on,' she said to the farmer.

'Eastern European both of them, can't remember his name, he disappeared a couple of weeks ago. She stayed on, said her name was Tracy, I think, but called in sick two days ago; reckon she's moved on, too. It's what a lot of them do, they can be a nightmare.'

'If it helps, she's not in any trouble.'

'And nor are you, yet,' Cath added.

'We just need her address and phone number if you have that,' Martin said.

'You'd better follow me into the office,' the farmer said, and headed towards the front door of the farmhouse. Martin grinned at Cath, quite the double act, as they followed him down the path.

***

Ten minutes later Martin and Cath were driving back down the farm lane away from Gosling's Farm. 'God, I enjoyed that,' Cath said, as Martin concentrated on missing as many potholes as he could.

'Yep, it worked well, special constable. Anyway, I'd no idea you actually had the tax office number in your phone.'

'I didn't.'

'Oh, nice one, then. Must admit, I thought he was going to face our bluff out.'

'Me, too, I was starting to panic a bit.'

'So who were you ringing? I heard the ringing-out tone before you put the phone to your ear, so knew you were making a real call.'

'My home phone, it'll all be on my answer machine.'

Both of them laughed and Martin said he looked forward to listening to it over a bottle of wine, as and when they ever got chance. He felt a lot of the pressure lift, getting out into the field with Cath had really given him a boost. He was ready for his next face-to-face session with Igor. He just hoped the woman, allegedly named 'Tracy' could give them some arrows to throw; anything could prove pivotal.

'Is it far?' Cath asked.

'Ormskirk is just down the road; it sounds like a bedsit, probably in a side street near the town centre, or above a shop or suchlike.'

'Do you think Gosling will keep his word and not ring her to pipe her off?'

'Not in his interests to do so. He'd only bring a world of pain on himself. But one thing does worry me.'

'What's that?' Cath asked.

'I know we threw in the modern-day slavery remark as a threat; but it's the exact type of place where that foulest of crimes can lie hidden.'

'When we are done, I'll pass on our potential concerns, just to be on the safe side. I know the ex-DCI who chairs the Pan Lancashire Anti-slavery Partnership.'

'Brilliant.'

'Gosling will love us.'

'I don't care; if he's got nothing to hide then he's got nothing to worry about,' Martin said.

'The grubby little man deserves some grief.'

'Okay, we are only a couple of minutes away now,' Martin said.

'How do you want to play this?'

'I reckon off-the-cuff again; it worked well enough before.'

'Deal,' Cath said.

Martin pulled in to a side street behind a row of shops. The address they were after was indeed a flat above a shop, at the end of the row. 'Come on, let's go.'

Chapter Fifteen

Martin and Cath approached the half-glazed front door to Flat 7B, which was accessed via a steel walkway leading from a fire escape at the rear of the building. It looked like a developer had turned the upstairs storerooms above the shops into apartments. Hence the doors being on a gantry at the rear. Looking from the street at the front, you wouldn't realise the upstairs were flats if you didn't know.

'These would make great safe houses.'

'Wouldn't they,' Martin said as he knocked on the front door. There was no initial response, but the sound of a toilet flushing inside the property could be heard. He exchanged a concerned look with Cath, before knocking again, only harder.

The door was then opened by a female in her 30s, tall and athletic looking with blonde hair tied behind her head. She spoke with an Eastern European accent, similar to Igor's, and said, 'I'm not buying anything.'

Martin produced his warrant card, and said, 'We are from the North West Regional Organised Crime Unit.'

'Police?'

'Yes, we just need a word, won't take up too much of your time.'

The female started to close the front door, but Martin put his foot inside the jam to stop her, 'Look, it's nothing to do with your work status, visas or immigration if that's what you are thinking.'

'What then?'

'It's just a word, Tracy, as my colleague has said,' Cath threw in.

Martin saw the name react on the woman's face.

'Word about what?' she asked, still keeping the door pressed against Martin's foot.

'Inside would be better,' he said.

'Why?'

'Because we don't want to chat about Igor in front of your neighbours,' Cath added.

'I don't know any Igor,' the woman said, and then tried once more to close the door.

But Martin was ready for her, he pulled his foot out of the way as he put his shoulder to the door and pushed hard. The woman leapt backwards as the door flung open and bashed against a hallway wall. He quickly pushed past her and Cath followed, closing the door behind them. They both took the first doorway off the hall which led into a small front room. They came to a halt and turned around to face the woman as she rushed in after them.

'Get out of my house, now,' the woman said, looking flushed and hostile.

'Not until you tell us your real name,' he said.

'You already told me it's Tracy, so you know my name.'

'But it's not is it?' Cath said.

'And we need to know how you ended up in this photo?' he added.

'What photo?'

Martin pulled the photo from his inside pocket; it was the same one he had shown Gosling at the farm. The woman took it and looked intently at it, and he saw a look of horror spread across her face. As she was studying it, Cath elbowed Martin and nodded towards a waste paper bin. He looked and could see what appeared to be a smashed up mobile phone in it. He nodded his understanding, just as the woman stepped forward with the photo in one hand whilst pointing at it with her other. She didn't look happy.

'How you get this?' she demanded. 'It is private.'

There was a long settee in front of them which looked to be the same as the one in the photo. It was facing a large window at the gable end of the property. He walked over to the window and looked out of it. He could see a yard at the side of the building with other commercial looking buildings in the foreground. He turned to face the woman whilst pointing at the glass, 'I'm guessing that the "how" was through this with a very long lens. You really should shut your curtains when you have company.'

'You bastards,' she spat.

'Granted; as it was private. Now your real name please?'

'Tracy,' she said, but sounded less sure of herself.

'No it's not.'

'Or maybe it's pronounced Tracyetsky.' Cath said.

The woman gave Cath a withering look, the ones that only women could give to another woman, and then said, 'Why the name?'

'We just need to understand who you are in relation to Igor,' Martin said.

Cath pointed to the photo still in the woman's hand, and added, 'And how you know him? Apart from like that.'

The woman gave Cath scowl number two and said, 'He's just a casual friend.'

'And you are?' Martin pushed.

The woman sighed and answered, 'Beramitch. Olga Beramitch.'

'I accept that the Olga bit is probably true,' Martin said.

'But your last name is Jakinsky, isn't it, Olga?' Cath interjected with.

She was voicing the same nagging concern that Martin had unsaid. Colin had told him that Six had warned that assets such as Igor often travelled with their real wives. They were also agents - of sort - albeit as a sleeping partner, so to speak. He tried to not smile at his own pun. He guessed it was probably supposed to add to their credibility and back story.

The woman looked genuinely surprised on hearing the name Jakinsky, and Martin said, 'But I think I'll just call you Mrs Igor.' It bothered him that she had chosen to use a different surname. If she was his wife, why not say so. Maybe Beramitch was her real name, but there was something else going on here. He was sure that she wasn't related to Volkov, be that by blood, or in-law; and that was just the start of his misgivings. Martin knew if they left without her she would most probably be on her toes sharpish. Maybe they had caught her in the act of fleeing;

hence the smashed up phone in the bin. He then pulled his rapid handcuffs from his pocket and snapped one end onto the wrist that was still holding the photo, which she then dropped.

'Hey, what is this?'

Martin heard Cath's phone ring as he said to Olga, 'Olga Jakinsky I'm arresting you for entering and remaining in the UK by deception, namely using a false identity. An offence under the 1971 Immigration Act.' He glanced at Cath and noted a stern look on her face as she looked at her phone screen.

'You say you are not interested in immigration,' Olga said, regaining Martin's attention.

'I lied. You do not have to say anything. But it may harm your defence if you do not mention when questioned...' he said, as he noted Cath had moved to the other side of the room as she took her call; she looked perturbed. '...something which you later rely on in court. Anything you do say may be given in evidence,' he finished off to Olga.

He then grabbed her free arm and cuffed that too, and told Olga to sit on the couch and wait.

'What is going on?'

'You have hardly been forthcoming so I've decided to continue our chat on our ground.'

'I've nothing more to say.'

'See what I mean.'

'You lied about immigration.'

'Look, it is just a means to an end; if you cooperate with us back at the station I can make this entering the UK under a false name thing go away. Now just wait there a sec.'

She didn't reply, and Martin quickly walked over to Cath and heard her whisper her intelligence security code into the phone as he neared. This sounded serious. She beckoned him to listen in, he realised that she couldn't put her phone on speaker mode with Olga sat a few metres away, but she turned the phone laterally so they could both put an ear next to the handset. He could hear the caller say, 'Confirmed: Cath, it's Gill here.'

'Hi,' Cath said.

'Where are you now?'

'Ormskirk, an hour from my office.'

'You need to get back there and ring me on a secure line.'

'What's up?'

'Er, we have received an authenticated message re your enquiry.

'Okay.'

'The thing that happened.'

'The B-thing?' Cath whispered.

'Yes. There *is* to be a second one.'

'Oh my God; when?'

'Day after tomorrow. Ring me when secure,' then the line went dead.

Chapter sixteen

Martin loitered with Colin in the main incident room at Preston police station, while Cath rung Gill in Manchester for a more open conversation. She joined them a few minutes later and Martin asked, 'Anymore?'

'Not really, it was the same as the original call, in so far as that a digital voice distortion device had been used. They are working on that, but it appears sophisticated,' she answered.

'Intel-wise?' Colin asked.

'Just the day after tomorrow at 12 noon.'

'Okay: quite a hunch, Martin, re Olga,' Colin said.

'It was after what you had mentioned about operatives often bringing their real wives with them. She sort of fit the image. Couldn't risk her doing one. And Cath was ahead of me on that one, too.'

'Must admit, the look in her eyes when you showed her the photos was striking,' Cath said.

'How do you mean?' Martin asked.

'Beyond annoyance; it appeared a deep personal affront; if it was just a casual thing, well that's one thing, but if she is Igor's wife, then perhaps she would feel the betrayal of her privacy a whole lot deeper.'

'Makes sense, good thinking. You've obviously read her well.' Colin said.

'I tried to; on a woman-to-woman level, but I don't think she likes me.'

'I could tell that; I saw the looks she gave you.'

'What the hell is going on?' Colin said.

'A good question; and only two people know the answer. How do you want to play this?' Martin asked.

'I reckon you should have a further chat with Igor.'

'Good for continuity,' Martin replied.

'And I'll have a quick word with Olga; I wasn't the one who locked her up, so that might help,' Colin said.

'Always the good guy,' Martin said, grinning.

'As it should be,' Colin replied with a smile.

'But why don't you take Cath in with you?' Martin said.

Both Cath and Colin tuned to face Martin. 'Not wishing to put pressure on Cath, as she's not trained in such matters, but she could be your silent partner, observing Olga's reactions. Plus, if she doesn't like Cath, as we suspect, it might give you an edge.'

Colin opened his mouth to answer, but Cath beat him to it. 'I'm in, sounds like fun.'

Colin followed with, 'How do we stand legally?'

'No issues: don't forget she was sworn in as a special constable this morning.'

'I'd forgotten about that. Let's do it.'

Martin rang down to the custody suite and arranged for the prisoners to be taken to adjoining interview rooms, and ten minutes later he parted company from Cath and Colin and headed to Interview Room One. He was glad to see the same two Rugby players dressed as cops stood guard.

He walked into the room with a manila folder under his arm to find Igor looking passive, ambivalent even, sat on his chair. He glanced up as Martin sat down, but no more. 'Look, Igor, I may have overstepped the oche a little before, expecting you to work for us long term. I got carried away. I'm sorry.'

On hearing the apology Igor looked up and said, 'I do what I have to do within the limits of what is allowed for me. But I will never turn traitor to become your bitch.'

'We didn't have the best start, but I don't dislike you.'

'You think me a fool?'

'Fair enough, but I do want to help.'

Igor just scowled at Martin.

'It's in both our interests, let's take out the emotion.'

'How is it in my interests to be a traitor?'

'Saves doing thirty years?'

'No problem.'

'Saves Uncle Nik seeing those photos?'

'Show him.'

'Or hearing what you think of him?'

Igor didn't reply.

'Ah, not so keen about that one.'

Igor groans.

'Look, it really will be just for twelve months so as to fit in with your evasion protocols.'

'Once on your hook, you'll never let me go.'

'Yes we will, think about it; after twelve months you'll be well past your sell-by date. Our friends at MI5 and MI6 just want you as a consultant; not an operative. You wouldn't be required to proactively do anything against Russia.'

'What use am I then?'

'We have nothing against Russia or its people, but we have a joint dislike of the people running the place.'

Igor seemed to consider Martin's last point with due respect.

'How can you prove your word?'

'Well, we won't send your wife back to Moscow for starters.'

Igor looked up with a pained expression. 'I already told you, wife is in Moscow.'

Martin opened the folder and showed Igor one of the original photos.

'Yes, yes, you already showed me the photo of the girl.'

'Not a girl, but Mrs. Jakinsky. We know she is your wife.'

Igor shifted in his chair and said, 'No, I told you, just a girl.'

'That's why you are not now bothered if we send the photos back to Moscow, though to be fair to you, you did a pretty good job of pretending at the start.'

'You are wrong,' Igor said, more loudly.

'As we say over here, "you have over-egged the custard" with your Volkov remarks.'

Igor then jumped to his feet.

Martin tensed, Igor had caught him off-guard, but he held his nerve and said, 'Sit down and calm down, I've something to tell you.'

Igor stared at Martin with one of his earlier hate-filled gazes, but then slowly retook his seat.

Martin waited a while and then said, 'We have a small problem.'

'Your problems are not my problems. Where is my new passport? I will not be your spy. I have done as asked, I told you about the bomb.'

'That is still very much open to you, but the problem may interrupt it.'

'What is this, you go back on your British word?'

'I'm honestly not trying to shaft you.'

'No?'

'It's just that you said there was to be no second bomb if the first was a success.'

'That is true,' Igor said, as he tuned fully towards Martin and laid his tree trunk sized forearms on the metal table. Fully attentive now.

'Trust me, I want to believe that.'

'You can believe it.'

'Just one problem on that front.'

Igor sighed and then said, 'Okay, go on.'

Martin told him about the coded second call. Igor reacted with temper and denied it, so much so, that the two guards came rushing in. Martin had to reassure them that he was fine, but told Igor to calm down, again. Once he had settled a little, Martin thanked the two cops and they slowly retreated. They looked disappointed.

'This is not a game?' Igor asked; his voice now back to normal levels.

'Why would it be? This is the last thing either of us wants.'

'Then, I have no idea what has gone wrong. But you can ignore it. I positioned the first bomb and I have not placed a second bomb.'

'What about Olga?'

Igor looked up with genuine surprise on his face which was quickly replaced with resignation. The same look he had when he told Martin where the first bomb was placed.

'You know her name so I will not try to bullshit you. I want you to believe me that there is no second bomb. I want my passport and I'm gone. Being your bitch was not part of our initial deal.'

'Go on.'

'She is my real wife; obviously not in Moscow.'

'We know, you know we know, and it's like I said, we will not send her back. But could she have placed the bomb, made the call?'

'Not possible, she is not an agent, she is just my wife. She knows I'm on a mission, but not what. She is just support to my story; that is all. And in any case, the first call was automated and I have been in here, so no second call. It can only be actioned by me. So if you have received another one, I can't explain it. A technical glitch maybe?'

'Okay, now don't overreact, but we have Olga in custody.'

'What?' Igor said, his voice rising again.

Martin put his arms up, palms open-faced, and said, 'Just while we confirm things then she can go, and you can follow her, later. I promise.'

'You have not told her why I'm here, for God's sake?'

'No, no of course not.'

'She just thinks I'm on a fact finding mission and then we go home. I told her that her uncle would not risk her on a dangerous mission. This is also why I can't stay for twelve months.'

'Surely she knows enough to realise if your mission goes wrong, or your ID is compromised you may have to go dark for a year. You must have prepared her for that eventuality?'

Igor didn't answer.

'I thought so. It could all work out if you agree to it. We would ensure her safe passage home and pretend to be none the wiser; just expelling an illegal, as far as she is concerned.'

Igor looked as if he was working out the logistics of what Martin had said, but didn't respond.

'But we could do with recovering your ordinance, and then there can be no more bombs, ever.'

Igor still didn't answer, he seemed to be wrestling with the last few remarks from Martin, and then he said, 'Trust me it is safe. I can't give you the hide; they would find out at some stage and then know a betrayal had taken place.'

'We could make up a cover story, we are good at those.'

'They would not believe you. It is safe, and there is no second bomb. That's all I can say to you.'

Martin accepted that the interview was over, for now, and got up to leave the room. Igor sought his word as he left, and he told him he would keep his promises. Volkov would never know he'd been their guest. This brought on another classic, unsolicited, and no doubt, unintended, but heartfelt remark on hearing Volkov's name. Martin smiled to himself, and then asked the cops to take Igor back to his cell. When he arrived back in their office, Cath and Colin were already there. He quickly told them how he had got on.

'You believe him?' Colin asked.

'Until I know different, but I can't help feeling we are being played,' he answered.

Colin nodded and Martin asked how they had made out with Olga.

'She soon confirmed our suspicions as to who she really is,' Colin said.

'What, she admitted she's Russian Intelligence?'

'No, but she could well be; she did that staring at the floor thing at the beginning.'

'GRU?'

'Or could be SVR, more spy-ish, but out of a choice of either, I reckon GRU,' Colin said.

'Why?'

'The staring at the floor thing seems more military, and GRU is military intelligence.'

'Okay, but what other suspicions did she confirm?'

'Just that she is Igor's wife.'

'And that she really doesn't like me,' Cath added.

'At least we can corroborate their relationship, now Igor has admitted he is her husband,' Colin said.

'Anything else?' Martin asked.

'Just that she is only his wife and not an operative. She claims not to know what his mission is, other than it was low key. She knows he has two automated calls in place and knows one has been activated, but she has no idea what the content is. She says the only person who can help us re that is Igor.'

'You believe her?'

Both Colin and Cath answered, 'No,' in unison.

'It does explain something though,' Martin said.

Cath and Colin turned to face him.

'I always thought he was too calm about us showing Volkov the photo. He knew it didn't matter. He was only playing along in order to protect his UK-based wife Olga.'

'He just went too far with his act, when he started slagging Volkov off.'

'Those bits were obviously real,' Cath said.

'Trying to add credibility to his words,' Martin added.

'Dear God; but for Igor overplaying his role and calling Volkov insane et cetera, he would probably have never told us about the first bomb,' Colin said.

Cath put her hand to her mouth, and said, 'Doesn't bear thinking about.'

'Though, you'd have thought that Volkov would have realised that his comments were all part of his ploy,' Martin added.

'Just shows how sensitive Volkov is to adverse remarks, even when he should know, or believe, that they are not meant,' Colin added.

'True, but I think it is more about Igor not wanting it known that he had been caught. Not yet anyway. But it gets better,' Martin said. 'I forgot to tell you, insult-wise, he added that "Volkov is a pencil-dick who can't keep it up". And before you ask, it's all recorded.'

All three laughed and then Colin said that he'd better organise some search teams. Martin said that he'd join Cath and have a go at Olga.

Chapter Seventeen

Colonel Pavel Popov was behind his desk wearing a dark blue suit. It came with his rank that he could choose not to wear his uniform some days, and he enjoyed these trappings of status, irrespective of how small they were. It promoted respect from others who could not enjoy such relaxations; added dignity to his position; respect was everything. Especially in Moscow, and more so in the Kremlin. There was a knock at the door, he glanced at the wall clock, it was getting late; 8 p.m. already, he wanted to go home but couldn't until he'd heard the update. He hoped it was son of Ivan at his door. He shouted an order to enter and in walked his staff officer, Sergeant Ivanov. Excellent. 'You have the update?'

'Yes Colonel.'

'Which is? Spit it out soldier.'

'Olga has been arrested.'

'For?'

'As far as we can tell just some immigration breach.'

'Good; for being Igor's wife, then.'

'It would seem so, Colonel.'

'Excellent.'

Sergeant Ivanov nodded politely.

'Pity we don't know what Igor has said, exactly.'

'He can be trusted, sir, he will stick to his brief, I feel sure.'

'But of course.'

'I trained with Igor; he is loyal in my humble submission, sir.'

'I'm just being nosy; it doesn't really matter what he says.'

'He can be very convincing; we used to play poker.'

'As I say, it doesn't really matter what he says, he can't say what he does not know.'

Sergeant Ivanov nodded again.

'He can only say what he does know, or should I say he can only say what we have told him.'

'Yes sir and I gave him his final instructions prior to deployment. He will be convincing because he firmly believes what he has been told.'

Popov smiled appreciatively and dismissed Ivanov, who turned and left. He had one phone call to make before he could head home. Everything was going to plan.

***

Colin got busy updating Rogers, the Home Sec. and CT Command, whilst Martin and Cath had a quick chat with Olga. He was starting to feel like he had too many chiefs and suggested to Rogers that he report to just one of them. But apparently, all three had already discussed this and had decided that they each wanted direct updates. Bothersome or what. He'd just ended the last call when Martin and Cath returned. 'You two weren't long.'

'Told you she really didn't like me,' Cath said as she took her seat.

'It's not that, Cath, she has had anti-interrogation training, no doubt,' Martin said.

'I'm guessing there is no more coming from her?' Colin asked.

'Says she is just his wife and has no knowledge of his "fact finding" mission. And she can't help us more. She is clearly trying to appear cooperative but without being so.'

'She's not just Igor's wife, that's for damn sure. She's taking the piss,' Colin said.

'Agreed,' Martin said.

'I've just come off the phone from the Holy Trinity and I am surer than ever that she is a player. Jeremy has confirmed that Russian assets only bring their wives in for cover on long term jobs.'

'Like an infiltration?' Martin asked.

'One example, but also when the job, even if short term, is of high level.'

'That fits our circs.' Martin added.

'But here is the thing, Olga came into the UK over a month ago, and Igor has only been here two or three weeks. So if they didn't travel together there is a reason for that.'

'I'm guessing that Jeremy thinks Olga is more than a dutiful Russian operative's wife?' Martin asked.

'He's not sure, but suspects so.'

Then Cath added, 'Do you want me to brief Gill at Five? As this is all home security stuff and we have a unilateral agreement.'

'Jeremy said he'd do it, he couldn't get off the party call quick enough. He's got a real boner on, as he reckons if Five had done some basic follow up after their day's surveillance, bla, bla, bla.'

'But with no intel to suspect anything in particular, they were nothing more than illicit strawberry pickers, what where Five supposed to do,' Cath said.

'He's obviously one of those blind-hindsight jockeys. I hope it doesn't blow back on your relationship with Gill,' Colin said.

Cath picked up the receiver from her secure desk phone and said, 'It won't if I get in first.'

'Do it; we'd be nowhere without the photos they took. And I reminded Jeremy of that too, but he wasn't listening,' Colin said, as Cath got busy on the phone.

Do you want me to have another chat with Igor?' Martin asked.

'Yep, and I reckon we should up the ante; perhaps mention the coming over to our side thing again a bit more.'

Martin nodded at Colin and then grinned, 'I've got an even better idea. These two think they are taking the piss out of us, well, maybe it's time we played them at their own game.'

Colin wasn't too sure what Martin meant, or indeed had planned, and wasn't overly sure that he wanted to know, so just nodded and watched him scurry off. Once alone he picked up the phone to give Superintendent Tom Wheatfield a ring; it was time to get busy with some more searches, just in case there was a second device. It didn't look like anyone was going home anytime soon.

Chapter Eighteen

Martin smiled as he re-entered Interview Room One. Igor was in his usual chair and Martin took a seat and said, 'Told you we'd get along, eventually.'

Igor looked up and smiled back. It was the first time he had let his face crack, a huge moment in the undercurrents between the two. Igor spoke first, another moment.

'I really can't give you the hide, and I can't work for you. I have done as you have asked. I just want my new passport. I don't even intend to use it, if that helps. I hope to make contact with my handlers and they will never be the wiser if they have accepted the bomb was a success.'

'Which they have,' Martin said, reconfirming the last point.

'I only want it in case I need it, a safety net. And I know you have to bring my wife into it, it's your job. That is if you even have her, which on reflection, I truly doubt, but you had me convinced for a while, I'll give you that.'

Martin was enjoying the new, more approachable Igor, but was also suspicious; was this also part of his training. Fake appeasement. He said, 'Oh, we have her alright. And I'm not won over that she is just your wife.'

'What does that mean?'

Martin decided to push his luck, even if he was enjoying this new détente. The thought of someone with a metal detector blowing themselves to smithereens made him shudder. The seriousness and heavy weight of expectation suddenly became very evident on his shoulders once more. 'We have her, she's not just your wife and even if we let you go, we may keep her; just for a while.'

Igor's face hardened. 'You bullshit me again, or try to. You haven't got her, so please stop this. You embarrass yourself.'

Martin wasn't sure, but he thought he detected something else in Igor's demeanour when considering Olga and her predicament. Concern. No, more that: worry, trepidation even. He pulled a remote control from his pocket and aimed it at the two-way mirror and pressed a button. The mirror went fuzzy before turning into a CCTV screen. 'Say hello to your beloved.'

Igor spun around to face the monitor as it cleared. The view was of another interview room which looked the same as this one. Olga was sat alone at a similar table. She looked up at her monitor as the live feed became clear. She looked surprised, and then her face toughened. Igor jumped to his feet and spun around to face Martin which took him by surprise. His face was full of aggression. 'GUYS, GUYS, GUYS, IN HERE, NOW,' Martin shouted.

The two guards rushed in and each slew to a halt at either side of the steel desk. This stopped Igor in his tracks who looked as if he was about to launch himself at Martin. His head spun on its axis between the two uniform cops. They were now the threat, and even if he got to one, the other would be on him.

'Sit down and calm down,' Martin said.

Igor hesitated a moment further and then complied, slowly. Martin asked the guards to remain in the room and they each nodded before backing off to either side of the door. Both keeping their gaze on Igor, both with one hand on their hips. Martin noted that Igor now looked almost embarrassed, as if he was angry that he had shown such a reaction to seeing Olga. It certainly didn't fit the narrative.

'Look, I'm sorry about that, I just didn't want my wife to know I was here. And now she is here, too, she will be mad with me. You understand?' Igor said.

Martin did, but didn't believe it. He didn't respond. After a few more seconds, Igor turned to look at the TV screen. Olga was just staring at him. Nothing was said between them. It was very surreal. Then Martin noticed a slight change in Olga's expression. He wouldn't even call it a nod, but some form of tacit instruction seemed to pass between them. As Martin was trying to decipher it, Olga suddenly spoke.

'Igor, listen and listen good; Промолчать,' she said.

Igor turned back around, jumped to his feet, and launched himself across the table directly at Martin.

Chapter Nineteen

'My God, you were lucky,' Cath said, and Martin knew that he was.

'Ditto,' Colin added.

They were sat in a quiet corner of the canteen, and Martin had just briefed Colin and Cath with the events of the last interview. 'I owe those two boys a pint or three,' he said.

'I know they are big lads, but I bet even they struggled,' Colin said.

'They didn't mess about, both Tasered him straight away.'

'I thought only one Taser was supposed to be used on a subject,' Colin said.

'I don't know the rules, but two worked a treat.'

'But he's still with us?' Colin asked.

'Yep, and it couldn't have worked out any better.'

'How come?' Cath asked.

'Once partially subdued, it meant that they could kick the oca out of him.'

'MARTIN,' Colin said, looking alarmed.

'They had to, to get the handcuffs on him. But he soon offered his hands up, so they stopped.'

Colin's flushed complexion started to subside. Then he asked, 'What did Olga say in Russian?'

'Just looked it up,' Cath said. 'It translates as "Say nothing".'

'How very old school,' Colin said.

'And not what you'd expect an innocent wife to say,' Cath added.

Colin muttered his agreement, and then Martin said, 'That's when I took my opportunity.'

They both looked at him curiously, and then he continued, 'I said that now he was cuffed it would make the next round of kicking much easier.'

'What?' Colin said.

'I was bluffing,' Martin said, and pulled the TV remote from his pocket. 'I would have muted the screen, but when I asked if

81

my guards wanted another go, they both eagerly nodded. One of their mates is having an operation on his pancaked nose today.'

'And?' Cath asked.

'It worked, she said she would play ball if we stopped and left Igor alone. And let them both go at the end of it.'

'That will never happen,' Colin said.

'Granted, but I gave her my word.'

'You'll never go to heaven, Martin Draker,' Cath said.

'Needs must and all that, as Jeremy would no doubt say,' Colin added.

'So this means she is an agent?' Cath asked.

'Yes, and she's effectively turned, it's just by how much, we don't yet know.'

'Excellent, work, Martin, truly exceptional. The Holy Trinity will be pleased,' Colin said.

'Just Igor to go now; once he's recovered,' Cath added.

Then Martin couldn't stop himself from grinning from ear to ear. He'd kept the best bit until last.

'What?' Cath asked.

'He's turned, too.'

'Never!'

'He had little choice once she went, and had to admit that they were both agents; a two-person team. But he'd seemed reluctant to talk about her, kept trying to make it sound as if she was a junior partner and knew little.'

'We need to know how little that amounts to,' Cath said.

Colin sat back and mused for a moment before he asked, 'Was it for real?'

'You mean are we being played, again?'

'Yeah.'

'I've been wondering the same, but the kicking thing was spontaneous by me, thinking on my feet, so to speak, and her reaction seemed immediate. Igor's response thereafter was one of resignation. Neither could have planned for that.'

'Incidentally, will the two uniform PCs be sound?' Colin asked.

'No problems, I had a chat afterwards and I'm happy mum's the word. If anything, they looked disappointed they weren't allowed round two.'

Then a uniformed officer made a beeline towards their table. Martin recognised him as the custody sergeant. Cath stood up and met him before he reached them and spoke to him. Colin beckoned Martin to move closer so they could continue, unheard.

'I guess the test will be the second bomb and the hide,' Colin said.

'I made sure she knew that - out of earshot of Igor - on the way back to her cell,' he replied.

'What did she say?'

'Now turned, she said there is no second bomb as the first one was successful.'

'God, I hope that's true, I've got every available cop out there searching,' Colin said, and then he glanced at his watch.

Martin instinctively did the same. It was nearing 10 p.m. now, and if the warning timescale was true, they had until noon the day after tomorrow. 'She maintains that only Igor had access to warning calls, of which, she now admits knowledge of their content. Claimed that they were pre-recorded and automated. Said we can ignore the threat.'

'Bloody easy for her to say,' Colin said.

'I've told her that we want the hide as an act of good faith.'

'What did she say?'

'I didn't get an answer as the guards brought Igor back into the custody area, after being checked over by the police surgeon. I need to get back in there and have a further chat with her.'

Then they both looked up as Cath returned to their table, smiling as the custody sergeant walked away. She must have heard Martin's last remark as she asked, 'What about the hide?'

'Just that we need to know where it is. I need to get back in there with her.'

'No need. The custody sergeant has passed a message for you, from Olga,' Cath said, as she looked at a piece of paper in her hand.

'Go on,' Martin said.

'She says that the hide is in a large field area on the outskirts of Ormskirk, next to a large tree. But Igor must never know she has given it up.'

Chapter Twenty

As it was fully dark, Colin said that it was pointless doing a full scale search of the given location until daylight. He therefore arranged for uniform to throw a loose outer cordon around the area and they would take it up at dawn. It also gave all three of them a chance for a few hours rest. Martin was looking forward to going home, but Colin insisted they stay local. He could be like that sometimes; he wasn't their boss when off-duty. And Martin really didn't fancy staying in the police headquarters training school barracks. He was sure Cath wouldn't want to, either. Plus, mentally he felt the need to get to his home surroundings, if only for a few hours. He would remonstrate with Colin as soon as he came off the phone. But when he did it was clear that he had booked them all in a city centre hotel, so he relented.

However, once in his room he was asleep in seconds and awoken a few hours later by his phone alarm in what felt like seconds; but he did feel suitably refreshed none-the-less.

He was now driving as Colin worked his phone next to him. Cath had headed to the police station so she could maintain a secure line with Gill at MI5 - who had thankfully provided a twenty-four hour contact number. Gill had told Cath that as soon as the hide was confirmed, and the MOD had done their bit, it would create a lot of public noise. Not least by the uniform police activity. That would allow the security service to monitor all mobile phone traffic in a tight geo-map around the location; just in case Olga and Igor had a local spotter in place. It made Martin shudder at the thought of the team being wider than the two they had in custody, and said so as soon as Colin finished his last call.

'You'd be surprised how many sympathisers the Russians have in place all over the UK. Not spies in the traditional sense of the word, but disaffected and disillusioned Brits ready to be told to "Watch a wood and inform on any unusual police activity" etc.'

Colin asserted. 'The tossers won't even realise the gravity of what they are doing; just blinded by a twisted ideology.'

'Who in their right mind, irrespective of how extreme their political views are, would agree to such acts?'

'You'd be surprised; but the recruiters are expert in their tactics.'

'Bunch of failed university politics student scum.'

'Not necessarily.'

'The next time I see someone buying a copy of The Morning Star, I'll look at them anew.'

'We need to be on the lookout for anyone turning up quickly and asking over-zealous questions.'

Martin nodded.

'Anyway, how did your quick chat with Olga, go? I appreciate that you didn't have long,' Colin asked.

'She confirmed what was on the note passed by the custody sergeant, but was quick to point out that she had never been to the hide. She could only describe it as Igor had described it to her. She claims that the whole mission was one designed to get a re-emerging IS to jump in and claim responsibility for the bomb. To direct NATO, and in particular, the UK's attention away from Russia.'

'I know the first part seems to have worked, but after what those bastards have done to Ukraine, it's a bit naïve to think anything will take the spotlight off anything they do from here on in.'

'Could be flawed thinking, or just arrogant reasoning,' Colin said. 'I had a quick chat with Counter Terror Command while you were talking to Olga, first thing. They said that the Russians had probably planned this whole thing some time ago, and would be reluctant to sack it in the light of any renewed view of its likely effectiveness. Apparently, they are like that; slow, or unwilling to adapt once a mission has been authorised.'

Martin considered what Colin had said as he negotiated the back roads of rural West Lancashire, which in any other circumstances would be an idyllic drive. And then said, 'Unless that's not the mission; or not just the mission.'

Colin turned to face Martin and said, 'The plot thickens, as everyone has once said. God forbid, but I keep feeling that we are still being played. We should keep awareness to the possibility, until we can prove otherwise.'

'Granted.'

'What was your impression of her under interview, compared with when you locked her up?'

'She has gone to a lot of trouble to affirm that she was just the supporting act and that Igor was the main event. Said she was giving up the hide as she just wanted it all to end.'

'You believe her?'

'The jury's still out, as everyone has also once said; but she did seem genuinely worried that Igor must never know that it was her who had told us.'

'Why all that "say nothing" bollocks in Russian, then?'

'I asked her that, she said it was what Igor would have expected, she said she was working to a script.'

'I reckon the last bit is more truthful than she probably intending by that remark.'

'Granted,' he said again, and then nodded at Colin's mobile phone on his lap and said, 'How did you get on with the MOD?'

'Fortunately, their barracks are in Cheshire, little more than an hour away with the blues and twos going, so they are en route. The super will be Tom Wheatfield - even though it's his day off - to keep it tight. And he is orchestrating local cops to keep the cordons in place until we get there, but they have not been told why, as such.'

'We can always say it's an old World War Two shell, or suchlike.'

'That's what sergeant Scanlon at Bomb Disposal said.'

Martin slowed down as they negotiated a railway level crossing at a hamlet named Hoscar, and as he accelerated away, he noticed a local with a dog waving his walking stick at him. He saw that Colin had seen him, too. 'I'm guessing that speeding drivers may be a local issue around these parts,' he said.

Martin then noted a number of handmade signs in the front of several gardens, reminding drivers that the speed limit was thirty miles per hour. He glanced at the car speedo as they edged above sixty. 'I've probably just spoilt that old boy's day,' Martin said, as he glanced in the rear view mirror to see that the dog walker was now stood in the roadway waving his stick above his head. 'Silly bugger will get himself run over if he's not careful.'

'He'll have more to worry about if that ordnance hide blows up,' Colin added.

For a moment, Martin envied the guy, nothing more to worry about, other than speeders passing through his one-horse hamlet; or should that be a one-dog town. As irate as the poor old guy was, Martin would eagerly swop his day for his. Then he shook himself from his daft musings as they approached their destination. It was only the brain taking five ahead of what was to come. He switched back on as he hit the brakes; he could see two livered police cars parked, so he pulled in behind them.

The Ring O' Bells pub was a large detached building set back from the road and had clearly been closed for some time. Half the car park, which bordered the east side of the pub, was fenced off and there was building work underway. It wasn't clear whether the place was being renovated or turned into something else, such as apartments. The road itself rose, just past the pub over a bridge. As soon as Martin and Colin were out of their car, he could see why. On the west side of the pub was a canal - the Leeds to Liverpool canal to be exact - which went under the road bridge. 'So far it's just as Olga described it,' he said.

From the car park at the front there was a narrow roadway which led to the canal. At the entrance stood a cop with a clipboard, they both identified themselves and signed in before continuing. As they walked down to the canal, the view opened up. Opposite were a number of luxury houses whose gardens bordered the opposite towpath. On the pub side, a number of barges were anchored.

'These will all need checking,' Colin said.

'I bet there is an empty one which no one knows much about,' Martin said.

'Just what I was thinking,' Colin added.

'What a great place to hide, observe, and extract from the hide to, etcetera.'

'I bet Igor made the bomb in one.'

'And what a great way to get about undetected, at ten miles an hour,' Martin added.

They were then joined by Tom Wheatfield who quickly briefed them that both inner and outer cordons were now in place.

'What about those barges?' Colin asked.

'All evacuated, and four of the five are accounted for and look straight, I've took the liberty of passing the details to Cath at your office for intel checks,' Tom answered.

Colin nodded, and then asked, 'What about the fifth one?'

'Appears empty and no one knows much about it. But one bloke reckoned he saw a huge guy entering it a couple of weeks ago.'

Martin and Colin exchanged a look, and Colin said, 'The boat will need preserving for forensics so we will need a physical guard. Plus, we will need to interview all the barge residents and show mug shots; especially to the guy you mentioned, but we will arrange that.'

Martin then scanned the area on their side of the canal. There was a farmer's field adjacent which opened up at the rear of the pub and ran for several hundred metres. A number of trees sporadically bridged the space between the towpath and the field, which itself was two or three feet lower down. But stood on its own in the field thirty metres from the canal, and a hundred metres ahead of them, was what Martin was looking for. 'There,' he exclaimed, as he pointed at the lone tree inside the field itself; which looked odd.

It was a traditional English Royal Oak tree, about twenty-five feet high and a similar spread covering the ground. It was a perfect mushroom shape and just as Olga had described. The three of them rushed over and slowed their pace as they approached.

'What exactly are we looking for?' Tom asked.

'Evidence that the ground has been disturbed, but let's keep our distance,' Colin said.

Tom nodded as they stopped several feet short. They then did a sort of slow May pole walk around the tree, and on the northern side hidden behind the trunk itself Martin saw something. 'Here', he shouted, as the other two joined him, and he gently knelt down about two metres away from the base. The grass was stood up a little. He noticed that they were leeside of a gentle breeze and that the surrounding grass was flattened one way, suggesting that the prevailing winds favoured one direction. But a square metre patch was fighting this and looked erect, albeit, the grass length was only three or four inches. The field was clearly pasture land, but Martin couldn't see any grazing animals around at the moment.

'What is it?' Colin asked.

'There is a square section of turf where the grass seems to be fighting the breeze, as if it's used to flowing the other way.'

'You mean turf has been lifted but placed back the wrong way around?' Colin asked.

'Exactly.'

'Wouldn't that be a basic error for the likes of our bomber?' Tom asked.

'Maybe, but maybe not. If the air was still the last time he lifted the grass, it may not have been obvious to him. He probably did it in the pitch black, too,' Martin added.

'Well, let's back off gently, we'll point it out to Sergeant Scanlon and let him decide,' Colin said.

All three of them gingerly backed off and made their way back to the pub.

'Is this where you think our bomber hid his kit?' Tom asked.

'It's where we think he got it from in the first place,' Colin answered.

Martin could see the pained expression of the super's face, so added. 'We think he got his ordnance from what is an old soviet era munitions hide.'

'Dear God. I've walked my dog across this field most days, and my kids used to play around here when they were younger. A lot of children still do.'

Chapter Twenty-one

Thirty minutes later the MOD Bomb Disposal van arrived. While they had been waiting Martin had spoken to two DCs from their unit who he trusted implicitly, and tasked them with interviewing the barge witnesses who were now en route to Ormskirk police station. They were briefed to tell them that they suspected a World War Two bomb was buried there. Sergeant Scanlon walked over to them, 'Hello chaps, rather disappointed to see your faces again.'

'Sorry we have to show them,' Martin said.

Colin took over and gave Sergeant Scanlon a quick rundown of where they were up to. He nodded and was joined by a corporal who didn't introduce himself. When Colin had finished Scanlon said, 'I'll be number one on this, as in lead expo and Corporal Jones here will be my number two.'

Martin had to stifle a grin, and wondered whether Jones was the corporal's real name or just an army nickname; he knew how much the army loved their nicknames. Even more so than the police. He turned to face the corporal - who didn't look anything like Corporal Jones from the old TV show, *Dad's Army* - and nodded to acknowledge him. He must have seen Martin stifling a smirk, as the look on his face was like thunder; as if daring him to make a comment about his name. Martin reckoned that it was no nickname; poor sod. He bet he couldn't wait to be promoted sergeant. Though, he would no doubt still be referred to as Corporal Jones, if only behind his back.

'Come on number two let's go and have a look,' Scanlon said, and then the two men slowly made their way towards the oak tree. Tom had disappeared, which left just Martin and Colin stood by the cordon next to the pub watching the two army experts enter the field.

'Brave bastards, aren't they?' Martin commented.

'Absolutely; they have to get it right every time. No margin for error, ever.'

Then Martin's phone beeped, it was an incoming call from Cath. He answered it and she said, 'Gill was spot on.'

'Go on.'

'GCHQ have intercepted a mobile, which has now gone dark, presumably destroyed, from within the geo-fence.'

'Bloody hell, that was quick.'

'Wasn't it. Apparently an outgoing call into a mobile somewhere in Moscow, which just said, "Police and Bomb Disposal are at my location", then the call ended.'

Martin instinctively looked around him, there were a handful of local people stood by an outer cordon at the roadside; all looked of retirement age. He was unsure if that meant anything. He then glanced across the canal at the posh houses whose gardens bordered the area. He told Cath about them and asked her to do intel checks on the addresses and the occupants.

'Will do, and I'll pass the details on to Gill. She reckons they have a list of some known sympathisers, so with any luck, a local will be on it,' she said.

Martin thanked her and ended the call. He then turned to Colin and updated him.

'I hope we can identify the treacherous bastard; probably some middle-class sycophant who has never seen the inside of a cell before,' Colin said.

'Be lovely if we can change that,' Martin said, before turning to the front again, just in time to see Sergeant Scanlon walking back towards them. Corporal Jones was still at the tree on his hands and knees.

A minute later, Sergeant Scanlon was back with them. 'Yep, this is the place alright. A munitions hide.'

'Excellent,' Colin said. 'Do you get many of these?'

'You'd be surprised how often they pop up, certainly not infrequent. But this is not a soviet one.'

'How do you mean?' Martin asked.

'Too new, and not very well buried, though, by the look of the box it has been here some time, just not decades.'

'Okay, but what does it contain?' Colin asked.

RED HERRING

'The stainless steel box was used to store explosives, small arms and ammunition, probably. The box was under the sod you identified, and we have checked that there are no surprises attached to its base before lifting it.'

'Crikey, you've got it out already?' Martin said, and then instinctively looked across the field towards the tree. He could see the steel box on the ground with its lid open. 'And you've got it open already.'

'Normally, we'd just blow it up, but I knew that you were concerned that there might be some intel inside, so we decided to have a peek.'

'Couldn't the lock be booby-trapped?' Colin asked.

'Fortunately, it was unlocked, and after having cleared its edge, we backed off and gave it a low velocity prod with no problems.'

'I must have missed that, I was on the phone,' Martin said.

'I saw you back away, but couldn't see clearly what you were doing as the tree was in the way,' Colin added.

'Well, there is good news and bad news,' Sergeant Scanlon said. 'The box is empty of ordnance, but there is a zip lock plastic folder with documents inside, some of which are clearly passports. And this is clearly a new addition.'

'Excellent, thanks sergeant, and we'll need the box recovering for forensic examination once you give us clearance,' Colin said.

'Sure, my number two is just retrieving the folder.'

Martin and Colin then both instinctively looked back on the scene and could see that Corporal Jones had moved the box up onto the towpath next to the canal. The lid was still open and he had donned his protective helmet and gloves. Martin watched fascinated as the corporal stood over the opened box and then pressed his chest. Immediately, Scanlon cupped a hand to his ear and moments later pressed his own chest and said, 'Roger, received; proceed,' before he then turned to face Martin and Colin. 'The zip lock folder is loose in the box and not connected in any way to anything so we are about to retrieve it.'

'Meaning there are no booby-traps attached to that either?' Colin asked.

Scanlon nodded. Martin watched intently as the corporal bent down and with both hands carefully lifted the A4 sized clear plastic envelope out of the box. He stood up straight and put one foot forward as he was about to walk towards them. Then he stopped in his tracks, still with one leg stuck out in front of him. He slowly lifted his head up. He was stood one-legged on the towpath right next to the water's edge. He then shouted, 'TAKE COVER.' But no one did. All three men were cemented to the spot, albeit from a hundred metres away, staring at the corporal. He then slowly lifted both his arms up to shoulder height and in one swift movement he let go of both sides of the folder at the same time. In the second or two that followed, the zip lock document case fell towards the floor as the corporal jumped feet first into the canal.

Martin watched the eerie scene as gravity acted on both the package and the corporal - almost in a synchronised way, like some weird Olympic event. The corporal quickly disappearing below the water's surface, and as his head was starting to enter the canal, the plastic document carrier hit the tow path.

It exploded on impact, and all three men hit the deck as a shower of earth flew in all directions, covering all three in debris as they landed on the ground.

RED HERRING

Chapter Twenty-two

Colin had rarely seen Martin so animated. Truth be known, he was more than rattled himself. The bomb had been a small incendiary device trigged by a mercury tilt switch - and according to Sergeant Scanlon, it was designed to destroy the document holder and its contents, and little else. Not that Corporal Jones could have known that when he spotted the trigger. In fact, the canal proved to be more of a threat than the bomb. It took all three of them to help the poor man out of the water before he drowned. Wearing full kit and a ballistic helmet, he almost looked comical as he fought to keep his head above the water. And he was one seriously pissed off expo when they did manage to free him from his would-be watery grave.

They were now back at Preston nick, and Colin was stood in the anteroom to Interview Room Two looking through the two-way mirror as Martin marched into the room on a mission. Colin had made a management decision not to temper Martin. It was time to up the ante as they were definitively being played. He just hoped his sergeant-at-arms, and friend, didn't go too far. On the journey back, Cath had rang with an update from Gill. The bang had been reported straight away, into the same Moscow handset from a different UK mobile number, which had gone dark again. As had the Moscow mobile. Gill had told Cath that both would be burners, and would probably not be used again. It made the task of tracing the watching sleeper all the more difficult, particularly, as Five were unaware of any known sympathisers in the Ormskirk area.

Colin had asked if they had pinpointed where the second call had come from.

Cath had answered, 'Well, that's the weird thing; Gill said it didn't actually come from our geo-area. Once they had the Moscow number from the first intercept, they monitored that in case it popped up again, and it did, but the incoming from the UK was not where the first one came in from, but from Manchester this time.'

'Manchester?' he'd said, perplexed.

'Weird, I know, but Gill said it didn't necessarily mean there is another sleeper active.'

'I bloody hope not,' he'd answered.

'Just that they can bounce a number around from many devices to disguise where it originates from, a bit like Wi-Fi's VPN, but a bit more elaborate.'

Colin could only hope that Igor didn't have an entire network out there. He leant forward and turned up the volume from the interview room live feed as he watched Martin sit down opposite a startled looking Olga.

'What the fuck are you playing at?' Martin started with.

'I've no idea what you mean. Didn't you find the hide?' Olga asked.

'Oh, we found it alright, along with your little present.'

Olga didn't answer and Colin had to admit that she looked genuinely surprised.

Martin went on to explain.

'Oh my God, look I'm sorry, I didn't know, was anyone hurt?'

'The explosives officer would have been but for his quick reactions. I hope you are not saddened?'

Olga threw both arms up into the air and said, 'Look, why would I give you the details of the hide if I knew it was booby-trapped?'

'To set us up. For a laugh. Who knows?'

'Please, I can see that you are rightly upset, but it would not serve my purpose, would it? I gave you details as I knew them because I want this to end. I want out of here. All this is not my doing. It's all Igor, he's the mission lead.'

Martin didn't answer straight away, and Colin thought Olga had made a valid point. Then he said, 'Okay, you've made a plausible point - unless of course this is all part of some wider plan?'

'It's not, I promise.'

'And you seem very quick to drop it all on Igor; not such a loyal supporting spouse are you?'

It was Olga's turn not to answer. And then she asked, 'Did you manage to retrieve any munitions; I'm gathering that the incendiary device in the document holder didn't ignite them?'

'Why do you gather that?'

'Well, presumably the explosion would have been far, far worse than you have described.'

Martin nodded, as if to acknowledge the point.

'So did you get the stuff?'

'No, but you knew that.'

'Why, was it stolen?'

'Interesting you ask that.'

'Look, I gave you the details to prove that there is no second bomb, so it should have had the stuff in it.'

Martin didn't react.

'Was it empty?' Olga said, almost pleading.

'You knew the location, and you knew it was empty.'

'No I didn't, maybe Igor moved the munitions. I keep telling you that there is no second bomb. The call was an automated one set up by Igor; he probably couldn't cancel it because you arrested him.'

Martin then stood up.

'You must ask Igor about where he has hidden his explosives; he must have a new hide.'

'Oh, I intend, too.'

'But remember, he mustn't know I have told you about this hide, and before you ask, it is the only one he ever mentioned to me.'

'What would he do if he found out?'

'He'd kill me.'

'God forbid that there is a second bomb, but if there is; our deal is off.'

'There isn't, I promise you.'

'We still need to track the stuff down though, whether made up ready, or still stored loose elsewhere.'

'You need to ask Igor.'

'So you keep saying,' Martin finished with, and then walked out of view as he left the room.

Colin's phone rang, it was Cath, he answered it, just as Martin walked into the anteroom. 'Boss, can you come back to the office ASAP?'

'Sure, what is it?'

'Things just got worse; a lot worse.'

***

Colonel Pavel Popov was sat at his favourite pavement café in central Moscow. He'd kept his coat on over his civilian clothes as there was a chilly breeze in the air. There was plenty of room inside the premises but he preferred the outside tables. He glanced at his watch; it was two in the afternoon which was midday in the UK. He looked up on hearing footsteps to see his friend and colleague Artem approach. A smartly dressed man in his fifties and a senior intelligence officer in the SVR. 'Good to see you again,' Popov said, as he gestured towards the empty seat opposite him. It was debatable who outranked who, but Popov always liked to assume that he was the ranking officer. Artem clearly didn't agree as he took a different seat from an adjoining table and turned it to face Popov. He smiled before calling the waiter over and ordering coffee for them both.

'Likewise, and thank you, though I haven't got too long, so forgive me if I have to leave my coffee. You know how things are,' Artem said.

Popov did, and smiled in understanding. 'Everything seems to be going well.'

'Indeed, but can I ask who else knows about Olga?'

'Only my staff officer,' Popov answered. 'Even Igor thinks she is GRU.'

'Good, he will therefore be convincing.'

'That is what we thought.'

'Are you still okay about Igor?'

Popov thought before he answered, and then said, 'He is a good operative, I would like him back,' and then he shrugged his shoulders and added, 'But the mission comes first.'

'Remind me to stay your friend,' Artem said, and then both men laughed as the waiter returned with their coffees.

Once the waiter had left and both men had taken a sip of their beverages, Popov asked, 'What of the low level asset?'

'Done what has been asked.'

'A shame that they may be expendable, especially after all the effort and loyalty,' Popov added.

'There may be a way to leave them alone, for now. It would be a lot to give away. But as you say, "The mission comes first".'

'A dirty business,' Popov said.

Artem smiled, took a sip of his brew, stood, and said. 'I have to go. I will be in touch.'

Popov nodded a reply and then watched his associate walk away.

Chapter Twenty-three

Martin and Colin rushed into their office and made sure that the door was firmly closed behind them. Cath was at her desk sat up straight all business-like.

'So what have we got?' Colin asked.

Martin was praying that a second bomb hadn't gone off.

'That was Gill from Five. The technicians at Thames House have been working flat out on the two warning calls trying to illicit as much information as they can from them,' Cath said.

'I thought sophisticated voice distortion had been used,' Colin said.

'It had, and initially they were just looking for background noises that may have given a clue as to where the calls were recorded, if not sent from.'

'Any luck?' Martin asked.

'Apparently not, they had been professionally done in a "sterile audio environment" to quote them. So they started playing around with the frequencies. We've not heard the tapes, but apparently they were from a male voice who spoke very slowly. Initially, they thought that was for two reasons: one, to ensure that the message contents were clearly understood by the recipient, and two, as English appeared not to be the caller's first language, they were naturally speaking slower as they concentrated on enunciating their words legibly.'

'Makes sense,' Colin said.

Martin grinned at Colin's unintended pun.

'That was until they played around with the speed.'

'What happened then?' Martin asked.

'They soon realised that the tape may have appeared to be pre-recorded - but that the speed *had* been altered - so in fact, was not.'

'Why alter the speed?' Martin asked.

'Well, once they were happy they had altered the tapes to the correct speed, as in the natural speed of the speaker, they made their *first* breakthrough. The caller isn't male, the voice is female. It's been slowed down to give it a male sound.'

'Are they sure?' Colin asked.

'Yep, and they definitely weren't pre-recorded.'

'Explain?' Colin asked.

'The distortion device itself slowed the diction down to a predetermined speed as the caller spoke through it.'

'Could have still been pre-recorded,' Colin replied.

'Apparently not, according to the boffins. And they are certain that the second call was made live when they received it. That was shortly before we arrived at Olga's apartment,' Cath said, aiming her comments at Martin.

'The smashed up phone in the bin,' he said.

'Exactly, and do you remember the sound of the cistern flushing as we knocked on the door?'

'I do, I wondered if it was drugs at first.'

'Probably the SIM card.'

'And the distortion device,' Martin added.

'So it has to be Olga who made that second call, at least,' Colin said. 'If not both.'

'She'll no doubt deny it,' Martin added.

'She can deny it all she wants; she made both calls; they have compared her real voice, and have managed to remove 70% of the distortion. It might be Russia's top tech, but our techies are better. The voice match is beyond doubt.'

'Well done, Cath, that's great work,' Colin said.

'Granted, but not by me.'

'I knew she was playing us; now we have some real ammo to go in hard and find out once and for all what is really going on,' Martin said, as he turned towards the door.

'Do you want me to come in with you?' Colin asked.

'Probably best you don't,' Martin answered.

'Why, what are you going to do?'

'Probably best you don't know,' Martin said, 'and probably best you don't watch from the viewing room, either.'

'Christ, should I be worried?'

'No, but she should be; I've had enough of this merry-go-round.'

'Go on; tell us what are you going to do?' Cath asked.

Martin stopped and considered for a moment, and then said, 'Come with me and you'll find out. She doesn't like you, we can use that. Just follow my lead.'

'You got it, Skipper,' Cath said, as she jumped from behind her desk.

It made Martin smile; she'd never called him that before. He glanced at Colin and noticed that his complexion was turning pink, and said, 'Don't worry, boss, what you don't know about, you can't have been a party to.'

'Just don't get us all sacked. But do what you have to do, as this could mean that the second bomb could be back on, and we now have less than twenty-four hours.'

'I know, she's been playing us all along with misdirection and deflection,' Martin said.

'She's the one in charge here; Igor's just the muppet,' Cath threw in.

Martin and Colin both nodded. Then Martin led the way out the office and Cath rushed after him.

Once inside the anteroom to Interview Room Two, he told her what he wanted her to do as they awaited Olga from custody.

Five minutes later all three of them were sat around the steel desk. Martin noticed that Olga's body language seemed to have stiffened on seeing Cath. She clearly didn't like her, but he had no idea why; maybe it was just an alpha female versus an alpha female thing, but it didn't matter. As agreed with Cath, Martin would do most, if not all the questioning and Cath would just look at Olga; weigh up her nonverbal responses and genuinely irritate her by her presence.

Ignoring Cath, Olga looked at Martin and asked, 'Did you ask Igor about the ordnance?'

'Not yet.'

'How will you tell him that you have found the first hide?'

'We'll think of something, it shouldn't be too hard.'

'You promised not to blow me out.'

102

'Interesting choice of words.'

'What do you mean?'

'I'll come to that, but firstly, we know that one or both of you are playing us.'

'Igor will be, not me.'

'My money is on you.'

'And mine,' Cath added.

Olga gave Cath her death stare, before returning her gaze to Martin. And this unexpectedly, gave Martin a glimpse into the soul of the real Olga. She had unwittingly dropped her façade in that petulant moment. It showed a scheming, intelligent and dangerous person lurking within. 'We are going to speak to Igor shortly, tell him about the hide we unearthed, and ask him several things.'

Olga didn't respond, and Martin pulled a remote control from his pocket and aimed it at the two-way mirror. A second later it flickered to life showing the inside of Interview Room One. It was positioned slightly behind Olga and she didn't turn around, not until the audio kicked in. Then she looked in time to see Igor being placed in his usual chair by the Rugby players, who then left him on his own. He didn't look at his mirror confirming that the feed was one-way, at the moment.

'What is going on?' Olga asked, turning back to face Martin again.

'Funnily enough, that's our question to you? Well, to both of you really.'

'I've no idea what stupid game you are playing.'

'Oh you will; and it's you who is playing the game.'

Olga just shrugged her shoulders.

'It may help your recall if I tell you that we know.'

Olga sighed, and said, 'Okay, I'll play your daft game; know what?'

'Know that it was you who placed the two warning calls.'

Olga threw her head back and laughed.

'You see, your top of the range voice distortion devices might be considered cutting edge in Russia, but our experts thought it was rather quaint. And as soon as we have the cleaned up version, we can play it to you, if you like?'

'You make all this up, play what you like.'

'Or perhaps we should play it to Igor, he'd like that wouldn't he?'

Olga then gave Martin the death stare, it was his first; he must be touching a nerve. 'But first we are going to have a chat and just tell him that it was you who rang in the warning calls, and probably you who "blew him out" - to use your phrase - when you reported a suspicious male which led to his arrest. See how all that sits with him. We'll leave the monitor on so you can watch his reaction. You won't have to take our word for things.'

'Say to him what you want, he'll not believe you.'

Martin then stood up and Cath followed his lead. And then he added, 'And if that doesn't work, then we can arrange a reunion.'

Looking less sure now, Olga said, 'What reunion?'

'I'll put you together in the same room; I know how passionate you two can get when you are alone.'

'He'll not believe you.'

'He'll believe you gave us the hide location at the very least, or he will when I show him these.' Martin then opened up his mobile phone and quickly scrolled through a few photographs he had taken of the hide at the Ring 'O Bells, ensuring that Olga could see them.

'You're bluffing; he'll kill me.'

'Why the fuck should I care about you. And when it comes to killing, you started it. Incidentally, the maintenance guy you slaughtered was called Simon Devlin; he had a wife, a daughter and a grandkid. So why should I give a damn what Igor will do to you. But we'll start off by letting you see his initial reaction on screen, and then we'll come back for you.'

'I'm going to enjoy this,' Cath said, and they both headed to the door.

'WAIT,' Olga shouted. 'What do you want to know?'

'What the hell is really going on would be a start; but I guess that can keep. Firstly, we need to know where all the outstanding ordnance is. You tell me now where that is, and I mean all of it, and I won't "blow you out" to Igor; and I'll even cancel the reunion. You've got ten seconds.'

Olga didn't reply for a moment or two, Martin could almost hear the cogs going around in her head, as he counted down from ten in his.

As he reached three, Cath grabbed hold of Martin's arm in an unscripted moment and said, 'Come on, you've given that ice bitch enough chances. She'd dreaming up her next bullshit line now; I can see it on her face.' She then physically pulled Martin towards the door, so much so, that he nearly lost his balance. Cath was very convincing. And by the look on Olga's face, she clearly believed it, and that was all that mattered.

'Okay,' Olga said, and then she told them what they had asked for, but it wasn't what Martin had expected to hear. Not by a long way.

Chapter Twenty-four

Martin ran into their office closely followed by Cath. Colin was at his desk and looked up as they rushed in. Martin had to take a second to catch his breath before he spoke. Cath made straight to her secure desk phone to presumably speak to Gill at MI5.

'Looks like you have news,' Colin said.

'Could say that,' Martin said, as his breathing started to return to normal.

'The missing munitions?'

'Yep, and unfortunately, they are made up.'

'So there is a second bomb; the bastards.'

'She's still laying it all on Igor, but we can chat later about that. You won't believe where it is.'

'Where?'

'Preston railway station.'

'That's not possible. That place was fully searched after the first bomb exploded.'

'The perfect place then, as in the last place we would look.'

'I get that, but I spoke to the MOD after the first went off, and they searched everywhere in case there was another device linked to the first.'

'Not their fault. You'll understand when you see where it is.'

'Okay, you can fill me in en route; I'll ring Sergeant Scanlon at Bomb Disposal while you drive.'

Martin nodded and grabbed a set of car keys from the hooks on the wall.

'Can you ring the super Tom Wheatfield for me?' Colin asked Cath, who was talking on the phone. She nodded an acknowledgement as she talked; she was clearly through to Gill at MI5. 'And I'll ring the Holy Trinity,' Colin added, more to himself than anyone else.

Five minutes later and Martin was driving like Lewis Hamilton's faster brother, while Colin held onto the passenger side grab rail and spoke to the MOD with his mobile in his other hand. He'd already radioed Preston Communications Room to get the outer cordon in place as soon as possible. As they drove up Corporation Street Martin had to slow as a uniform cop was busy closing the road with ticker tape. He quickly flashed his warrant card out of the driver's window before accelerating again. If the original intel was correct they had twenty-four hours, but Martin knew they couldn't rely on that; no matter how much Olga promised that it was true. Her confession about the second device left a litany of further unanswered questions, but they would have to wait.

He drew up outside the Fishergate entrance where the taxis' drop-off and pick-up egress was. They both ran to the station's main entrance and were met by Charlie the station manager. Martin could hear the tannoy on a loop telling everyone to clear the station.

'This has to be a mistake,' Charlie said.

'Only wish it was,' Martin said. 'Can we ensure that Platform One is cleared first?'

'Sure,' Charlie replied, turned and left.

While Martin and Colin caught their breath, Martin asked how Sergeant Scanlon had taken the news.

'Defensively, very defensively, until I iterated your comments, but I told him I didn't know the exact location myself, which I don't. Didn't want to keep him on the phone in a debate. Said we'd show him as soon as they arrived.'

Martin nodded.

'So where is it?' Colin asked.

'Built into a wall. This is why no normal search would have found it.'

'How did they manage that?'

'She said she didn't know, just that Igor had done it, probably when he placed the other one. She claimed he told her about it briefly. She also said it was a much bigger bomb than last time.'

'None of this makes any sense.'

'I know.'

'So if the first bomb was a success, they were just going to leave the second?'

'Totally improbable, and as you say, it makes no sense.'

'While we await the MOD I'll have to give the Holy Trinity a ring, give me something I can tell them by way of a part explanation,' Colin said.

Martin really didn't envy Colin making those calls. But before he could answer, they both had to stand aside as members of the public came rushing out the station. After the events of the other day here, no one needed telling to evacuate, twice. 'What I can tell you is that I truly believe that she is shit-scared of Igor. Knowing we had worked out that it was she who had made the warning calls was a good softener, but the sickener was when I said she could watch Igor's reaction via the CCTV as I told him it was her who had betrayed him. I also hit her with a promise to put them together for a reunion.'

Colin turned to look at Martin, and said, 'And would you have put them together in the same interview room or cell?'

'Good question. I would have certainly had to go through the motions, right up to marching her down the corridor to the room he was in. But it's moot for now. Though, we can still use the threat to find out what the hell is really going on, once we are done here.'

'As long as she still believes it,' Colin added. 'You've done brilliantly Martin. Not to be underestimated.'

'A team game as you said; we've all done okay.'

Colin nodded before taking his phone from his pocket, taking a deep breath and wandering away from the background noises of the people fleeing, to make his calls. As he did so, it gave Martin a moment to reflect. He was surer that ever that Igor believed the bombings to be his mission, and nothing more. Probably always planned a second blast, specifically designed to have maximum casualties after the first, smaller device had done its limited worst. Probably intended to increase the public's terror that way. People would wonder if there weren't more bombs. And if so, where and when. And as time went by, the threat of the unknown would add to the panic, as would the pressure the public would put on politicians. That's how terrorism worked. But this didn't explain what Olga was up to. Or was he overthinking it. Maybe she did just want out. Maybe she was just Igor's wife supporting the mission, which is why she had broken. Not an agent as such. Or maybe, something entirely different was in play. If so, he had absolutely no idea what.

***

Colonel Popov was a passenger in a departmental car driven by his staff officer Boris Ivanov. They pulled up in a quiet suburban street in a residential area on the outskirts of Moscow. The buildings were mainly apartment blocks built long ago in the soviet era. Therefore they all looked the same, with their drab stained concrete frontages. Some were still state-owned, but many were now privately possessed. Popov couldn't tell which were which. As far as he was concerned the whole district was one big shithole, and he wanted out of there as quickly as he could. 'And you say the widow had returned to her hovel,' he asked Ivanov.

'Yes sir,' Ivanov started with, as he nodded to a black van parked in front of them. 'They watched her enter thirty minutes ago and she remains in there alone.'

'Let's get this over with then,' Popov said, as he reached for the door handle.

Both men were dressed in civilian clothes, though Popov's were a lot smarter; he was dressed in a long flock coat covering his smart casuals beneath. The overcoat alone cost more than the old dear would earn in a month.

They crossed the road to the block they were interested in, and three men alighted from the van to join them. They were all dressed similar to Ivanov, jeans and sweaters with roll-up necks. Ivanov told one of the men to stand guard and prevent anyone else from entering the building. He told the other two to follow them, but to wait in the corridor outside the flat until they were called inside.

The apartment they were after was thankfully, on the ground floor not far from the building's entrance. Popov had little desire to climb several flights of stairs and even less desire to use the piss-drenched elevator; or so he imagined it would be.

The old dear answered the door and Ivanov - as arranged - identified himself and did all the speaking. Popov had no desire to enter into a conversation with the old hag. He was merely there for effect.

The old woman was in her sixties but looked eighty. She wore the dowdy clothes of a low-paid worker, with a nylon apron on top. This almost made Popov smile, her clothes were hardly worth protecting. Ivanov showed the woman his identification and she invited them inside. Once in her kitchenette, Boris told her that their visit was concerning the national interest. She put her hand over her mouth and looked stunned.

'So you see I can't explain everything, but you must come with us for your own safety,' Ivanov said.

'But why? I am of no interest to anybody. And I am a loyal supporter of our motherland.'

'This is why the motherland wants to protect good comrades such as you.'

'Protect me from what?'

'As you know, your daughter does important work.'

'I know she works for the state, she is working away at the moment.'

Ivanov nodded towards Popov and said, 'We know, the Colonel here is her superior.'

The old lady got to her feet from the kitchen chair she had just slumped on, and replied, 'A Colonel, here in my humble home. My daughter must be doing very important work.'

'She is, and is valued, though her work may take a long time, but for now, she wants us to make sure you are well. Not that we have received any direct threats or the like; it's just a precaution, you understand,' Ivanov finished with.

The old woman nodded, though Popov was certain that she understood nothing.

'Where will we go?'

Ivanov turned towards the front door and nodded, and in walked the two men from the corridor. He then turned back to face the woman and said, 'We will take you to a nice resort on the Black Sea coast, where you will have your own private villa for a few weeks and everything you could possibly need. These gentlemen will look after you.'

'Oh my, that sounds too grand for me. And what of my work?'

'Your job will be safe and waiting for you on your return.'

'My daughter must be a very important woman, I had no idea.'

Ivanov nodded a reply.

'Whenever I ask her what it is she actually does, she just says that she is an analyst.'

'Do you need any help packing?' Ivanov asked.

'No, it won't take me long. I've never been on holiday to the Black Sea before.'

Ignoring her, Ivanov gave their farewells and then they left her with the two other officers, as she headed towards the flat's only bedroom. Popov couldn't wait to get outside and breathe in some fresh air.

'In fact, I've never been on any holiday before,' he heard the old nag add as he and Ivanov headed through the front door.

Chapter Twenty-five

Martin watched as the Royal Logistics Corp Bomb Disposal wagon pulled up near to the station's main entrance. Sergeant Scanlon alighted and marched straight towards Colin and him, while his corporal disappeared to the rear of their truck.

'I'm getting sick of the sight of you two, no offence,' Scanlon said, as he arrived where Martin and Colin were stood.

'None taken, and likewise,' Martin retorted with.

'So what have we got?' Scanlon asked.

Martin then quickly told him what he knew.

'Thank fuck for that, the Major would have had our bollocks on his desk in a Newton's Cradle had it been any different. I told the station manager to keep all the bins sealed for seven days, and to ring me if any were disturbed.'

Martin couldn't supress a grin as he thought of one of those executive toys duly adorned. He might have to nick the expression and use it himself.

'I'll be Number One, and my corporal will be Number Two, we'll go in and have a quick recce first.'

Colin and Martin both nodded.

'Come on Jonesy,' Scanlon shouted over his shoulder, and was quickly joined by Corporal Jones. Martin and Colin nodded a greeting as he jogged past them with a rucksack on his back.

***

Sergeant Scanlon quickly prepped Corporal Jones with what DS Draker had just told him.

'Do you want to kit up first?' Jones asked.

'No, let's take a quick peek and assess, first.'

Jonesy nodded and Scanlon led the way.

Five minutes later, they approached Platform One of an eerily quiet, deserted railway station. The atmosphere was surreal. Scanlon was relived to notice the bins all looked sealed but wanted to make sure that they didn't just look sealed, and turned to Jonesy, 'Can you check the bins and I'll have a closer look at the wall.'

RED HERRING

Jonesy nodded and they parted. The wall was in the centre of the platform structure separating platform one and two. It was made up of various things such as a shop and café, and a toilet block. But as he progressed along the lengthy platform, the walled area became more prevalent the further along he walked. He was re-joined by Jonesy who reported that none of the bins had been tampered with, so they could ignore those. He joined in with Scanlon's search, taking the lower half of the wall, while Scanlon perused the upper part; easier on the back and privileges of rank.

They were nearly at the end of the platform when Jonesy came to a halt and said, 'Here.'

Scanlon bent down to join him and could see that the mortar between the bricks was a lighter colour than elsewhere. It covered an area about two metres wide and one metre high. Scanlon took a metal spike from his pocket, similar in size to a ballpoint pen and gently offered it to the edge of where the mortar changed colour. Firstly, on the darker stuff; this kicked back. It was as it appeared, old, hard and solid.

He then gently touched the outermost edge of the lighter coloured grout and the point immediately gave way. It was fresh, very fresh; two or three days' old fresh, he guessed. It had hardened some, but the spike cut into it with minimal effort. It may even have been a weak mix; which told its own story. He looked at Jonesy and raised an eyebrow. There was no way they would have found this had the intel update from the cops not driven them there. He quickly tested the rest of the mortar in a similar way at several randomly chosen places. He was happy that the whole 2 x 1 metres area was fresh, albeit with the original bricks having been replaced as they had been originally set, no doubt.

'Do you want to kit up, now?' Jonesy asked.

'In a minute, let's have a proper look first.'

Jonesy nodded and took the rucksack from his back and asked, 'X-ray or probe?'

'Probe first, then we can X-ray if there is something there,' Scanlon said. He touched the first spot he had used his spike on and his fingers confirmed the pliability of the grout.

Jonesy passed him a probe which was a slender device, not unlike his spike, but longer with a glass lens at one end and a wire at the other. The wire was connected to a small handheld device with a screen which Jonesy was holding. Scanlon looked back at the device as Jonesy played with its controls, the screen suddenly lit up with a green hue showing a wandering view of the outer wall. 'Ready?' he asked.

'Ready,' Jonesy replied. It might have seemed like he was asking the obvious, but in their game everything had to be confirmed and nothing was ever left to supposition.

Slowly, and very gingerly Scanlon pushed the business end of the probe though the soft mortar in a twisting motion like a hand drill action. He did not want to push a dollop of the stuff through into the unknown. As soon as he was in, he pulled a lever on the side of the device to make it swivel in all directions to give Jonesy a 360 view of things.

'Stop,' Jonesy said.

Scanlon did.

'Ninety degrees right.'

Scanlon moved the probe head accordingly.

'Stop,' he said, again.

'Still, still, still.'

Scanlon held the device as stably as he could.

'Recording, recording, recording…and ended. You can withdraw now, Sarge.'

Scanlon slowly did so in a mirror movement to that which he had done on the way in. As soon as he saw the end of the probe fully out of the wall, he stated, 'Clear.'

He then jumped to his feet as Jonesy played with his monitor's controls, and asked, 'So what have we got?'

'We've got a secondary alright, a big one with a timer on top. No sign of any trip devices or motion switches, just a big fuck off bomb with a timer trigger attached.'

Scanlon leaned in to get a good view as Jonesy replayed the short recording to him. It was as he had described it. When he had watched it a couple of times, Jonesy asked him how he wanted to proceed.

'We'll fully kit up, and used the robot to fire a low velocity round into the lower wall underneath it. Confirm that there are no motion, or other anti-handling triggers, and if not, we'll slowly remove the bricks and deal with it.'

'Roger,' Jonesy said.

Both of them then hurriedly made their way out of the station.

Chapter Twenty-six

Martin watched the entrance avidly awaiting the MOD chaps, while poor Colin had wandered off to a quiet corner to ring the Holy Trinity. Martin glanced at him as Colin finished his call and ambled back towards him. 'How did it go?' he asked, as he arrived.

'Be bloody easier having to ring just one of them, let alone play to their politics; like walking on eggshells.'

'What do you mean?'

'Big egos having a dick waving contest, and the one with the biggest dick is the one without a dick.'

'The Home Sec?'

'Yeah.'

Martin grinned at his boss; Colin wasn't one for the funnies normally, Martin liked to think that that role sat at detective sergeant rank. This only reinforced how frustrated Colin must be feeling. 'I love it when you get driven down to my level,' he said.

Colin laughed, which Martin hoped helped ease the pressure on him a little. 'I've got Susan Jennings - Counter Terror command - being held back on a short lead by the Home Sec. - Miranda Daniels - who in turn clearly has Jeremy from MI6 nibbling at her ankles. And then the chief constable, Don Rogers is clearly feeling that his nose is being pushed back.'

'I guess we should be grateful it's not the Holy Quartet.'

'MI5?'

'It is a home UK threat after all.'

'I get the impression that the Home Sec. is speaking on their behalf. At least we have a direct back channel into them via Gill from Cath.'

'Small mercies.'

'Yes, but they want a full briefing from us after we've dealt with the immediate threat here.'

'Sounds like fun.'

'And you are invited to this party whether you want it or not.'

RED HERRING

Martin inwardly groaned and was about to attempt a witty response, but his attention was drawn to the entrance as Sergeant Scanlon and Corporal Jones emerged at pace.

The two MOD officers quickly briefed them and then set to work unloading the robot from the rear of their van. They'd asked for the cordons to be extended due to the size of the device, which Scanlon said would 'make a mess of half the station'. Colin got the uniform super, Tom, on the case, and they in turn decamped to the end of the entrance driveway where it joined with Fishergate - the road which passed the front of the railway station.

It was fascinating to watch both bomb disposal officers in the rear of their van operating the robot as it started to slowly enter the station. Both men were scrutinising a screen in the back of the van. It looked like Jonesy was at the controls. Martin was dying to see more and glanced at Colin, who nodded. They quickly made their way to the back of the van, fully expecting Scanlon to bollock them, but he invited them inside. 'Cheers, there could be vital intel we can pick up about who constructed the device,' Martin offered weakly. He knew they would be recording all the images.

'Yeah, yeah, yeah,' Scanlon said, in a singsong Beatles-esk way. 'Just keep still and silent.'

Both nodded.

Martin watched intently at the green-hued images on the control screen - which Jones was working - and could see the robot's view as it descended the ramp to the main platforms. He wanted to ask what happened if they had to endure stairs but kept his mouth shut. The thing was driven by tracks and had a large rifle-like weapon on its top. Eventually, it made its way to an area of wall three-quarters the length of the platform, and swivelled on its tracks to face it. The area on the screen was at forty-five degrees and Martin couldn't tell how far the robot was actually away from the wall. He guessed it was some distance, but was it a safe distance. He wanted to ask whether the robot could be at risk, it must cost a fortune, but again kept his own counsel.

He didn't have to wait long to get the answer to his question. The robot deposited a small tripod onto the platform which had what looked like a dart on top. He could see a green blinking light atop it. Then the robot withdrew, and a few minutes later came rumbling out through the main doors of the station.

The screen they were all huddled around went dead and then it kicked back into life. They now had a clear view of the wall again. The tripod thing must also have a camera attached. Jones looked at Scanlon who nodded. Martin then watched as Corporal Jones flicked a black hooded switch on his control consul. It hinged upwards to reveal a red rocker switch underneath.

'Firing,' Jones said, and then flicked the red switch.

Martin was mesmerised watching the screen above the switch and noticed the green LED atop the dart turn red momentarily before it sped off the top of the tripod and hit the wall close to the ground.

The monitor was awash with dust and debris, but as it slowly cleared, Martin realised what he was seeing was the exhaust gases from the projectile and not debris from an explosion. As the images cleared, the wall could clearly be seen as it was; intact with no detonation having taken place.

Sergeant Scanlon turned to Martin and Colin and said, 'Okay gents, the show is over. Now the hard work starts.'

'What actually happens next?' Colin asked.

'We slowly remove the bricks, one piece at a time to fully expose the device and then we deal with the fucker.'

'Big fucker,' Corporal Jones, added.

'Yes, thank you Corporal Jones, "big fucker", I should have said.'

Martin had nothing but unbridled admiration for what these guys did, day in, day out. He thought his job could be hard, shitty, and dangerous sometimes, but it was nothing compared what these two had to do on a regular basis.

'Come on, let's get out of their way,' Colin said, and they both wished the MOD guys luck and made their way back to the outer cordon.

***

RED HERRING

Colonel Popov was back in his dated office behind his desk when Boris Ivanov knocked and entered. He'd noticed that he had taken to doing that more and more, rather than knocking and awaiting the order to enter. He'd have to have a word with him about that; he couldn't have junior ranks taking liberties; even if it was his trusted staff officer. But he'd do it later, perhaps at the end of the day so he could sleep off the bollocking. He didn't want to have him moping about now, not when things were getting interesting.

As Ivanov approached, Popov asked, 'Is the old hag settled into her temporary new home by the sea?'

'Yes sir,' Ivanov answered, as he came to attention in front of the Colonel's desk.

That was better he thought, and said, 'Stand easy.'

Ivanov did and Popov asked, 'And did they get the photograph I asked for?'

'They did, sir, but had to wait until she was asleep so as to take it unseen.'

Popov nodded his understanding, and then told Ivanov to show him. His staff officer then took out a mobile phone from his pocket, it wasn't the private one he knew he had, but a departmental one with a large screen. He watched him play with the controls before he turned it around to show him. Popov could see a picture of an old woman sleeping which then became a short video. The images moved around the bed and then zoomed in to clearly show the face of the old hag who was sleeping on her side. She could be heard snoring loudly. The image then retracted and turned to show the operator who was one of their men, but he was now wearing a balaclava mask, and in his other hand was a handgun. The gun was pointed at the old nag. The images showed the handgun in the background with the woman in the foreground as the operator approached the sleeping body - and the gun was put right next to her head.

Then the images withdrew and turned back to face the hooded-clad man. The balaclava had cutaways for the eyes and the mouth, and it was obvious that the wearer was smiling an evil grin. Then it ended.

'Excellent, Ivanov, you have done well, that is indeed what I wanted, and more, if I'm being honest. That is first class.'

'Yes sir,' Ivan replied, and looked very pleased with himself. He asked if the Colonel wanted anything else and Popov said that he did not and dismissed him. As he watched him leave his office he decided to postpone the bollocking, for now at least. Then he reached for his desk phone. It would be his turn to feel very pleased in a few minutes.

Chapter Twenty-seven

'Come on Jonesy, we need to work fast. I know we could use an angle grinder to remove the mortar, as there are no motion sensor switches, but I'd rather do it by hand,' Sergeant Scanlon said.

'Agreed, and hopefully once we get a couple of bricks away, it should be easier,' Corporal Jones replied.

Both bomb disposal officers worked using a hand implement with a sharp end, each working on the same brick, but from different ends. Both were fully kitted-up, and it was making progress slow. The gloves in particular. As if reading his mind, Jonesy asked for permission to remove his helmet and gloves. It was a personal choice really, but if this thing went off, the blast suits they were wearing would not offer a huge amount of protection. Plus they were hot things to wear even on the coldest of days. Scanlon answered Jonesy by taking off his gloves and helmet, the rush of cooling air on his face was a welcome tonic. Jonesy did the same and the two of them upped their speed.

Once they had the first brick away - always the trickiest - the next followed more quickly. They had started at the outside of their marked area and slowly worked inwards. It wasn't long before they caught their first actual glimpse of the bomb. And as Jonesy had put it, it was a 'big fucker'. It was made up of military grade explosives, and must be at least three or four times larger than the first. On the top of it was a digital clock. It didn't show a countdown, just the current time. That was not to say that there wasn't a non-displayed countdown going on behind the screen somewhere. The other way it could be detonated would be by a radio signal sent from a mobile phone, though on inspection, Scanlon could not see the remnants of a receiving cell phone unit.

No matter, they would deal with the detonator first ensuring that the explosives could not be activated, and then they would take the whole thing away. But to be safe, before they had approached he had activated some kit in the back of their van which had sent a signal jammer out covering their immediately vicinity.

It didn't take long before they had deactivated the device and released it from its housing. They carefully laid the explosives on the platform and had a further look at it.

'Well, the intel was correct,' Jonesy said.

'Absolutely, and not only is this definitely a classic Russian military configuration, but I reckon it's been constructed by an experienced bomb maker. Look,' Scanlon said.

He pointed to some of the wires connecting the timer to the detonator, the certain way in which they were bent and tidied up, was to his eyes, a signature. 'What do you reckon?'

'Agreed; it's as if the bomb maker has done this so many times, they don't even see the way they do it now. I mean, there is nothing in a wall cavity which is going to snag or interfere with those wires, but they are wrapped up none the same. All neat and tidy.'

Scanlon pulled his mobile phone from his pocket and took several photos. He turned to Jonesy, 'Whilst, the signals are down, I'm going to have a good look around just to make sure there aren't any more surprises, if you can babysit this one.'

Jonesy nodded.

'As soon as the jammer is off, I'll have the Major all over me like a baby's vomit.'

'Understood, Sarge.'

'We've got away with this one, as it was so well hidden, but if the devious bastards have hidden a further device...' Scanlon said, leaving his sentence unfinished.

'If you like, I'll take this to the van and secure it, and update the detectives.'

'Cheers, and maybe borrow one of the coppers to guard the van and then join me, it could take us a while.'

'Will do.'

**

Martin and Colin were anxiously awaiting news by the MOD van and were joined by the uniform super, Tom Wheatfield, who looked uber stressed.

'What's up? Colin asked.

'The bloody press that's what. I've had several officers keeping the pack back, but as soon as we are clear here I'm going to have to front them. And they will have a party.'

'How come?' Martin asked.

'They will say we should have found the second bomb after the first one, and how many more are we going to miss and all that shite,' Tom said.

Martin heard footsteps and turned to see Corporal Jones approach with a large narrow package. 'I'll just secure this in the van and then I'll brief you. Could do with a PC to guard it while I go back in,' he added.

Five minutes later, the device was somewhere in the back of the MOD van with its doors locked, and with a PC stood guard. The officer didn't look entirely happy.

'Don't worry, it's totally safe now,' Corporal Jones said, as he walked back to where Martin, Colin and Tom were stood. After the update, Jones jogged back inside the railway station.

'Well, that should help calm the pack,' Tom said.

'Not that there should be a third device,' Martin said. 'It doesn't fit with what we know.'

'I hope you are right, God forbid,' Tom added.

'And while they finish their search, it'll keep these damn things quite a bit longer,' Colin said, holding up his mobile phone handset as he spoke.

'Once they are back on, they will go metal,' Martin added.

They were interrupted by a PC running to join them. As soon as he caught his breath, he addressed them all. 'Sirs, I've been on the outer cordon on Corporation Street, and have received an urgent message from the NWROCU office analyst, Cath Moore.'

'I'm not a sir, but go on,' Martin said. This drew a bollocking glance from Colin. Fair enough; not the right time for flippancy.

'Your officers have been going through the CCTV from the station, the PC said.

Martin knew that they had had two trusted DCs trawling through all the CCTV, starting from the time the first bomb went off, and working backwards. He'd done his fair share of such work when a DC himself, and knew how mind-numbingly boring it was. But also knew how easy it was to miss something extremely important. A lack of concentration for even a split-second could miss the most critical of evidence. He'd buy them both a beer or two when he next got the chance.

'And they've found something?' Colin asked.

'Yes sir, they are asking for you to return to your office as soon as you are able to.'

'Thank you officer, much appreciated,' Colin said.

'Yes, well done,' Tom added.

As the PC jogged away, Martin felt like asking why Tom had said 'well done'. Well done for what. For jogging here and passing a message. But he kept his gob shut.

Chapter Twenty-eight

Having left Tom to deal with the press, Martin and Colin made their way the short distance back to Preston Central police station. As soon as they reached the bottom of Fishergate Hill, near the river, their mobile phones burst back into life. Each with a succession of tones and noises, though Martin noticed that Colin's had the most. His brief respite from the Holy Trinity was over. And as essential as the phone jammer was, he couldn't but wonder about the level of disruption that the device had caused to the locals. A necessary evil.

They parked their car in the rear yard and were walking towards the rear entrance when Colin took a call, which was obviously from Sergeant Scanlon. The fact that he was using his own mobile to ring Colin signified good news. As soon as he'd finished the short call, Colin turned to face Martin, smiling.

'He's as certain as he can be that there are no more devices. He's checked all the walls and structures; he's even walked the tracks of each platform looking for any disturbance. So unless we want a painstaking fingertip search doing with fully trained search teams, which will take days, he's as confident as he can be.'

'What about an explosives dog?'

'They did that the other day, but as good as they are they can't sniff through enclosed brickwork.'

'I guess not.'

'And according to his major, "unless intel directs differently, we consider the scene clear".'

'What do you reckon?' Martin asked, glad that he was not Colin.

'I've agreed, but who knows whether one of the dick wavers will disagree. I guess it's up to Susan Jennings, the CT boss,' Colin answered, and then showed his phone handset to Martin, signifying that he'd better report up the chain. Martin said he'd leave him in peace and make a brew while he rang the powers that be.

'That's a good result,' Cath greeted Martin with, as he entered their office.

'And here too, I'm guessing,' he answered, as he picked up the kettle, which was hot.

'Already done it, they are over there on Colin's desk,' Cath said, as she pointed to two steaming mugs of beverage.

'Cheers,' Martin said, and then asked, 'So what have you got?'

'Those two detectives you put on the CCTV have done brilliant. You owe them a pint or three.'

'Defo.'

'I've cropped it into a working copy so as to preserve the integrity of the original as a potential exhibit,' she said, as she turned her computer monitor around to face away from her desk. She then joined Martin stood in the middle of the room as they awaited Colin.

He joined them a few minutes later and said that the Holy Trinity had agreed to release the railway station as a scene as soon as forensics had finished examining the area where the bomb had been. But added that Jennings had said that, as Colin was acting as Bronze and Silver Commander on the ground, she concurred the decision in the light of any intel to the contrary.

'So she is saying that she agrees because you are on the ground and she is not?' Martin asked.

'Pretty much, so if the Hole in the Wall Gang have placed a third device, she can point her finger away from her own acquiesce, and in my direction.'

'Bitch,' Cath said, and added, 'Sorry.'

'Don't apologise, she is,' Colin said, which surprised Martin nearly as much as Colin's 'Hole in the wall' gag.

They quickly turned their attentions to Cath's monitor which was showing a paused video, which in turn was a still image of Platform One.

'They have not had much luck with the platform where the first bomb was placed, as it was in a litter bin and several people have legitimately used the bin. Some can be clearly seen and are not known to us. Just members of the public. Some have hoods up whose faces aren't facing the cameras, so remain unknowns. It's going to take the tech boys some time to play around with those images, and it all may be to no avail.'

'Granted,' Colin said.

'So they have left that for now and widened their search to other areas and have started to go backwards in time as well.'

'Makes sense,' Martin said.

'And then they didn't.'

'How do you mean?' Colin asked.

'They figured that bombers may be a bit like arsonists; they enjoy watching the aftermath of their evil acts. And in this case, as we are not totally aware of who else might be out there as part of the team, they decided to have a look going forward after the first bomb, and in particular, to see who came in after the station was re-opened.'

'That is inspired detective work,' Colin said.

'Indeed,' Cath said. 'And also a bit of luck. The two detectives doing it are the same two who were on the knocker in Latham looking for a potential sympathetic spotter; which got them to thinking.'

'Still inspired,' Colin said.

'What I'm going to show you is a clip from yesterday morning. They started their scrutiny straight after the bomb had exploded for continuity reasons, expecting nothing until the station was re-opened later in the day.'

Martin and Colin both nodded. It made sense.

'But they didn't get that far. This is what they've found,' Cath said, and then activated the video.

Martin watched the images which he noted were of good quality and in colour. It showed a general melee taking place with lots of people rushing around. The station was still closed, so all who were there were operating in an official capacity. Then a workman came into view carrying a rucksack on his back, and a rolled up item in one hand; the item was red and white striped and looked like it belonged outside a barber's shop.

Cath pointed to the figure and said, 'This person stops right by the wall where the second bomb was found and sets up a work place.'

Both Martin and Colin watched intently and Martin soon realised that the Sweeny Todd sign was in fact one of those pop-up red and white work tent things which you often see on the street when repairs are being made. 'Cheeky bastard,' he said.

'You could say that,' Colin added.

'Best time to do it, if you think about it,' Cath added.

'Didn't anyone challenge him?' Martin asked.

'Apparently a security officer did, and the individual just said that they were there to repair the wall and check the cavity for damp,' Cath said.

'That takes some front,' Martin said.

'In all the drama going on, no one questioned it further, they were all too busy clearing up the mess and getting the station ready to re-open as quickly as possible.'

'What of the security guard?' Colin asked.

'The two DCs had a quick chat with him on the phone and have gone to see him to take his written statement as we speak.'

'Any description to be going on with?' Colin asked.

'Not much, apparently the guy was wearing a fluorescent jacket, hard hat, goggles and a dust mask, so no chance of an ID.'

'Course he was,' Martin said.

'And once he was inside his tent, he's out of view,' Cath added, as they all watched the individual put the tent up, put his rucksack inside, have a quick word with the security guard before then disappearing inside the makeshift bomber's hideaway.

'And of course, yesterday morning Igor was in custody,' Cath added.

'If there is a third active member, it will put us back to where we started, potentially,' Colin said.

Martin didn't answer; he felt queasy at the thought. He really had no idea what was going on now. All his working theories were flying out the window. He sat in depressed silence with the others as they watched the rest of the clip. Approximately an hour later, the workman appeared from the tent with his back to the camera. He took down the cover, rolled it back up, and made his way off the platform with his rucksack. The wall looked no different, though it most certainly was. He also noticed that the way the workman pulled the rucksack onto his shoulders gave it a different looking displacement. He'd initially taken it off slowly, and with some effort, but now it looked as light a feather; which it would do minus a bomb. He didn't say anything as it would be stating the obvious, plus he didn't have the energy. He felt deflated. He knew Cath and Colin were, too, it was evident on their faces.

'Okay, let's go through it all again,' Colin said.

Martin wanted to argue, but knew Colin was right; it was just the thought of doing so that was so energy-zapping. Cath played around with her computer controls and then rolled the tape from the beginning.

Martin did his best to concentrate as the show repeated. He saw the first sighting of the workman as he appeared on the screen. Rucksack on his back, and with the rolled up tent in his right hand. He must be right-handed.

'Shit, look,' Cath spat.

'What?' Martin and Colin said together. Martin's attention now reawakened.

'I didn't notice that before,' Cath said.

'Notice what?' Martin said.

'Hang on I need to make sure,' Cath said, who then played around with the controls. The workman walked backwards out of shot and then she pressed play again. Only this time Cath had slowed things right down, and the tape ran not much quicker than a few frames at a time.

'There,' she screamed.

'Where?' Martin said, and glanced at Colin. He looked as nonplussed as Martin was. They both turned their attention back to Cath's monitor as she ran the video again, but even slower this time. Then she froze the tape and pointed again, but Martin was still none the wiser.

'You know how breezy railway station platforms are,' She said.

He did, and said so.

'Well, look here; just as our bomber first appears on the screen, a gust of wind must have hit him and made his fluorescent jacket flap open, if only for a moment. A millisecond earlier, and the camera would have missed it; he would still have been out of view. They watched it again, and Martin saw what Cath had seen, but not the relevance. Just as the man appeared in the shot his coat had blown open, and then shut to a moment later.

'Don't you see it?' she asked.

Both Martin and Colin had to admit that they didn't. There was nothing shown by the brief opening of the coat, but for a black sweater of some kind underneath.

'Men!' Cath exclaimed, and then she increased the image size, and also stopped the frame in the moment when the jacket flap was most open. It took her a couple of seconds to get it right.

'Pretty slim waist for a man, wouldn't you say; even a skinny man,' Cath said, now grinning.

My God, she's right, Martin thought, now seeing what only Cath had spotted.

'And "*he's*" got a pretty decent rack under that sweater, too,' she added.

'The Bomber's a woman,' Colin said, joining the party.

'The bomber's that bitch Olga; must be,' Cath finished with.

'And this was only a few hours before we went to her flat,' Martin said.

'No wonder she was in the process of legging it. We got lucky,' Cath finished with.

Chapter Twenty-nine

Martin entered the interview room to find Igor sat in his usual place. He looked calm, and before Martin could take his seat opposite, the big Russian spoke.

'Sorry about my reaction last time; I know I haven't helped.'

This took Martin a little by surprise, but accepted his comment as genuine. 'Fair enough, but what I have to say to you shortly will do nothing to calm your mood, so don't overreact, well, not with me, okay?'

'More games?'

'No games.'

'Okay then.'

'But firstly, I want to say that we believe you when you say that there was to be no second bomb if the first was a success.'

'I'm glad about that.'

'And I understand your reticence at giving up your hide.'

Igor nodded.

'But you have to understand that we had to find it and deactivate it.'

Igor shrugged his shoulders and said, 'You'll not find it.'

'We already did,' Martin said, and then sat back in his chair away from the desk.

Igor looked more stunned than angry.

'And don't worry; we'll come up with a plausible explanation to keep your handlers happy. I told you before that we are good at making up stories.'

'How did you find it?'

'I'll come to that in a mo.'

'Well, if you found it you must have triggered the booby-trap?'

'Yes, you could have warned us.'

'You weren't supposed to find it.'

'Fair enough.'

'And it was only ever intended to destroy my document cache.'

'Hmm; the jury's out on that one: could have still caused significant injury, but you'll be pleased to know that no one was hurt.'

Igor shrugged again. Martin put his hand in his jacket pocket and took hold of the small TV remote, but kept it there for now. He also instinctively glanced over his shoulder to the door, and immediately regretted it. He didn't want to give Igor any none-verbal clues. He'd already primed the prop forwards on the other side of the door, just in case.

'At least you have the ordnance now, so I can go soon, no?'

'We'll come to that bit later on, but first, I want to answer your first question, and I want your wife to know.'

Igor sat up in his chair and narrowed his eyes quizzically. Martin took the remote control from his pocket and activated the CCTV capability of the two-way mirror. Both men stared at it as its screen went fuzzy, before clearing to show a picture of Olga sat in the other interview room, alone. She looked up at her screen, which indicated that she could see them, too. 'Olga, glad you could join us,' Martin said, raising his voice. She didn't react. There are two things I want to share with Igor. But I'm only going to disclose the second one, once I've shared it with you, first, in private. But I do want you to see Igor's reaction when I tell him the first bit. And trust me, what you are about to hear is nothing compared to the second bit.'

Olga didn't say anything; she just started straight into the camera.

Igor said, 'What is this? You said no more games.'

'I can assure you Igor, this is most definitely not a game,' Martin said directly at Igor. 'I may have to let you two have a reunion after all,' he said, and glanced at the monitor. He could see Olga's eyes widen. 'Igor,' he started, getting the man's undivided attention. 'You asked how we found the munitions hide.'

Igor nodded, but Olga shouted, 'No, you promised.'

Igor's head spun around to look at Olga and then back to face Martin, and he said, 'No!'

'I'm afraid so. Your wife told us, and she also told us that you were in total charge of it, so as it was empty, it's all on you. She also tried to say that you were in charge of the automated warning calls, which we now know was her.'

Igor didn't launch himself at Martin this time, much to his relief, but just sat for a moment looking stunned and obviously processing what he had just told him. Igor slowly turned to face the screen and said, 'If this is true, you know what will happen...'

'Now, as regards the second bit: it comes in two parts - one bit Olga already knows, as she told us - but she doesn't know the second bit. And as I'm true to my word, I'll speak to her first, before I share it with you, Igor.'

Martin wasn't too sure if Igor was listening, as he was now staring at the monitor. He then jumped to his feet and put his face right up against the screen on their side, and said, 'I'm going to kill you.'

Martin quickly cut the connection before Olga could react. 'Sit down Igor, please.'

Igor slowly turned around and stared at Martin for what seemed like an age, but eventually did as he was asked. 'That's not a nice way to speak to your wife,' Martin added.

'She is not my wife. She is a senior Russian Intelligence officer, and she is in charge of the mission.'

Martin had long guessed the latter, and had wondered about the former. But to hear Igor confirm it so easily now, surprised him. It was his turn to look genuinely stunned.

'The mission was as I have always told you it was, but it seems that Olga is up to something else. And if I knew what it was, I'd happily tell you. I'm guessing she made the first call and arranged my arrest.'

Martin nodded.

'So she has totally betrayed me?'

Martin nodded again.

'Please let us have the reunion you have threatened; it will only take me a second. Then I want to go home.'

'The reunion may happen, and you will be on your way as promised, once we have sorted it all out.'

Igor's shoulders dropped, he looked totally bemused. Then he looked up, and asked, 'What is the second thing?'

'I can't tell you yet, but I will.'

Igor just nodded and slumped back into his chair.

RED HERRING

Chapter Thirty

Martin and Cath walked into the second interview room to find Olga prancing up and down on her side of the desk. She stopped and glared at Martin, which was a rarity as she usually saved those looks for Cath. 'You total bastard,' she shouted.

'Shut up and sit down if you know what is good for you,' Martin said.

'More threats,' she spat, still standing. 'Or what, are you going to beat me like Igor now wants to?'

Cath said, 'No, he won't, but I would love to slap that arrogance from your face, so shut up and sit.'

Martin raised an eyebrow at Cath and had to surprise a grin. He wasn't sure if she meant it, but she was certainly believable. Olga sat down. As did Martin and Cath.

'Why, why did you tell him about the hide, and the calls?' Olga said.

'Because as bastards go; you are it. You have been taking the piss from the start,' Martin said.

'How do you reckon that? I told you where the hide was.'

'But not about the little surprise.'

'I told you where the second bomb was: what more did you want?' she spat, still irate.

'You didn't tell us that you are not Igor's wife,' Cath said.

Olga turned to face Cath full on with one of her death stares.

'Or, that you are really a top Russian Intelligence Officer.'

The death stare continued.

'Or, that you are really running the show.'

The stare intensified, if that was possible. Martin was starting to worry that Olga might attack Cath, and prepared himself to intervene quickly if she did.

'Or, that it was you who actually placed the second bomb.'

Olga threw her arms up in the air and said, 'Now hang on. That bit was always true; Igor was in charge of making the bombs and placing them.'

'I'm sick of this bullshit, and I'm sick of being played by you,' Martin said.

'It's true,' Olga said.

'I don't know what your agenda is; perhaps you are just trying to protect your true status. After all, if you are a senior intelligence officer, your value just went through the roof.'

'Okay, you are right; I was just trying to protect my true status.'

'It's more than that; because it was you who placed the second bomb, probably both of them for all we know,' Martin said.

'I keep telling you, Igor is the munitions expert.'

Martin glanced at Cath, which was a prearranged gesture. He then turned back to face Olga and said, 'I've not yet told Igor that you placed the second bomb - while he was in custody - and no doubt, against the mission objectives. Well, as far as he was concerned.'

Olga didn't respond.

'But I will tell him, just to see how he'll react. Just before I leave you both alone.'

'He'll not believe you,' Olga said, weakly.

'Of course he will you stupid cow,' Cath said. 'If he knows he didn't plant the bloody bomb, who the fuck else could it be.'

Olga's attention was back on Cath now, but the death stare had gone.

'Plus, we have you on CCTV,' Cath said, and before you consider that you were hiding yourself quite convincingly; what you do not know is that a gust of wind blew your jacket open to reveal your slim figure.'

Olga opened her mouth to respond, but Cath beat her to it, and continued, 'And the image also reveals your black sweater and your chest. So unless Igor has grown a pair of tits, stop taking the piss.'

Martin was truly impressed. Cath might lack any formal interview training, but more than made up for it with natural gusto.

'We can show you the video clip if you like, before we show it to Igor that is.'

Olga didn't respond.

'Well?' Cath said. 'Do you want to watch it; we could show you both together if you like.'

Olga slowly shook her head, and said, 'That won't be necessary.'

Martin thought that she genuinely looked broken down now, and added, 'So tell us what the hell is really going on?'

Five minutes later, it was Martin and Cath's turn to look truly stunned with what Olga told them.

'Do you believe her?' Cath asked, after they had left the interview room.

'God knows; we are due to meet the Holy Trinity later with Colin, we'll see what they reckon?'

'What now?'

'I'm not going to tell Igor this, obviously, but I just want to double check his story, or his belief. Can you brief Colin; I'll only be a few minutes.'

Cath nodded and left Martin as he approached the first interview room. He quickly told Igor that they had proof that Olga had placed the second bomb which was why the hide was empty. He kept back the rest of it. Igor looked truly astonished, and quickly confirmed that she was the bomber, but he had no idea why she had placed the second device, especially as she was the one who then gave it up. Igor insisted as he always had, that if the first bomb was considered a success, then it was a waste of munitions to do a second one. Getting ordnance into the UK, and hidden, was not an easy task, so to waste it was totally counterproductive. And not conducive to the mission. That mission being as he believed it. Martin was as happy as he could be now with Igor, he believed him. He also believed him when he said he had no idea why Olga had betrayed him.

'Crikey, that's quite a story,' Colin greeted Martin with as he entered the office and re-joined him and Cath. Martin nodded.

'Excellent work,' Colin added.

'Not me, boss, it was all Cath who did this; I bet she's not mentioned that.'

'Sorry, no she didn't,' Colin said, before turning to face Cath and congratulating her.

Cath's cheeks reddened momentarily and she smiled and nodded.

'Come on,' Colin said. 'Let's see what the powers that be make of it all.'

Chapter Thirty-one

Thirty minutes later, Martin, Cath, and Colin were on the top floor of Force HQ walking towards the chief constable's office. Inside, Don Rogers, who was dressed in his usual uniform in shirt sleeve order, was waiting for them with an array of screens set up on his conference table. His door was answered by ACC Susan Jennings, the North West of England's Counterterrorism Commander; she greeted them with a warm smile and looked younger than Martin would have guessed. She appeared in her early forties, slim, tall, with her brown hair in a bob, wearing a powder blue two-piece business suit. She nodded a familiar nod at Colin who had met her before, and he quickly introduced Cath and Martin. Introductions over, all five took a seat at the conference table. Martin could see that two of the screens facing them appeared live, each showing a desk in front of an empty chair. A sticker above one of the screens had the words 'Home Sec.' written on it, and the second had a note saying 'MI6'; Miranda Daniels, and Jeremy.

'Before the others join us, I just want to congratulate you all on the successes you have somehow achieved so far,' Rogers said.

'Here, here,' Jennings added.

Martin and Cath nodded, and Colin said, 'Mainly down to these two,' nodding towards Cath and Martin.

'A team game,' Martin added.

'Colin has briefly outlined where we are, and in particular, what Olga has now said; and he has also updated the Home Sec., who will have spoken to Jeremy,' Rogers said.

'And I have kept Five in the loop,' Jennings said. 'And we are hoping that Gill, their analyst can join us, but if not, I'm sure Cath can fill in for her.

'Will do, ma'am,' Cath said.

Then the 'Home Sec.' screen burst into life as did the 'MI6' one, as Miranda Daniels and Jeremy took their seats. Rogers M.C.-ed and handled the further introductions before Daniels addressed them all.

'First class job so far by your team, Colin, but for the sake of absolute clarity can we have a detailed update. Forgive me if I make notes as you talk, as I have to attend a COBRA meeting shortly afterwards and need to brief the PM first, who will be chairing it.'

Colin cleared his throat and spoke for several minutes, starting from when they had arrested Olga, to the discovery of the hide and the second bomb. The fact that Olga had planted it; having probably prepared both devices. Although, Igor must have placed the first. Martin was impressed with the way Colin was able to grasp a complicated narrative and break it down to its important salient points, clearly and concisely. He went on to brief all on the fact that Olga made the warning calls; she must have been the one to blow Igor out, leading to his initial arrest. He then explained what her true status and position was in it all.

Jeremy was the first to respond as Daniels caught up with her notetaking.

'I'm pretty sure I could find a job for you guys if you ever get tired of working for the police. Top result and much thanks to you all, the pressure is now off. I take it that we are happy that there can't be any further devices?'

'As sure as we can be,' Colin replied.

'And you are happy with Igor, now, at least, I'm guessing?'

'Over to you, Martin,' Colin said.

Martin hadn't been expecting to be asked to speak so soon, so sat up and took a second to consolidate his thoughts before he did; conscious of the need not to over-state things. He knew from past experiences, that once you put your reputation behind one point of view, how quickly that can all turn on its head and then the 'should've squad' appear from nowhere and jump all over you.

'In the absence of any intel to the contrary, yes, I'm happy with him. He seems to truly believe the mission was as previously stated, which is why he showed genuine surprise when we told him that a second bomb had been placed.'

'Perhaps, he knew; maybe that was why he was reluctant to give up the munitions hide,' Jeremy probed.

'Had been wondering the same,' Jennings threw in.

The 'should've squad' were already preparing their own defences in case it all went tits up, Martin thought before he answered, 'He was truly shocked, and once he knew that Olga had blown him out, he reacted violently. If he could get his hands on her, he'd kill her. As far as he's concerned, she has betrayed him - and Russia - for reasons he can't fathom.'

Cath threw in, 'And please don't forget that it was the threat of putting them together, that opened Olga up.'

'On the threat of putting them together, I'm not sure I heard that,' Daniels said.

'Nor me,' Jennings added.

'Well, I did, and I thought it was a splendid ploy,' Rogers said, and then quickly added, 'But I have forgotten it already,' and he gave Martin a reassuring smile, for which he was grateful.

'Like I said; if you guys ever fancy a career change...' Jeremy added.

'Moving things on,' Daniels said, taking back control. 'The million dollar question is of course with regard to *why* Olga went to all this trouble; just to scupper things. What are her true mission objectives?'

All eyes were back on Martin and Cath: Martin cleared his throat and continued, 'She claims that up until now, she has being playing to a detailed script.'

'We always got the feeling that we were being played,' Colin said in support.

'Her mission - if we believe her now - is to infiltrate Jeremy's mob. And in order to give herself credibility, she was to blow out Igor; tick. Then she was to reveal the details of the second device in a third warning call.'

'We just got to her before she could do it,' Cath added.

'So she had to improvise. It may not have been part of the plan to give up the munitions hide, but she claims that our interventions forced her to. She obviously knew it was empty which would then lead to her "eventually" rolling over and appearing to give us the location of the second bomb through gritted teeth.'

'It's all a bit elaborate, no offence,' Jeremy said.

'Which is why we can't be sure that she is not still trying to play us,' Colin said.

'She lost control of planned events once we had her in custody. She clearly hadn't anticipated what could happen then. Or the threat from Igor, once we outed her to him,' Martin added.

'Don't get me wrong, you guys are doing a remarkable job; but how do we know that declaring her mission to infiltrate us isn't actually part of her original ploy?' Jennings asked.

Jeremy was nodding.

Daniels said, 'Exactly, she could very well still be loyal to, and working for the Russian Federation.'

'A double agent,' Rogers joined in with.

'It would be a very daring plan, if that was what is happening,' Jeremy added.

'We need to test her. We need to be sure before she is handed over to Jeremy and exposed to potentially damaging intel,' Daniels said.

'I guess just knowing what you look like is sensitive intel in its own right?' Martin asked.

'He's not that ugly,' Jennings threw in.

'Yes thank you, Sue, how very funny,' Jeremy said.

'That is why I want Colin's team to stay with things until we are surer of what is really going on,' Daniels said. 'I don't want her exposed to anything secret until we are sure.'

'Agreed,' Jeremy added.

'Under your oversight, Sue and Don, obviously,' Daniels added.

Both Rogers and Jennings nodded their agreement.

'I suggest that we share our misgivings with her,' Jeremy said. 'Blame me, if it helps keep your relationship sweet with her, and let's see what she comes up with.'

'Failing the value of anything she says, we could also put her to task, and see how that goes?' Jennings said.

'Excellent, it sounds like we have a plan. I'll leave the tactical details to you lot as I have to go and see the PM now, and bring him up-to-speed prior to the COBRA meeting,' Daniels said.

'Just one question, before you go ma'am, if I may?' Martin quickly threw in.

'Yes, what is it?'

'What do we tell Igor? He still thinks he will get a new passport and a choice of whether to go home or disappear - with our backing.'

'Jeremy will brief you on that.'

And then the 'Home Sec.' screen went blank.

'Okay,' Jeremy said. 'As we now know that Igor is indeed married to Volkov's niece - who is not Olga - and is therefore still worried about his remarks, we can use that to our advantage. This is what I want you to tell him.'

Chapter Thirty-two

Martin was glad that Colin sent him and Cath home for an earlier night. At the meeting, the Holy Trinity had become the Holy Quartet. Though, Colin said he hoped Jeremy's presence would be ad hoc. 'It should be Sue Jennings's job to liaise with Jeremy,' Colin had said as they left the Force HQ's building.

'It sounds like they have clashed before,' Cath threw in.

'Yeah, he didn't look too pleased with her "he's not that ugly" jibe,' Martin added.

'Probably, the only way to deal with an ego as big as his; take the craic when one can,' Colin finished off with.

They dropped Colin at Preston nick to collect his car, and then stayed in one motor and headed back to Manchester. Cath had invited Martin to stay over and he was looking forward to some quality down time. They collected a takeaway on their way, and thirty minutes after that, were both sat on Cath's two-seat settee, refuelled and with a fresh glass of wine each. Martin stretched his neck until it cracked, and he felt a lot of tension leave him.

Colin had been right to send them home early; the time pressure was off now the second bomb had been dealt with. They could start afresh with Olga and Igor with renewed vigour in the morning.

Cath suddenly upped and reappeared ten minutes later in a silk dressing gown. Martin raised an eyebrow at her as he felt other parts of his body start to stir. Cath responded with a smile and said, 'I need an early night for more than one reason; but let's finished that bottle first.'

Martin leaned across and quickly filled Cath's wine glass.

'What do you think Igor will say?' she asked.

'Not sure; he could take it either way, I guess. I'll just have to be at my best in putting a positive spin on it.'

'Yep. Can't wait to speak to Olga again.'

'Me neither, but let's leave those machinations until tomorrow.'

'Agreed. Come on, we can finish that bottle in bed.'

RED HERRING

Martin didn't need telling twice, and was quickly on his feet. 'I'll just have a quick shower first,' he said, as he pretended to sniff one of his armpits.

'That would be preferable,' Cath said, with a glint in her eye as she stood up and then made her way to the bedroom.

The following morning, Martin was up and dressed first and was glad that he'd previously left some clean clothes at Cath's, it would save them loads of time in not having to call in at his on the way in. They were both ready by 7.00 a.m. and on the road by five past, hoping to avoid the worst of the rush hour traffic. Though it would still take them an hour and forty-five minutes to do what should be a forty minute journey. They eventually got out of Manchester's suburbs and joined the M6 north trundling along at between 40 and 50 m.p.h. They'd be okay just so long as there wasn't an accident or breakdown ahead of them; then it would be carnage.

As if reading his thoughts, Cath said, 'So what do you think about moving somewhere more central to the region?'

Martin kept his gaze ahead as he watched the traffic, the guy in front was a power on, brakes-on merchant, constantly; and he wanted to give him some space. But also needed some room to think about what Cath had just said. Not about being able to sack this dreadful commute to Preston, thirty miles north of where they both lived, every day, but the unsaid within her remark.

Most of their worktime was spent within a thirty mile triangle between Manchester, Liverpool and Preston, and at their satellite office in Preston. Somewhere equal distant between the three points made sense, probably favouring the Preston point slightly. But that wasn't the issue. He hadn't been going out with Cath that long, and even though he spent as much time at hers as his own place, it sounded like she was alluding to the next step; moving in together. He wasn't against the idea, but didn't want to buy something with her just yet, in case it all went tits up. He was also very aware that the longer he took to answer her, the worse it looked.

He decided to ask a qualifying question before he answered her properly, and asked, 'Are you suggesting that we rent somewhere together, say, in southern Lancs?'

'Look at me, scaredy cat,' she said.

Martin turned to face her and was relieved to see that she was smiling.

'Of course I mean rent somewhere. Christ, I'm not ready to buy a house with you, yet. What if you turn out to be a complete nob head?'

Martin was mightily relieved, and laughed as the tension eased.

'No, I would suggest that we both keep our Manchester homes on the go for now, and just rent somewhere to live that's rural and central. We can still use our homes for weekends or nights out in Manchester. After all, together we should be able to afford to rent somewhere, and keep our homes.'

'That sounds like an excellent plan.'

'I'm glad, and you sound greatly relieved.'

Martin then spent the next five minutes trying to dig himself out of the hole caused by his misunderstanding. But eventually threw his hands in the air in submission, as he realised that the hole was only getting bigger.

'My bad,' Cath said. 'I was probably just testing you. I'd love to share a home with you, but we still need to take things slowly, I feel.'

'You mean you were just checking in case my needy alter ego had returned?'

'Something like that. We've both been hurt before, and there's no rush.'

'Yep and yep,' Martin said.

Then they both sat quietly for the rest of the journey which seemed to pass in no time, now. Even the brakes and accelerator idiot in front of them wasn't annoying him anymore.

Chapter Thirty-three

'I hope you have had a better night's sleep, now you have unburdened yourself?' Martin asked.

Olga shifted restlessly in her chair in Interview Room Two, and asked, 'How long before we can move to somewhere more comfortable?'

'It shouldn't be long now.'

'I hope you mean that.'

'We do, the police want their police station back.'

'What are you grinning at?' Olga asked, aiming her remarks at Cath who was sat next to Martin - they were in their usual seats.

'I was just thinking, that this is the first time you have not started off by giving me the death stare.'

'So?'

'So, was that all part of your act, too?'

'And you wonder why I don't like you.'

'She has a valid point, Olga.'

'Meaning what?'

'Meaning that you could still be a loyal Russian double agent. You blowing Igor out and stopping the second device could still all be part of your script to infiltrate us. Pretending to out yourself could just be part of things. I'm not saying that we don't believe you, but we have to be sure. Surely you can understand that?' Martin said.

'I want to speak to someone at the top.'

'This has come from the very top,' Cath added.

Olga went quiet for several moments where she looked to be in a state of genuine contemplation, before she eventually looked up and said, 'What is it that you want?'

'Proof,' Martin said.

'I want some assurances.'

'What assurances?' Cath asked.

'Things didn't go quite as planned. You arresting me saw to that.'

'We gathered as much,' Martin said.

'And putting me in with Igor gave me no choice but to declare. I know he would have killed me long before I could have explained the real mission to him.'

'Why didn't he know what the true mission was?' Cath asked.

'He is just a brute force grunt. He is not skilled enough for higher aims, plus he was supposed to be believable in what he thought the mission was about once captured.'

'See, that's part of the problem, you claim that you have only really come over to our side to save yourself from Igor. But that is not a willing act. And what happens when you and Igor are separated?'

'I see that. But having flipped, I am no use to Russia, so I have little choice. If I go home with the mission failed, things would not be good for me.'

It was Martin's time to reflect. Olga had actually made a fair point; if it was true.

'What assurances do you seek?' Cath asked.

'That you will under no circumstances put me anywhere near Igor. I have seen him in action before; he would kill me in an instant. If we even passed under escort in a corridor, it would be enough. Brutal and lethal force with no conscience is his skill set.'

'Agreed,' Martin said.

'Then we must do things to keep the subterfuge alive; Moscow will expect contact at some stage.'

'Go on,' Martin added.

'If I have been accepted as a fake defection, then I will be allowed my liberty, even if I am under heavy surveillance, no?'

'You'd have to be on a tight leash until fully trusted, I guess.'

'By now a phone will have been left for me at a dead drop, for me to contact my handlers in due course. I am expert in counter surveillance, and will be expected to visit the drop in a way that can be checked that you are unaware. Only then, will Moscow fully believe that my false infiltration has been a success. If you Brits were to know of this, then Moscow would know that I am not believed by you, and the mission has not yet been successful. Maybe even fatally flawed.'

Martin glanced at Cath and she returned a puzzled look. How on earth would she be able to make that call, and more pointedly, how the hell would Moscow know she was doing so free from prying, unbelieving eyes? Then it hit him. Shit. He looked again at Cath and saw it on her face, too.

'Please tell me that you are not saying that there is a third member of your team wandering about out there?'

'Not exactly,' Olga answered, 'but I will need to visit the drop and not use the phone.'

'What?' Martin asked, still puzzled. And then Olga explained.

**

Colonel Popov was sat relaxing on his own in the Officers' Mess when there was a knock at his door. He recognised the swift double tap done lightly; it was his staff officer Ivanov. It seemed there was no hiding place. 'Come,' he shouted. And in rushed Ivanov. 'You have news?'

'Yes, Colonel,' he replied.

'Report.'

'Several things have happened very quickly, some official, some not.'

'Official, first.'

'The Ministry of Foreign Affairs have been contacted by the British.'

'Ah; Igor?'

'Yes sir, they are not stating how they have arrested him or what he may have said, but they do not want him and they are asking if we would consider an exchange.'

'Excellent. He was always going to be a great loss to us. I'm glad we are to get him back. Who do they want in return?'

'They claim that we are holding two aid workers and two mercenaries who are all British nationals seized by us from Ukraine.'

'They want four for one?'

'Yes Colonel.'

'Typical of the British arrogance. They can have one. I shall take personal control of those negotiations.'

'As you see fit.'

'And what is the unofficial news?'

'This is not good news, sir,' Ivanov said, and then he told him.

Chapter Thirty-four

Martin and Cath had nipped into the back yard of the nick to catch a breath of air when they saw Colin walking back towards the rear door. He had just come off his phone. Martin quickly told Colin about their interview with Olga.

'Let's run through the last bit again,' Colin said.

'According to Olga, Moscow will not know whether her infiltration mission has been accepted until she is allowed some freedom.'

'To presumably report in with the Russians?' Colin asked.

'Yes, but not directly. A phone, will by now, have been hidden at a dead drop site by a sympathiser,' Martin added.

'Five need to get their act together on these sympathisers; they seem to be everywhere,' Colin said.

'It may well be the same one from the Ormskirk area who was watching the hide,' Cath said.

'Let's hope so,' Colin said.

'Anyway, the sympathiser will visit the drop every day between noon and one o'clock. Olga will be expected to only visit between these times so that her visit can be monitored, and more importantly, it can be seen that she is alone.'

'Ah.'

'But as she is still under compromise protocol, she is not to use the phone as all signals are banned in case we are monitoring them. If they need to get a note to her, it will be left at the dead drop by the sympathiser.'

'So what does she suggest?'

'She has to be seen to visit the site at the correct time, and to do so alone. Then Moscow might consider lifting her compromise protocol, where after she can use the phone to call in.'

'And by so allowing her to do so, will mean that they accept that her mission to infiltrate us has been a success?'

'Exactly.'

'Do we believe her?'

Cath took over while Martin took a swig of water from a bottle he was carrying, 'Well, she didn't have to tell us about the sympathiser watching, or the strict approach timings. She could have either; left evidence that she had visited the site at a different time, or visited it at the correct time, but when not alone. Either way, would have sent a subliminal message to her handlers that she was under suspicion, and not trusted by us.'

'She really didn't have to tell us those bits, I agree.'

'The other red flag would be the arrest of the sympathiser too soon.'

'Too soon, how do you mean?'

'Until the compromise protocol is lifted, the sympathiser is active and necessary. Once lifted, he or she will stand down and any arrest can thereafter be done by us. But she suggests with a plausible cover story when the time is right; just to be on the safe side.'

'I was thinking more of a plausible fatal car accident for the bastard,' Colin spat.

Martin grinned, but was not entirely convinced that Colin was kidding.

'So she wants to go there unsupervised?' Colin asked.

'She knows that is a no, no, but we could watch from a discrete distance and insist that she wears a mike. A closed circuit one so it doesn't give off any radio signals or microwaves, just in case the sympathiser has any scanning kit with them. She says she is comfortable with that,' Martin added.

Colin sat in thought for a moment and then asked if either of them had anything extra to add, before he rang the Holy Trinity.

'I suggest a full surveillance team, but to hold back with a wide geo-fence encircling the area. We can take her to a designated outer RV and let her approach on her own. Then after she leaves, hopefully, the outer surveillance cordon can pick up the sympathiser as he or she leaves,' Martin said.

'The sympathiser will be off guard during their exit and all we need to do for now is to follow them away, house them, and then identify them. We can take further action against them at a time of our operational choosing,' Cath threw in.

'Sounds like a decent plan, we'll have to run it past Sue Jennings, and Five in particular, to get it green lit, but it sounds good to me,' Colin said, and then pulled his phone back out of his pocket.

Cath said that she would speak to Gill at Five, and Martin said he would make a start on the written surveillance authorities. Then he would have to speak to Igor and tell him his fate. The bastard was still escaping a murder charge, so he should still consider himself very lucky, but no doubt would not. Martin would be glad when this job was finally over and they could get back to some honest detective work. The murky world that intelligence and the security services operated in, would make him ill if he had to do it long term. It was a filthy, immoral, grey world, where seemingly anything goes in the name of national security.

***

Igor sat in quiet contemplation, once the two thugs guarding him had returned him to his cell. He saw the look of surprise in the girl detective's eyes when he'd told him his fate; and he didn't kick off. He actually surprised himself. His natural reaction would be to launch himself across the table and to rip the detective's throat out, but that would of course be counterproductive. He still couldn't understand why they didn't keep him shackled in the interview room; the Brits were riddled with strange rules. It would be very different in Russia.

'On the plus side, you get to go home and not be charged with the murder you committed' the girl detective told him. This of course was true. But returning to Moscow this way meant that his masters would know that he had been captured, and the mission was not a success. Plus, he would face severe scrutiny as to why he had allowed himself to be caught, and what he may have told the Brits under interrogation.

The first was easier to deal with as he was betrayed by that bitch, Olga, but would they believe him. She would no doubt put her own spin on events once she was, too, similarly returned; presumably also in an exchange. He just wished he could get his hands on her whilst they were still in the same building. It wouldn't take long, and his truth could thereafter never be challenged.

But overriding everything for Igor was the humiliation of being sent home this way. It was career suicide. If the Brits had been true to their word, then he could have returned under his own terms; classed as uncompromised, with the safety net of a British Passport if he needed to disappear. But this way: he was little more than a commodity which had passed its use by date.

He was seething.

Chapter Thirty-five

Martin had been glad to get out of the interview room without the need to have Igor Tasered. But he knew Igor was a deep-rooted bastard, and so he'd warned the guards to stay vigilant around him. They all seemed mightily relived when he told them that he wouldn't be there much longer. He would soon be escorted to an MI6 facility to await his repatriation once the negotiations were complete.

Colin had briefed the Holy Trinity - as he still referred to them as, even though there were now four when they all joined in - and they had all given the plan the go ahead. Though, Sue Jennings had insisted on them using an MI5 surveillance team from their Manchester office backed up by her Counter Terrorism department's specialist firearms officers. Martin and Cath were to escort Olga to a forward RV and then Olga would run in to the drop site unescorted. But - unknown to her - CROPs - Covert Rural Observation Posts - officers would dig themselves in overnight and would be able to provide a live commentary as she approached. Once they had run the plan - excluding the CROPs bit - past Olga, she said that she was happy and disclosed the location. Cheeky bastards; it was a hundred metres infield from where the munitions hide had been near the Ring 'O Bells pub.

All three of them had no option but to stay the night in training school bedrooms, which Don Rogers had previously given them the use of. Accompanied by a drink free night. And a sex free one, though Martin couldn't really comment on how Colin spent his lone time.

The main briefing the following morning had taken place at Force HQs at 5 a.m. with the exception of the MI5 surveillance team who didn't want to put their faces on show. Sue Jennings had orchestrated their briefing separately.

All the teams had headed out early so as to get themselves established in plenty of time just in case the sympathiser did a few early recces each day. They had no idea how professional he or she was, and Martin was worried that Olga was holding back a bit. They had plenty of time to kill and were spending it in a quiet corner of the HQ's canteen. Colin had left them to take up residence in a command centre near the main HQs building. It was known colloquially as 'The Pizza Hut', as it resembled the restaurant chain's buildings' design. Eventually, Martin voiced his disquiet, 'I'm finding it harder and harder to believe that you don't know the identity of the sympathiser?'

Olga spun around on her chair and looked intently at Martin.

'It would save us a lot of time if you could tell us, and add to the proof that you are now on the side of the righteous,' Cath added.

'Righteousness can always be defined differently, depending on your point of view. But I honestly do not know who the local sympathiser is. The system is designed that way, so that they can be used over and over again. If there ever was an absolute need for us to meet, then the operational imperatives that demanded such, would override that rule. But that would be very rare.'

'I must admit, that's what Gill told us,' Cath said, to Martin.

'Who is Gill?' Olga asked.

'Doesn't matter, and it won't be her real name, anyway,' Cath said.

'Ah, an MI5 analyst,' Olga said.

'Why did you say "analyst"?' Martin asked.

'An obvious guess. Anyway, the sympathiser won't show her or his self, but they will be there.'

'And you can give us no clues?' Martin asked.

'None; look, I could even have met her or him and wouldn't know it.'

'It's a pretty impressive network; worryingly,' Cath said.

'We are not as unprofessional as you would like to think.'

Martin noticed her use of the word 'we'; it still worried him as to Olga's true allegiance. But he guessed only time would tell. Let's get today out of the way, first, he mused as he looked at his watch. It was nearly time to go.

It was only a thirty minute drive to Lathom, the rural outpost near Ormskirk - which was a medium-sized market town in West Lancashire where everywhere was very flat. This was obviously why the area was so suited to arable farming, along with munitions hides and dead drop sites, obviously!

The road in from a hamlet named Rufford was a quiet lane and any tail would have stood out a mile. They weren't followed. They pulled over about a mile from the Ring 'O Bells pub where another vehicle had been left for them. Cath and Martin would wait there and could listen to the radio feed from the CROPs officers that Olga didn't know about. At 11.45 a.m. they prepared to leave Olga, and as they were starting to get out of the car Olga asked a strange question.

'What is to stop me fleeing?'

'An MI5 surveillance team, for one,' Martin answered.

'You think I could not pass through them like a hand through water?'

'They say not.'

'What is to stop me finding out?'

'I guess nothing; but it shows that we are starting to put our trust in you, doesn't it?'

Olga smiled; it was as if she suddenly appreciated the confidence they were showing her. But Martin felt duty bound to add caution to her, and said, 'Plus, if you do change your mind, and have a go, but end up making a splash with your hand, I can't guarantee that you won't be shot.'

Cath stared at Martin in disbelief. But Olga did not; she laughed, and said, 'Now I feel at home, see you soon.'

Martin and Cath climbed into the stationary car and Martin quickly found the handheld surveillance radio set which had been left for them under the driver's seat.

Cath said, 'I don't recall that part of this morning's briefing.'

'It won't do her any harm to believe it,' he said, as he turned the set on.

A couple of minutes later, a voice announced the arrival of Olga in the car. Martin had done surveillance many times and there was a regimented way of doing it, supported by a strict glossary of terms and radio discipline. But the MI5 team seemed to have a far more relaxed approach, no call signs, for example.

RED HERRING

It was all a bit 'Bill and Freda'; like a relaxed chat. But he was sure it was far more professional than it sounded to his cop's ear.

The commentary switched and effectively followed Olga's movement up to a tree a hundred metres past where the hide had been. A further voice described the row of barges tied up, none of which had apparently displayed any movement within them.

Then a final voice described Olga lifting a sod of grass at the base of a Sycamore tree. The area was otherwise deserted. She pulled out a self-sealing clear plastic bag and opened it. From within she took out a mobile telephone, appeared to examine it, check the bag for anything else and then put everything back as it was. She checked her wristwatch which made Martin instinctively check his, 12.10 p.m. Then she slowly walked away from the tree in the same direction she had approached.

The first voice jumped in and put her back in her vehicle before announcing that she was driving away in a reciprocal route.

Everything had gone as planned and nothing unexpected had happened. Then the lead voice took over again, telling all teams to remain vigilant, and to move onto a predetermined inner cordon, in order to see the sympathiser leaving.

Then silence for what seemed like an age. Olga returned, and Martin asked Cath to jump in with her and wait a little while. He was loathed to leave the radio in the car, but couldn't take it into their car in front of Olga. He'd give it a couple of minutes; hopefully, the sympathiser would soon become self-evident as he or she drove or walked away, after having broken cover. Martin hadn't seen another vehicle the entire time they had been there. In fact, he hadn't seen another vehicle since they left the main A59 road at Rufford on the way in.

A couple of further minutes passed and he knew he would have to leave soon, and leave the MI5 teams to do their job. But just as he was about to turn the radio off and store it back where he'd found it, it burst back into life.

One of the dug-in CROPs officers saw a male figure appear from behind thick gorse and walk down the canal path. He hadn't seen him arrive, but such things could be easily missed, Martin knew, especially when you had spent hours looking at nothing through a sort of mini-periscope. But thank God he'd seen it now. The figure must have been secreted behind the hedgerow for some time. Excellent.

Then it turned to rat shit.

The male continued along the towpath, and then boarded one of the barges, and moments later chugged off along the Leeds to Liverpool canal making his or her escape at four miles an hour. He'd have to leave it now, and just hoped the surveillance team were able to somehow follow without blowing themselves out. If that happened, then the whole job could be knackered. It was time to trust to their undoubted abilities, and get Olga out of there.

Chapter Thirty-six

As soon as they set off back, Olga confirmed to Martin and Cath that there were no messages left with the phone, which she did not turn on; as per protocol. Cath asked if she saw or heard the sympathiser, and she'd answered not. This had been confirmed anyway, by the CROPs officers. 'Do you think the sympathiser was there?' Martin asked conscious of not giving anything away.

'Not as such, but he or she would have been watching. Did your watchers see anything?' Olga asked.

'Not heard, yet, which I think we would have if they had, but let's wait and see,' Martin said. He noticed Cath's head drop a touch, she obviously believed him, but he couldn't share anything with her in front of Olga.

'I suppose we are going back to the cell in Preston?' Olga said.

'We are, but not for much longer,' Martin said.

'It was nice to be outside once more,' she said.

'I bet it was, and I'm glad you didn't try to extend your trek,' Cath said.

'It was tempting, but as you English say, "I know which side to butter my bread".'

Martin and Cath both laughed at Olga's slight misquote and it eased the atmosphere in the car. The rest of the journey passed quickly, and an hour later they were back at Preston nick and Olga was taken to her cell. Martin was relieved to notice that Colin's car was already there, he could hardly wait for any update. He'd quickly briefed Cath on what he'd heard on the radio as they walked from the cells.

'Shit, shit, shit,' she said. 'Making his escape at four miles an hour; how clever.'

'We should have considered the possibility,' Martin replied as he opened their office door.

'I take it that following a barge is not easy?'

'Not when unplanned. Only the foot units can deploy, obviously, and if the barge chugs beyond 4 or 5 miles an hour then they can't keep up without running, and even if it stayed at walking speed, they'd stick out like a uniformed cop with a sandwich board saying, "I'm not really following you, honest".'

'What about a jogger?'

'Can work, short term, but with limited reach. Even if you keep changing the jogger, it will look wrong very quickly.'

'So what will they be doing?'

'The best they can do will be to concentrate on being "ahead and waiting", by putting people on any bridges and such like, ahead of the barge with the vehicles taking a parallel route and hoping that he or she doesn't hop off where they can't be seen.'

'Quite,' Colin said, as they took their seats behind their desks.

Then Martin realised that Colin not being in the 'Pizza Hut' probably didn't mean good news.

'Apparently, the team were frantically trying to plot the route along the canal and cover all eventualities. All eyes had been on the row of gardens opposite where the barges were moored,' Colin started with.

Martin knew that they had all been guilty of that, after all, the houses there afforded a fantastic spread of view. It was where he would set himself up if the roles had been reversed. It was this assumptive thinking which had been their undoing.

'And as they were sending teams all over the place, they identified a long stretch of canal between bridges, where the canal bends slightly keeping any long term visual out of range. So when the barge didn't reappear as expected, they sent a foot unit along the tow path as a jogger, only to discover that right in the crook of the bend was a boozer which backed up to the canal. Obviously, a popular watering hole for the "four miles an hour club".'

'Bugger,' Martin said.

'I'm guessing our sympathiser's barge was moored there, with him nowhere to be seen?' Cath said.

'Got it in one.'

'This is clever,' Martin said. 'This shows not only a high level of planning, but someone with a good knowledge of surveillance and counter-surveillance.'

'Indeed,' Colin said.

'But hopefully, we may find something inside the boat which may identify him?' Cath asked.

'I wouldn't bank on it,' Colin said.

'But at some stage, when they deem it safe - bearing in mind that the sympathiser doesn't know that they've been followed - they'll go back to it, and move it,' Martin said, suddenly feeling more upbeat. A plan was forming. All they had to do was monitor the barge, and even put a tracker on it, if possible, and wait for their target to return and then carry on as planned. He voiced his thoughts.

'That's what Sue Jennings said, however it will be tricky to get a tracker on board until things there quieten down. Too many folk sat in the pub's beer garden. But nevertheless, it's not all lost,' Colin added. And then he asked how they had got on with Olga, and Martin let Cath fill him in whilst he put the kettle on.

Brews suitably made and served, he asked Colin what their next step should be.

'Well, once we have identified the sympathiser, and the resultant background work on them is done, then at a time deemed appropriate by the Holy Trinity, we can nick them with a suitable cover story. But Five are keen to let him or her run once they have control - in an intelligence gathering operation.'

'Bug his home?' Cath asked.

'Bug his home, car, phone, and anything else that moves. They want to know when he goes for a dump; it could be quite educational what comes from that. Apart from the dump bit, obviously,' Colin said.

There he goes with that humour thing again, Martin thought.

'What about Igor?' Cath asked.

'Yes, let's discuss him,' Colin said, and then turned to face Martin.

'It's like I said, he took the news far better than I would have expected. Well, to qualify that, he didn't overtly react, but behind those sunken eyes I could see some rage.'

'Because we reneged on our promise to let him go with a new identity if he wanted one?' Colin asked.

161

'Partly, I reckon, but mainly as he now knows that his bosses are aware that he had been captured, and there will be ramifications to that, no doubt.'

'But the bastard has got away with murder,' Cath said.

'I know, you'd think he'd be more appreciative, he's just too self-centred to think like that. I'll be glad to see the back of him.'

'Won't we all,' Colin said, and then he took a large gulp of his brew.

'How's it going on that front?' Cath asked.

'According to Jeremy at Six, negotiations through their backchannels are underway, and as soon as they have managed to get as much as possible from the Russians, the exchange will take place in a neutral location,' Colin said.

'What are we asking for?' Martin asked.

'He won't tell me exactly, says that bit is classified, but he is happy that they can get several of our citizens back. The threat he is using, is the murder charge hanging over Igor, exacerbated by the value of Igor. It takes years to train operatives like him.'

'Won't he be blown, now?' Cath asked.

'As he stands, yes. But Jeremy reckons the Russians will change his appearance. They have intelligence that the two monsters who committed the Salisbury outrage have already had "Identity realignment" as he put it.'

'I'll be glad to get back to normal investigative police work,' Martin said.

'Me too,' Colin added.

'Me also, I guess, though it is fascinating,' Cath said.

Martin and Colin both turned to look squarely at Cath, just as Colin's phone rang. Martin and Cath watched silently as he took the call, He didn't say a lot, but started to smile before he closed the call by saying, 'Wow, that's excellent, thanks for letting me know.'

'Sounds like good news,' Martin said.

'We could do with some,' Cath added.

'Good news indeed. As Five were setting up the new plots around the barge and the pub, their command car had been going through the footage of video and stills taken by their various operatives, and in particular, the CROPs teams.'

'Go on,' Martin said.

'And they have managed to capture a clear front on shot of the sympathiser's face. And as the loggist in their car was uploading the images to their office for further checking, the guy doing the uploading is fairly sure he recognises the face. Reckons he has seen him on a previous surveillance. Gill is on it as we speak.'

'Let's hope he is right, just in case our sympathiser has decided to abandon his barge. He's probably got more than one way to cover, and egress from the dead drop site,' Martin said.

'The last bit is a cheery thought,' Colin said.

Then Cath's secure desk phone started ringing, and Martin and Colin watched as she answered it. It must be Gill at MI5.

It was Cath's turn to listen, smile and then give a heartfelt thank you. She ended the call and turned to face them.

'Gill?' Colin asked.

'Oh yes,' Cath confirmed.

'And?' Martin asked, it was like interviewing Igor he mused; well, not quite so, but the suspense was palpable.

'Their surveillance officer was correct. Gill has face-matched the image with one on their system. We now have the full identity of the sympathiser, and all the powers of the state are being mobilised against him as we speak.'

'That is great news,' Colin said. 'The intel they can potentially learn from him could be gold dust.'

'I just can't wait to nick the bastard, when we are allowed to move on him,' Martin said.

'Me neither; it will be nice to see his smug face again, but under our terms,' Cath threw in, grinning like a Cheshire cat who had just won the national lottery.

'Again?' Martin and Colin managed to say in perfect unison.

'Oh yes,' Cath said. 'The Russian sympathiser/sleeper or whatever you wish to call him is none other than Derek Gosling.'

It took a second for the name Gosling to hit Martin. 'The farmer, Gosling?'

'That's the one. That objectionable little letch who employed both Olga and Igor to pick his strawberries.'

Chapter Thirty-seven

The custody sergeant had left the flap down on Igor's cell door when he had taken his meal dishes away. Thankfully, they had stopped spitting on his meals now, so at least he could eat what they called food. And they were being more civil. He'd no idea why, but wondered if someone had spoken to them to temper their behaviour. Perhaps the 'Girl Detective' had done him a favour after all. The benefits of having the flap down were two-fold; it allowed for better air circulation, and he could peer out through it from time to time. Not that there was much to see, as it appeared he and that treacherous bitch Olga, had the place to themselves.

He was trying to stay positive, but as with any custody situation, he had far too much time on his hands. He was still at a loss why Olga had betrayed him. He would have half-understood it, had she just done so once she had been locked up. But the more he chewed it over; it could only have been her who put the call in as soon as he had placed the first device in the bin at the railway station. As per *her* instructions. And if she had always intended to blow him out, why did she not say where the second device was before the first exploded. And if she placed the second device after the first had gone off, it made even less sense. Then he heard the gate to the cell complex being unlocked, so he put his head on one side so he could peer through the flap opening in his cell door.

It was Olga being led back down the corridor to her cell at the far end of the complex. She must have been interviewed again. He shuddered at what else she may have fessed up to. He glared at her as she was led past, but she didn't look in his direction. He thought about shouting something to her in Russian, but decided not to. He needed to stay calm, for now. His main concern was getting out of here without facing a murder charge. Then such a musing led him to think about how he would be received by his masters back in Moscow; he shuddered. He'd face that ordeal when he had to. But for now, he had to compartmentalise his thoughts as he lay back down on his wooden bed. The first mental box was all about getting out. He didn't expect to be interviewed again, could see no profit in it for them, and he wondered how the exchange negotiations were getting on. Then, he returned his focus to mental box number one, with half an eye on what would become box number two.

He was fed again, so now knew it was early evening - the custody sergeant had previously removed the wall clock in an infantile act of spite. He also closed the cell flap again. He wasn't sure why they'd closed it, but didn't have to wait long for an answer. He heard the gate being unlocked and then the sound feet shuffling to a standstill outside his cell.

A voice he recognised as the custody sergeant said, 'He's in this one. I don't suppose you want a two-for-one deal?'

A deep voice he didn't recognise, answered, 'Just this one for now thanks.'

Then the cell door was opened and in walked the sergeant followed by two men in casual clothes. Both with dark hair, in their forties, one short, and one tall; both slim. Initially, he wondered if they were counter terrorism police, but there was a different air about them from the girl detective.

The tall one spoke, it was him who had spoken just before, 'My name is John, and this is Ian,' he said, and pointed to the smaller man. 'And we are here to escort you to a safe neutral location.'

Igor nodded and said, 'Am I on my way back to Russia?'

Neither man answered, but the taller one - John - looked at the sergeant, who said, 'I'll be in my office when you are ready.' He then turned and left.

John seemed to wait for ages before he answered, Igor. 'Yes, a deal has been struck. Our job is to simply get you out of here as a first stage. You are at the first part of your journey home, so there is no need to do anything other than to thank your lucky stars that you appear to be worth more than a dog turd in your bosses' eyes.'

Funny man. But Igor decided not to rise to the insult, it would be counterproductive. He just had to play the game now, and get the hell out of this shit hole. 'I understand,' he did say.

John nodded at Ian, who then produced a pair of rigid handcuffs. Igor put his hands together in front of himself and allowed Ian to snap them on. They were tight and hurt so he said so. John nodded at Ian, who then backed them off a notch. He thanked them both. John was clearly in charge.

'Are you MI5 or 6?' he asked, as Ian took hold of the rigid centre of the cuffs between his wrists, and started to lead him out of his cell. He wouldn't miss this place.

'Six,' John said, 'but you already knew that.'

He guessed he did, and decided to keep quite. Five minutes later he was led by Ian out of the rear door of the police station, to a black Range Rover parked a couple of feet away. He was put in the back seat and was soon joined by John, the boss, who slid in next to him from the other side. Ian got in behind the wheel, in front of Igor, and they were off. It felt great to be back on the outside. He hoped he never saw Preston again. He knew from his own pre-mission reconnaissance that they were only about ten minutes away from junction 31 of the M6 motorway. From there he could be taken to Manchester, or even London. Or God knows where they planned to take him. He doubted that he would be taken straight to a military airport from where he could be flown home. He suspected that he would be taken to a holding facility first.

Box number one was now empty. It was time to consider the contents of box number two.

'Always remember your training' was a mantra that was drilled into him, and the training he now needed was in box two. It related to a course he had done a few years ago with Chechen Special Forces. Igor mentally opened box two and peered inside.

He then looked out of the passenger window. They were leaving Preston and had started to descend a hill towards the M6 motorway junctions at Samlesbury. Using his peripheral vision he could see that John was glancing left out of his passenger window. Looking ahead he could see that Ian was concentrating on keeping the vehicle speed down, as they approached a fixed roadside speed camera. It was now or never.

Igor launched his left elbow at John, swiftly and silently, and used his shackled right hand to push and aid the acceleration of his attack. Their mistake was not cuffing his hands behind his back. The elbow struck John's right temple with practiced pinpoint accuracy. John slumped forward. He was unconscious and wouldn't know what had hit him.

Igor turned his attention back to the front, as he saw Ian's eyes in the car's rear view mirror, as he started to react. But he was slow. These were not military trained men. Another arrogance by the Brits, sending desk-jockeys to escort him instead of soldiers. Their bad, as their American friends would say.

Igor reached over the driver's seat head restraint and put his cuffed hands tightly over Ian's head using the rigid nature of the manacle's middle section on Ian's throat. He was fairly confident that he had the applied pressure on the man's laryngeal prominence - Adam's Apple - and as he pulled back sharply. He used his feet against the driver's seat backrest to accelerate the crushing of his windpipe.

Ian was dead or near death in seconds, as the car swerved but continued its downhill run. Gravity helping to keep it in a straight line, but Igor knew that it would not last long. He shoved Ian to one side and reached further over the head restraint. He quickly knocked the manual gear selector into neutral, before taking hold of the steering wheel. A car behind hit its horn as their vehicle slowed to around twenty miles per hour, but speed soon picked up as the vehicle started to coast now it was out of gear.

At the bottom of the hill, the road bent right towards the motorway roundabouts, but there was a large grass verge on the left which preceded the entrance to a hotel.

Igor aimed the car towards the verge and it soon ran to a juddery halt in the soft sod. He let go of the wheel and stretched through the central console area and quickly found the handcuff keys in Ian's jacket pocket. Once released, he took over the driver's seat and ploughed the car off the turf and onto the hotel carpark. He located a large up-and-over commercial waste bin at the far side of the hotel, and quickly transferred his passengers into it. One minute later, Igor was minus his load and heading up the M6 towards Lancaster.

Now it was time to open box number three.

Chapter Thirty-eight

The mood was sombre in Chief Constable Don's Rogers office when Martin and Cath followed Colin through the doorway. Inside was Rogers behind his desk, and Sue Jennings was pacing up and down. Martin noticed that one of the multi-screens was live on the conference table with Jeremy's face on it. He was also sat behind a desk and looked strained. As soon as they all had taken a seat, Rogers brought the meeting to order.

'This gathering is not to decide any blame, either on our hands, or Jeremy's men's, but to evaluate what has happened and why. The "should have" squad can have their time later,' Rogers started.

But for the seriousness of the situation, Martin would have allowed himself an inner smile at Rogers's comments about the 'should have squad', as he was usually one of its lead members.

'And we must not forget that one man has sadly lost his life, and another is in hospital with a fractured temple and concussion,' Rogers added.

Rogers then asked Jeremy for an update, and he gave the room a full briefing as to his personnel's statuses. John was apparently single and would eventually be okay. Ian sadly leaves a widow and two young children. It was the last bit that really dug deep on hearing it.

After a moment's reflection, Jeremy continued, 'We need to try and evaluate what Igor will do next. And Colin, your team are the ones who know him the best, what is your assessment?'

Colin - as pre-arranged - turned to face Martin, who said, 'What I think is all guesswork.'

'Granted,' Jeremy said.

'Well then, I don't believe that he will continue his mission.'

'Agreed, but why do *you* think not?'

'The mission - as he believed it to be - is outed, so it would serve no purpose to blow anything else up as the rationale for so doing is no longer there.'

'Also, agreed,' Jeremy said.

'But I suspect he feels greatly humiliated that his masters now know that he had been arrested.'

'So he'll want to mitigate it?' Sue Jennings asked.

'Yes, and by escaping, he already has in part. He is returning to Russia under his own terms, which incidentally will negate the need for Jeremy's Moscow counterparts to exchange anybody.'

'Unfortunately true,' Jeremy said.

'So he is currying favour?' Sue added.

'Yes. He is a loyal machine of their state, and notwithstanding that he was compromised by Olga, he will be keen to get his narrative to his bosses before she has chance to do so,' Martin said.

'Let's not forget how top-down driven the Russians are. Igor will be very aware of getting it in first, given that Olga has seniority over him,' Jeremy threw in.

'Makes, sense; which means he will be keen to get out of the country as quickly as possible.' Sue said.

'Will he not try to make contact with his handlers, first?' Rogers asked. 'Given what you've just said.'

Cath answered, 'According to Gill at Five, he won't risk doing that; conscious that we will be on hyper alert and his signals could be intercepted.'

Jeremy added, 'That's also correct. We have GCHQ on it as a priority; and those boys and girls could hear a mouse fart in a field of farting rats.'

'So how will he attempt to leave the country? We already have an All Ports Warning in place, and Border Control are briefed and on full alert,' Colin said.

'Unfortunately, he will have access to at least one other hide,' Jeremy said.

'So he'll have access to various ID documents?' Rogers asked.

'Yes, so your job, chief constable, just got a whole lot harder, I'm afraid,' Jeremy said.

'And it means we can consider him armed, too,' Sue threw in.

Martin groaned.

'As must you be once you leave here,' Colin said, aiming his remarks at Martin, who nodded.

'Why only *one*?' Cath asked, aiming her remarks at Jeremy.

'Sorry?' he replied.

'Why only "one other hide"?'

'Ops security, so he can't blow out the location of more hides if arrested, balanced against his potential need for access in an escape and evasion situation.'

Martin felt angry, had they known about this, they could have pushed Igor on it during interviews. Plus, it might have explosives in it. He asked Jeremy why he hadn't shared this with them before now.

'Our Ops security, I'm afraid; you didn't need to know,' he answered with an arrogance returning to his voice.

'We are on the same side.' Martin said.

'Quite,' Jeremey said.

Jeremy's flippant reply did nothing to lower Martin's hackles, but he knew now was not the time to take on this supercilious man. He took a breath and asked, 'Well, what about any explosives?'

'An emergency hide will be small, it's a back-up, and it'll have ID docs and probably a handgun, and not much else.'

'That's very specific,' Martin said.

'Trust me; I know what I'm saying.'

'Pity you didn't trust *us* before now; we could have pushed for that intel previously, and be staking it out now.'

'Nothing personal, old boy.'

Martin had to dig even deeper not to tell this sanctimonious man what he really thought of him, but held his tongue, again, as he noticed Colin glaring at him.

Cath jumped in with, 'Will Olga know where it is?'

'Probably,' Jeremy said.

'Then we could do with asking her PDQ,' she said.

Martin looked at Colin, who looked at Rogers, who responded with, 'Yes, Colin, you'd better crack on, soonest. Plus, it'll be another chance for her to prove her allegiance. Off you three go, I'll finish up here with Sue and Jeremy.'

Colin nodded and all three quickly got to their feet.

As they headed towards the door, Sue said, 'As soon as you have a locale, I'll have an armed surveillance team ready to cover it.'

Colin thanked her and they continued out of Rogers's office. As they rushed along the corridor, Martin said, 'I'm sure that twat makes it up as he goes along.'

'Not now,' Colin said. 'Just give me the car keys, I'll drive and you two can run in when we get there.'

'Point taken.' Martin answered with. 'I'll ring ahead and get Olga taken to an interview room ready.'

Twenty minutes later, they pulled up at the front entrance to Preston police station and Martin and Cath quickly alighted, leaving Colin to sort the car parking out. Five minutes after that, they entered the interview room with Olga sat in her normal position. They quickly took their seats opposite.

'This looks serious,' Olga said.

'We need to know where your second hide is.'

'Your emergency back-up hide,' Cath added.

'I don't know what you are talking about.'

'Yes you do, and we need to know where it is, now.'

'You want us to believe your intentions, well, this will go a long way to establishing the trust we both need,' Cath said.

'Has something happened?'

Neither Martin nor Cath answered.

'Something has, hasn't it?'

Ignoring her question a second time, Martin said, 'We really don't have time for this. We know that you have access to a second hide in order to facilitate escape and evasion.'

'Well, you will also know that it will have no explosives in it.'

'But it will have a gun,' Cath said.

'Trust me, no child will find it.'

'If you are good to your word, then why won't you tell us where it is? Or was giving that up not part of the script?' Cath asked.

'I suppose so, I mean I am; "good to my word" that is. It's going to take a little while to get used to this; you have to understand that.'

'I suppose so, too,' Martin said.

'Okay, but first, you tell me what has happened.'

'Nothing has happened,' Martin said.

'You talk about trust; it works both ways, you know.'

'I know that. But it has to start with you.'

'Well, tell me when I'm getting out of this shithole. It's not fair you have moved Igor first. Or is he on his way back to Moscow already?'

Then as Martin was considering his next comment, Cath made a fatal error. It was not her fault of course, considering that she was not interview trained, or experienced in doing them. In fact, she had done brilliantly up until now. But all interviewers make mistakes - even trained and experienced ones - and sometimes they drop howlers. This was a howler.

Cath said, 'He's not gone anywhere; he's still in his cell.'

Olga seized on this, 'Then why haven't you asked him. He was the technician; I was always more the brains of the outfit.'

Martin turned to face Cath, but before he could stop her, she said, 'We have, but as you know, he's not friendly like you.'

'I passed his empty cell on the way here, in fact, I passed all the cells, and they are all empty. As are the other interviews rooms; all the doors are open.'

Martin knew it was too late; they'd been caught in a lie. He jumped in, 'I could try and bullshit you by saying he is on his way home.' He noticed Cath looking at him puzzled.

'You could, but I would then ask why you had not said that in the first place.'

'Yes you would,' Martin said, and then noticed the penny drop by Cath's expression. He turned to face her and said, 'No biggie, Cath, I know you were just trying not to worry Olga.' Cath smiled, appreciatively.

'I don't like the sound of this,' Olga said.

'Okay, time to be honest. Igor has escaped his escort,' Martin said.

'How on earth?' Olga asked.

'That's not important at the moment. But now you know, I guess we can ask you what will he do?'

'Well, apart from killing me, you mean?'

'He can't get at you in here.'

'The fact that he knows where I am is half the intel he needs. I want moving.'

'What else will he do?' Cath asked, after recovering her voice.

'He'll want to get home under his own terms - after killing me, of course.'

'The second hide?'

'You'll move me?'

'It was always part of the plan, so yes,' Martin said.

'Give me a pen and paper; it'll be easier to draw.'

'On it,' Cath said, and then jumped up and rushed out of the room.

Whilst they awaited Cath's return, Olga leaned across the table to Martin and said, 'No one must know where you take me.'

'That goes without saying,' he answered.

'I mean no one outside you and Cath and your boss.'

'It would only ever be a "need to know" thing.'

'No. Not good enough,' Olga said.

Martin wasn't too sure why, but she seemed very agitated all of a sudden.

'You have to understand that the Russians have eyes everywhere, so it is safer not to trust anyone.'

Martin guessed she was talking about the network of sympathisers. He was looking forward to getting the full angle on these maggots from Olga, once things were more settled.

'Remember, they could be anywhere. They go about daily life as normal until activated. The woman in your canteen, the man who washes your cars, who knows? They could be anywhere.'

Martin took a gulp. He'd not considered that they could be infiltrated by these traitorous rats and said so.

'Not infiltrated, they are not operatives like me, but they do all have day jobs, which could be anywhere. That is all I'm saying, so safer to assume that, and trust no one you don't have to.'

'Point taken, but we are going to have to know much more about them at some stage.'

'Once safe, I'll tell you what I know, but it is not everything. The system is designed that way so no one person knows too much.'

Martin nodded, he understood that and believed her, but was nevertheless looking forward to hearing what she did know.

'I'm a bit jumpy knowing Igor is on the loose, probably being a bit paranoid. But my point is that these sleepers are just normal British citizens, so therefore will be woven throughout all walks of life. Not to spy, just to do their day jobs and lead their normal lives. They are only supposed to spy on orders for a specific reason, like watching the hides when they are active.'

The description 'normal British citizens' rankled with Martin. These termites were anything but, but he took her point and further reassured her. Then Cath returned with a pen and paper and handed them over to Olga.

She took them and paused, before saying, 'You will not like this.'

RED HERRING

Chapter Thirty-nine

Colonel Popov was preparing to leave early for the day. He wouldn't arrive home for hours yet, indeed he wasn't expected until early evening, but he had a grace and favour apartment which his wife knew nothing about. In it living rent free was a man half his age; a very good looking man whose company Popov enjoyed once or twice a week. It always surprised him how his country seemed to accept that men in positions of power - such as him - often had a concubine. That was fine, even wives accepted it, well; some did; though he knew that his would not. But when it came to affairs of the heart between couples of the same sex, it was very much frowned upon. A complete hypocrisy. And an illustration of how far Russia had yet to come when it came to genuine equal rights. Not that Popov paid much heed to human rights in other areas of life. Torture and manipulation were part of his department's daily staples. That said, he knew that even if the day came when Russia caught up with most of the world and accepted same sex relationships, his would still be frowned upon. Not just because of his position, but he had another vice; a far darker one. It was matched only by his black soul. He enjoyed hurting his lover; it somehow eased his guilt. Transferred the blame onto the pitiful wreck he would leave in the apartment once he was sated.

He knew that his own self-serving narcissist psychoses were his one area of weakness, and it had to be guarded at all costs. So when he granted entry to the knock on his office door and saw that it was his staff officer Boris, he immediately stopped tidying his personal effects from his desk. It was an act he did every day on leaving. And as if on cue; Boris had asked him if he was finished for the day, to which he lied that he was simply off to a meeting but was neatening his desk. He knew his answer was shallow, and Boris simply smiled and said, 'Of Course, Colonel.' Popov knew that Boris already thought that he had a lady friend, so he smiled back. It would do no harm for him to continue to think so. How loyal Boris would still be if he knew the truth, he wasn't sure.

'I just need a couple of minutes of your time, sir,' Boris said.

'A problem?'

'Maybe, sir. Our watcher followed a car carrying Igor—'

'What!'

'I'm afraid so.'

'How the hell did that come about?'

'He claims he saw activity in a beer garden where he left the barge after leaving the phone at the dead drop.'

'He's being paranoid, surely. Did he see anyone follow him to or from it?'

'He says not, he says that he is sure that he was not followed, particularly when he left in the barge. Just felt uneasy at some people in the beer garden after he moored it.'

'He is being overly suspicious. He is just a farmer. These sympathisers watch too many James Bond films.'

'I agree, and I told him that they could not have known that he would leave in a barge, or more importantly, where he decided to stop and moor it.'

'So your assessment is?'

'There was no one at the dead drop. He is seeing shadows.'

Popov knew that the untrained often saw things when they were nervous. Even trained operatives were occasionally guilty of seeing what was not there. It meant that all was well with the true mission, and that Olga was being accepted by the stupid arrogant Brits. That was the main thing. But how had the sympathiser ended up following Igor? He asked Boris to explain further.

'Because of his concern at the dead drop, he decided - without permission - to park up near to the police station where Igor and Olga are being held. Just in case he could see anything. And as it happens, soon after he parked up, he saw Igor being driven away in a plain car by two men in plain clothes. The idiot decided to try and follow.'

'They were obviously preparing to repatriate him. I hope the farmer hasn't messed that up.'

'Well, it might have turned out okay.'

'Go on.'

'The farmer was conscious of being spotted, so he tried to follow from a distance. He claims that he did not have much of a view of the car, but as he headed towards the motorway junctions he saw the car leaving a hotel car park. It was being driven by Igor, and he was alone.'

'And how is this okay?'

'I just thought, sir that we will not have to free any prisoners in order to get Igor back. He will go dark and make his own way home.'

'Yes he will. But we have no way of contacting him, or controlling him. We don't know what he might choose to do. Do we?'

Boris went silent as Popov's comments sunk in, and he could see him register them. A pause, then he said, 'He might want to, but he'll not be able to get anywhere near her. This mission will be safe.'

'I hope you are right, Boris; you know Igor well, you trained with him. What do you think he will do?'

'He might want to, but he's not stupid, sir. He'll revert to escape and evasion protocols.'

'I hope you are right, Sergeant, or we'll both end up in Siberia. Dismissed.'

Boris saluted, turned and left. Popov sat in silent contemplation for a moment and then picked up his phone; he had two calls to make: one, to cancel this evening's arrangements, and two, to arrange to meet Artem of the SVR instead. He'd tell him that they had ordered the sympathiser to keep watch - damage limitation. Artem would be annoyed, after all, foreign intelligence was his remit, and he would probably regret giving them direct access to the sympathisers. But what was done was done. He just hoped that ultra-loyal Igor didn't ruin things hereon in. That said; what could even Igor do on his own without proper kit or intel. He may know where Olga is, but he couldn't get at her. It should all work out as planned.

All operations had to allow for the unplanned, and this was no different. Plus, they would eventually get Igor back once he had put his escape protocols into effect. He was a highly trained operative, and Boris was right; they'd now get him back at no loss to them. The Brits would be seething. Plus, Artem had other assets in place which might prove fruitful once knowledge of Igor's escape filtered out, as it would. It would be good to get quality feedback. But if he knew Igor, which he obviously did, his escape would leave a trail of destruction in its wake. Popov allowed himself to smile at the thought.

Chapter Forty

Martin pulled the car into the same spot they had used when they were last here with Olga. Cath, in the passenger seat, said, 'Cheeky bastards.'

'We should have guessed that they'd use the same locale for both hides, and the dead drop,' Martin said.

'How come? Even Gill at MI5 seemed shocked.'

'Think about it, it all makes good operational sense, really; one watcher can cover all three.'

'I guess so.'

'We'll have to make sure the entire field is properly searched.'

'Won't that be tricky without being seen?'

'They'd do it at night with CROPs trained operatives using infrared kit.'

Then the handheld surveillance radio lodged between Cath's feet kicked into life announcing the arrival of the MI5 surveillance team in their usual "Bill to Freda" way.

'But for now, we wait and watch?' Cath asked.

'Yep. I know we don't have to be here, and if it drags on we can leave it with them.'

'I hope it doesn't run long, I'd love to see the shock on Igor's face but won't he sus that Olga will have told us?'

'That's the weak bit, but he is low on options, and is arrogant, so he may think he can clean the plot first, and if he doesn't clock the team, he may be driven to go for it,' Martin said.

'Let's hope he does.'

'I know, because if he doesn't, then he's running free and we have no idea where.'

They both sat in silence as the whispered radio chatter continued. Observation Posts were set up by the CROPs officers, who were not happy having to do so in daylight hours, but needs must. In fact, this could work in their favour as Igor might not want to approach until it was fully dark. On that point, Martin discussed with Cath that they should at least wait until half an hour after darkness before jacking it in.

Time passed slowly after the remainder of the surveillance team reported that they were in position. It didn't take long as they were all used to their plot positions from the other day. They even had a couple in the beer garden at the pub this time as a bonus, and they had already reported that the barge was where it had been left by the sympathiser. It appeared empty at the moment, but could be an attractive prospect for Igor if he turned up. They were prepared for that too, this time, as they had three armed operatives further up the canal on jet skis. They were not MI5 operatives, but a special forces intercept team. MI5 had their own barge there too in case a covert follow was needed.

Martin drove into nearby Ormskirk at one stage to grab some food and find a toilet. By the time they returned it was going dark and the only radio chatter they had heard was the occasional 'No change' from the OP with the visual. The visual being on a second tree further in-field from the first. They must like using trees.

***

Igor waited until it was fully dark before he made his approach. It was nearly dark already, so he could risk a few more minutes wait. Once he was happy that nightfall had fully arrived, he silently left his hiding place and carefully did a full recce of the area to check for any signs of a surveillance team. The Brits thought that they were world leaders in this particular dark art, but that was just their inbred egotism kicking in. Let them believe so, such limited thinking was one of their weaknesses.

Once Igor was satisfied that he was alone, he started to make his approach. The area was very rural so it didn't take him too long to clean the plot. He had no compass with him so had had to navigate using the stars; fortunately, it was a clear night. But the moon cast little in way of illumination opposed to what a new one would. Twenty-four hours earlier it would have been full; he was doubly lucky. He'd had to take one risk though, and he hated taking avoidable risks; it smacked of unprofessionalism. It was too British for his liking. But it had gone okay; he knew that bitch would no doubt tell the enemy the details of the second hide, so knew he had to get there before they could respond. This was why he'd gone straight to it even though it was daylight. He'd done a quick recce first, and knew that it would be easier to spot watchers at this time of day, and there had been none.

That had been hours earlier, and he now patted his jacket pocket to feel the reassuring outline of the Glock pistol, next to fake IDs and a credit card. Then he smiled to himself as he thought of the British amateurs, who were probably sat in the darkness watching an empty hide. He peered inside his mental box number three; he knew he had work to do before he could move to the next task. He was just grateful that he knew where he was headed; it was an address he had not shared with Olga on purpose. It was always prudent to hold some things back, even from those you think you trust. Just in case. He knew that his mark did not live at the address known to Olga. It was a front. The mark lived elsewhere, nearby, but elsewhere. The cops already knew the address known to Olga, but not the importance of it. Though a search of the place would reveal details of the house he was now looking at from its rear garden. He would have to be quick

The downstairs lights were on, and the curtains were closed. He decided the none-subtle approach; he didn't have time for anything else. Plus, he knew the mark lived alone.

A quick crawl around told him that the television was on in the front lounge, so he approached the rear kitchen door. Then just as he squared up to it, the light in the kitchen came on. Perfect timing. An expert at rapid entry he was through the door in seconds.

Stood before Igor next to a breakfast bar was a shocked looking Derek Gosling.

'You nearly gave me a heart attack. And what's with the door?' Gosling asked.

'I am short on time so I need you to say things quickly.'

'What things?'

'Are you a double agent, too?'

'What nonsense is this?'

'Because if you are, your treachery has backfired on you.'

'I've no idea what you mean. And how did you know that I actually live here?'

Igor ignored the farmer's question, and said, 'It was you who gave the police Olga's address.'

'Yes, but not because I'm a double agent as you allege, but they were threatening me with tax inspectors. I had to give them something,' Gosling said now losing his attitude. He started to back away towards the doorway, which presumably lead into the front room.

'Stay where you are,' Igor demanded, and Gosling did. 'But you betrayed us by giving them a true address.'

'No, I knew she would be gone by the time they arrived, I texted her to tell her to leg it.'

'Why not give a fake address?'

'They would have bounced straight back at me and brought the tax inspectors with them.'

'So, self-first?'

'No it wasn't like that.'

'She never got the text.'

'How do you know that? When I checked the flat later it was empty, and her stuff was gone, so I initially assumed—'

'You assumed wrong.'

'I realise that now.'

'Did you not know that you were blowing out another double agent?' Igor said, and then laughed at the irony of it. 'She betrayed me, but had already been betrayed by you. Then she betrayed us both to the police.'

'Look, you are getting this all wrong. I've no idea how you got arrested, and I didn't betray Olga, not really. And as for her being a double agent. Never.'

Chapter Forty-one

'Shit, shit, shit,' Martin said, as the eyeball confirmed that the second hide was empty. The surveillance team had deployed a dog walker to stroll past the plot. There were two other dog walkers using the tow path which would make their walker invisible. She quickly reported in that the ground had been disturbed so they bit the bullet and had a proper look. The hide consisted of a plastic biscuit tin, and it was empty. They were too late.

'What next?' Cath asked.

'According to the other surveillance team there is no sign of life at Gosling's farm, so I'm not sure,' he said, as his mobile rang. It was Colin. 'You've heard the bad news already,' Martin started with.

'Yep, and because of it, a decision has been made by the Holy Trinity to lift the sympathiser Gosling. He is our only possible source of intel as to where and what Igor might be or do next,' Colin said.

'I'd love to be there to nick him when he returns home,' Martin added.

'That's the real reason why I'm calling. The MI5 surveillance team have done a covet entry to the farmhouse hoping to pick up some information.'

'What about the flat?' Martin interjected with.

'Being watched and empty at the moment. Anyway back to the farmhouse.'

'Any intel?' Martin threw in, as Colin took a breath.

'If you'd let me finish.'

'Sorry.'

'Not regarding Igor, but they are of the distinct impression that Gosling doesn't actually live there. They have found correspondence addressed to him at an address in the area. I'll text you the details.'

Martin fired up the car's engine and said, 'We are on our way.'

'No need for stealth, but wait until the ARVs arrive before you go in,' Colin said, and then cleared the line.

Martin pulled out of the layby and quickly told Cath what Colin had said, and threw his phone onto her lap. It beeped and he asked her to read the incoming message,

'Ormskirk,' Cath shouted, above the car's highly revving engine.

Martin nodded and thought 'excellent'; Ormskirk was only ten minutes away.

***

Igor had heard all he needed to, he didn't have the luxury of hanging about. He knew that sooner or later the cops would be led to the farm, thanks to Olga, and then even the girl detective would find something to send them here. But exactly how long that process would take, he didn't know. He was just glad that he'd beaten them here as well as to the hide. Amateurs. 'Okay, give me your car keys.'

'Look, I can drive you anywhere you want to go,' Gosling replied.

'I just want your keys, now.'

Gosling reluctantly pulled a car key from his pocket and slid them across the breakfast bar. Igor saw the VW logo on the key which matched the logo on the hatchback in the driveway.

'This is all wrong, Igor, there is no way Olga is a double agent,' Gosling said.

'And you base this on what?'

'Just, that she can't be, she is a high ranking official. She outranks you, even.'

Gosling's last remark really pissed Igor off, as if he needed to be reminded that the traitorous bitch was his senior. It was a joke. She'd probably shagged her way up the ladder.

'You only find her treachery hard to believe because it is you who caused her arrest.'

'I told you, I texted her to warn her.'

'You are a traitor, but you didn't know that she was, so you inadvertently betrayed a fellow betrayer without knowing it. It is that which upsets you so, no?'

'Just take the car and go, and take your daft conspiracy theories with you. I have never been anything but loyal to the motherland. As far back as the glorious Soviet years. So why would I betray beloved Russia now. I have helped more operatives than you have ever met. I texted her, but I also knew she was leaving anyway. I actually thought she would be long gone by the time she received my text.'

Igor hesitated. He was aware how long Gosling had been a sympathiser and he also knew of some of the serious operations he had assisted with. All of which had been apparent successes. So why now. Perhaps he was reacting to the threat of the tax inspectors. The idiot should not have put himself in that position in the first place. He'd made himself vulnerable through his greed. And as loyal as all these sympathisers would always claim to be, they never sent their pay cheques back. They were all greedy. 'Show me the text, and be quick,' Igor said. He then followed him into the front room. Gosling muted the TV and then reached underneath it, and a few seconds later he pulled out a pay-as-you-go mobile phone. He fired it up, pushed a few buttons and then handed it to Igor. It was open on a sent text message via WhatsApp. He recognised the number as one of Olga's, and the warning written in the message was clear. And it had been read by the recipient. It seemed that Gosling was telling the truth. Though Igor still considered him a risk. A risk he would not need to use again. He would tell his masters that when he arrived back in Moscow. But for now he would believe what Gosling had said, and leave him be.

Then time sped up as he handed the phone back to Gosling, and everything changed. He saw blue flashing lights sweep through the thin curtains and wash the walls in a disco-like hue. Time to go. Then the lightshow stopped.

***

Martin turned the car headlights off as they approached the address. It was situated in a quiet residential area. The house was detached and sat on a corner, where a T-junction had a further road running past. He pulled up short and then turned off the engine.

'I can see light emanating onto the front lawn. Hopefully, he's in,' Cath said.

'Yeah, especially as the decision has been made to move. We don't have the luxury of time to watch. Igor's on the loose getting further and further away.'

'Damn,' Martin said, as he saw a blue light flashing in his driver's mirror. 'They were told to make a silent approach.'

'Well, I can't hear any horns,' Cath said.

Then the lamp was extinguished as the marked ARV pulled up behind them and its headlamps were also turned off.

'See, no harm done,' Cath said.

Martin grunted and they both alighted and had a quick chat with the two armed officers who joined them in between the two cars. Martin pulled out his own handgun and checked its action before replacing it in his shoulder holster.

The older of the two firearms guys spoke, 'We should really just contain the property as best we can, until further units arrive and then go by the manual.'

Martin knew the guy was correct, but he was just desperate to get his hands on Gosling. To watch the colour drain from his objectionable face when they hit him with what they knew.

'I guess you're right. I'll take up a position at the front aspect, if you two cover the rear.'

Both uniformed officers nodded.

'We all on comms?'

More nods and Martin replaced his radio earpiece as the armed uniform officers slowly made their way towards the property.

'You can wait in the car, Cath; I'll duck down behind a neighbour's wall with a view on the front.'

'Bollocks to that, I'm coming with you, I'll be safe behind a wall.'

Martin didn't have time to argue and guessed the wall would be as safe as anything. Two minutes later they were in position crouched down at the end of the next door neighbour's drive. God knows what the householders would think if they suddenly appeared.

'I can't see a driveway at the target property,' Cath said.

Martin risked a glimpse over the wall and saw that she was right. 'It's a corner house; it's probably around the other side,' he said. He then checked over comms that the other two were in position. They said that they were, with a good view of the rear. The kitchen light was on but the back door looked like it had been forced. It was ajar and not sitting straight. This changed things.

A moment later Martin heard what sounded like a muffled pop.

He looked at Cath, and although he knew she was not used to firearms, even she asked, 'Was that what I think it was?'

Before he could reply his radio earpiece kicked into life. It was the older of the two officers, a PC 1222 James Grantham. 'Firearm discharged within the property.'

'You sure James?' Martin asked.

'One hundred percent; saw the muzzle flash through the thin rear room curtains. We're going in.'

'I'm right behind you,' Martin said, into his radio transmitter behind his coat lapel.

'And so am I,' Cath shouted.

'No,' Martin said, but he knew he couldn't stop her and had no time to try.

Within seconds they were in the back garden and could see the back of James and his mate as they went through the kitchen door. Martin and Cath joined them moments later. All three armed officers had their weapons drawn and held in a two-handed firing position.

Martin dropped his arms as he took in the scene. Midway between the doorways from the lounge to the kitchen laid the body of Derek Gosling. He was lying face down with a burnt gunshot entry wound at the back of his head. Point blank range discharge. Dark crimson blood was pooling away from his face. His head was on its side, and half his face was missing from the exit impact. He put his arm out to halt Cath, as he slowly stepped backwards as his crime scene protection head kicked in. James and his mate had continued through the house, and he could hear 'clear' being shouted several times.

After a minute, Martin and Cath were re-joined by James and his partner. James said, 'We can only have just missed the bastard.'

Martin nodded and said, 'We need to get out of here and limit our disturbance. Can you two check the back garden just in case he's in the bushes, but be careful.'

'Aye, aye Skip,' James said, and both men rushed off.

Martin opened the front door and he and Cath walked outside. He was glad to breathe fresh air, and be away from the grizzly sight of Gosling. And the metallic smell of fresh blood. He asked if Cath was alright and she said that she was, though she looked a little shaken.

He walked down the driveway at the far side of the house and pulled his phone from his pocket, but before he could dial a number, Cath prodded him. 'What?'

'When we ran in, there was a car on the drive. I noticed its nose sticking out beyond the building line. We couldn't see it from the wall. And now it's gone.'

'Shit, shit, shit,' Martin said, for a second time.

RED HERRING

Chapter Forty-two

Martin, Cath, and Colin didn't leave the meeting in Don Rogers' office until late, and all headed home to get some rest. The details of the car owned by Gosling had been circulated nationally with a 'report location, but don't approach' marker attached. Current thinking was that Igor would dump the car as soon as he could. A full search detail would be working through the night to hunt outwards from Gosling's house in ever increasing concentric circles.

The crime scene at the house was being forensically examined, and the body would be moved to the mortuary as soon as the scientists were happy for it to be disturbed. The dead drop box had been searched, and a mobile telephone had been recovered and would be examined as a matter of urgency. Though nothing would happen until the following morning.

Olga was horrified to be told of Gosling's death, particularly as it made her feel all the more vulnerable. She was anxious to be moved as soon as possible, and that the movement and the address of the safe house be kept secret. Martin had reassured her again of this when they had a quick chat to inform her of Gosling's death, prior to the meeting at headquarters. This caused much discussion between the three of them and the Holy Trinity. Jeremy said he could offer them a safe house in the region, with a team of two SAS troopers present at all times. Sue Jennings said she could provide a covertly armed 'gunship' to back up an MI5 surveillance team to follow Olga from Preston police station to the safe house.

The Home Secretary Miranda Daniels asked Colin, if Cath and Martin could continue as liaison and interviewers with Olga as they had the relationship. It would only need to remain so whilst the threat with Igor continued, and until such time as Olga's true allegiance had been proved. There was still some doubt, though both Martin and Cath had said that they were becoming more and more comfortable with her.

As the midnight meeting drew to a close, Jennings asked Martin and Cath, 'Olga seems very concerned about the safe house.'

'She is really scared of Igor,' Martin said.

'Granted, but from what you have said, she seems concerned that its location could become known beyond those who need to know.'

Cath answered with, 'She has more than hinted that there is an extensive network of sympathisers whose day jobs could be anywhere. Even in supporting roles within the police and elsewhere.'

'A jolly thought,' Jeremy threw in. 'Can't wait to fully debrief her about those, when we get the chance.'

'She claims not to know many details due to the cellular design of the system, but I'm sure she can give you the scope of the network, if only in generic detail,' Cath said.

'Well, it does us all no harm to make sure it's kept tight, Jeremy?' Daniels said.

'Only I, a maintenance team from MI5, and the SAS troopers will know the address. The surveillance and armed escort won't be told. After all, their job is to follow and protect; wherever that leads to,' Jeremy answered.

'What about us?' Cath asked.

'You simply head towards Manchester and you will receive text updates en route.'

'So how many people in total will know,' Rogers asked.

'The SAS will work shifts, so eight in total there. The safe house maintenance team consists of two, and me. Five will give me a list of ten addresses but won't know which one I'll pick. This is all standard, it's as tight as it can be,' Jeremy said.

'What about the following teams?' Martin asked.

'Normal procedure is for them to be stood down as you approach the final estate where the house is, you'll run in the last bit alone. It'll be three or four minutes, maximum.'

'It all sounds tight enough,' Rogers commented.

'Hmm, a shame in some ways,' Jeremy said.

All eyes in the office stared at the screen with Jeremy's face on it.

'Explain?' Daniels said from her screen.

'Well, if we could find a way of leaking the details of the address in a manner that would ensure it reached Igor's ear...'

'Not happening. You are not using my officers as bait,' Rogers said.

'Agreed, chief constable. I hope you are listening Jeremy. That is not going to happen, or do I need to get the Foreign Secretary to tell you?' Daniels said.

'Just shooting the breeze, Home Secretary, but understood. We'll just have to rely on you lot catching Igor ASAP. And in any event, Igor will be incommunicado, we suspect.'

That had brought the meeting to an end and had left Cath and Martin slightly unnerved. They had decided to bunk down in the police training school for the night, and discussed it as they walked the short distance to the accommodation blocks.

'You don't think Jeremy would actually contemplate such a leak, do you?' Cath asked.

'I wouldn't put much past that snake, but in this case, no. The Home Sec. made it clear. Plus, notwithstanding Igor's thirst to get at Olga, he's not stupid. He'd suspect any intel as flawed and a potential set up, surely.'

'If you say so. I Know you know him better than me.'

Martin could see that Cath looked reassured. He just wished he felt as she looked. He shook it off and said, 'Come on, let's get our heads down, we've got an early start.'

Chapter Forty-three

Igor had intended to leave Gosling be, having been partly
persuaded by him of his loyalty. That was until he saw the blue
lights wash once around Gosling's front room and then stop. He
crawled out of the front door on his belly to get a quick view, and
saw the police car parked up behind a civilian car. He was
withdrawing when he saw the girl detective alight from the
civilian car with a woman and huddle in close to the uniformed
cops. That had sealed Gosling's fate. He reverse crawled back in
and closed the door. He didn't bother confronting the farmer
again, no point, and no time. He had to act quickly.

He used a cushion from the settee in the front room to supress
the discharge from the Glock. It had been effective, but not as
much as a proper flash eliminator would have been. It had only
taken one shot, and he knew he had to move fast in case the
police had heard it. Conscious that the uniform cops, who would
be armed, may already be at the rear, he crawled out the front
again. Just in time to see the girl detective, and the analyst
woman running towards the house. He half hoped that they
would approach the front; they would get a surprise if they did,
but they flew down the side of the house towards the rear.
Probably for the best. He jumped to his feet, closed the door and
headed to the VW Hatchback parked at the far side of the house.
It fired up straight away and he drove away as quietly as he
could.

Every sinew in his being was screaming at him to floor the
accelerator. He resisted the urge until he had joined the main
road, which ran past the side of the property, and was out of
sight. Plus, he knew that the daft British cops would be making
loads of noise shouting their "armed police" warnings. They
really were amateurs. Once he had safely put some miles
between them and him, he knew he would have to dump the
motor quickly. He found a small hamlet on the east of Ormskirk
called Bickerstaff. It was near a junction for the M58 motorway.
This linked Liverpool with the main M6 motorway, which ran

north to Scotland, and south to the Midlands. He hoped they would find it quickly and assume that he had hitched a ride onto the motorway.

In fact, he yomped across the fields for several miles easterly, until he found himself on the outskirts of a small town called Orrell, near the larger town of Wigan. It was also near the M6 motorway. It had felt good to do some proper exercise again after days of being locked up in that tiny police cell. His initial plan was to steal a car from a house that was unoccupied. His thinking being, that if he broke in and grabbed the car keys, the owner would not know until they returned. It was holiday season, and he soon found several residential addresses where the curtains were all open and no lights were on. He realised that could mean anything from, the occupants being on a late night out, away overnight or being on a four week cruise somewhere, or suchlike. He had no way of knowing.

He was in luck, the first house he entered, which had a decent motor on the drive, had the keys hung up in the kitchen next to a 'going away to-do-list'. He'd no way of knowing how long the owners were away, but he only needed a couple of days. His escape plan, thanks to his assortment of fake IDs, was to get a ferry from the Lancashire town of Heysham as a foot passenger at the busiest part of the day, to the Isle of Man in the Irish Sea. He knew that even with a fake British passport, facial recognition could be his undoing. This is why he chose the Isle of Man. It was part of the UK so he wouldn't be passing through an international border, so hoped that security would be less acute. Also, the world famous Isle of Man TT motorcycle races were due to start, so the ferry port would be manic. He knew that enthusiasts flocked from around the world onto the tiny island.

Once on the isle he could get another ferry to Belfast in Northern Island, which of course was also still part of the UK. Once more the security at the port would not be the same as with an international one. From there he could simply walk or drive across the unpoliced border with Southern Ireland. Then his fake Irish passport would come into play. As Ireland is part of the EU, he would have unfettered access to all twenty-seven countries of the bloc, from where he could easily cross into Russia.

As he drove away from Orrell, in the newly stolen BMW saloon, he had one more task which he desperately wanted to complete. But knew he had no way of doing so, and even if he could, he would be taking a huge risk. His training was telling him to stick to his escape plan, which he thought was a good one. Plus, with every day that passed, more and more risk would be attached to it. He'd have to leave that last task locked away in box number four.

He joined the M6 and headed north. It didn't take long before he started to pass the turnoffs for Preston. He knew from pre-operational reconnaissance that there were five possible exits from the M6 to Preston, and as he passed each one the temptation to leave the motorway increased. He knew where she was, but that was all. What could he do? As he passed junction 32, which was the Broughton exit and link to the Blackpool motorway, he muttered, 'One day bitch, one day.'

Igor then shook Olga from his mind and headed north towards Heysham. He had plenty of time to kill, and had one last detour to make. He knew of another hide. It was a secondary backup hide, so wouldn't contain weapons or ordinance, but it may have cash, or additional resources. He pretty much had all he needed from the Ring 'O Bells second hide, but it would be remiss not to check it. It was in Williamson's Park in Lancaster, which was actually not a detour at all; it was en route to the port. He'd no idea if this hide was even still active, as it had not been part of his brief for this operation. But it was worth a visit whilst it was still dark. Plus, he knew one hundred percent that Olga had no knowledge of it, so it was safe to approach. He'd used it on a previous intelligence gathering operation a couple of years ago, and had only just recalled it as he settled into his drive north.

RED HERRING

Chapter Forty-four

Martin and Cath were at Preston nick by 5 a.m., Colin was already there. Stood next to him was a tall slim man in his thirties wearing smart casuals. Colin introduced him as Bill; he was their driver for the day from MI5. He was trained in all manner of surveillance, high security escort, mobile evasion techniques and more. Introductions over, Bill passed Cath a pay-as-you-go phone and explained that the updates on directions would come through it. She was to keep him briefed.

'Of course,' Cath replied.

'Martin, as the warranted officer, you can ride in the back handcuffed to Olga.'

Martin was about to agree, when he remembered that Cath as a newly sworn-in special constable could do his role. He explained this and added that Olga would probably prefer to be manacled to Cath rather than him. Cath agreed, and so did Bill. Cath handed the phone to Martin and he added, 'I'll ride shotgun with you up front.' Bill nodded.

'So who exactly will we have behind us?' Martin asked.

'A full surveillance team from our Manchester office is currently plotted up around the police station. A covert, armed response vehicle, courtesy of Counter Terrorism, will ride permanently behind the rearmost vehicle unless it's called forward. The surveillance command vehicle - call sign, Alpha One - will be in charge at all times. Well, until they are called off in the final minutes as we approach the safe house, which has the call sign, Sierra Hotel 7,'

Martin remembered what Jeremy had said about there being a list of ten safe houses in the region, and guessed that Sierra Hotel 7 was number seven on that list. Colin wished them luck and said he would be available on his phone if needed.

Martin and Cath got their stuff together and then roused a sleepy Olga in her cell. When they told her what was happening she displayed a mixture of relief and gratitude. And a comment about 'hot baths' and 'a proper bed'. The relief on the face of the custody sergeant was off the scale. 'Thank God, we can try and return things to normal, now.'

Martin and Cath smiled and once Cath was handcuffed to Olga, he led them out the rear steel door from the custody office into the back yard of the nick. Idling a few feet away was a Range Rover with blacked out rear passenger windows. Cath and Olga got into the back, and Martin jumped in the front next to Bill. Martin noticed that Bill was wearing a radio earpiece, so he put his own in his left ear. Obviously, Bill didn't want the radio chatter to be heard by Olga through the vehicle's speakers. This was confirmed when Martin saw Bill throw an innocuous looking rocker switch to its down position; speakers to earpieces.

Then Bill pressed a button on the steering wheel and said, 'Bill to Alpha One, we have the friendly.'

Martin heard Alpha One acknowledge Bill, and then turned to face Cath who had taken the hint and was fitting her own earpiece.

'Still don't trust me, eh?' Olga said.

'It's not that,' Martin said. 'Just radio commentary. Standard procedure. Have you heard how loud car speakers are when you are sat in traffic next to some tosser on the phone on hands-free?' This was actually true, and Olga smiled.

Bill set off driving briskly out of the police station compound onto the streets, and headed towards the city's inner ring road. Martin knew this was the general direction towards junction 31 of the M6 - the main access to or from Preston central. He pulled the pay-as-you-go phone out of his pocket and placed it in a dashboard recess in front of him.

He nestled into the car's sumptuous chair, and listened to the surveillance team's commentary. A comms check confirmed everyone's presence, including Foxtrot One which he assumed was the Counter Terrorism Unit's armed car; or 'gunship' as Sue Jennings had referred to it as. And notwithstanding an added formality with the use of some proper call signs, the chatter was still relaxed. But that probably just hid their confident professionalism.

Olga broke Martin's musings, with, 'So, what happens once we are settled in our new home?'

'We carry on the de-brief for a while until we are told not to,' he replied.

'What more can I tell you?'

'As much as you can about the network of sympathisers, would be a good start,' Martin said, and noticed Bill suddenly showing interest in the chat.

'I don't know much more.'

'Just all you do know will do for now.'

'Then what?'

'At some stage you will be handed over to the security service or secret intelligence services' handlers, long term, and our role will be over.'

'Will you miss me?'

'No offence, but probably not.'

'Nor me,' Cath threw in.

Martin noted that they were now on the M6 southbound headed in the general direction of Manchester, which was as much as anyone involved knew of their intended destination.

'Will our driver Bill be one of my handlers?'

'Sorry to disappoint, but I'm not an agent handler,' Bill said.

Then the pay-as-you-go vibrated on the dash interrupting the chat, and Martin grabbed hold of it. An incoming text from an unidentified number. He read it out loud, 'Do a recip at the next exit.' Martin knew that recip meant reciprocal, and was surveillance parlance for an about turn. Bill reacted as they passed the countdown markers for the exit at 29, Bamber Bridge, south of Preston. The timing suggested that the sender of the message knew exactly where they were. He guessed the motor probably had a tracker wired into it. He listened as the surveillance chatter responded to their movement. They left the motorway, crossed over it, and then circumnavigated a roundabout before re-joining it, and headed back the way they had come.

Five minutes later things became even more interesting; they were directed to do another recip, and then to leave the motorway at junction 29 and head down a dual carriageway towards the centre of Preston. Martin knew that at least half the surveillance convoy would have been temporarily lost during the manoeuvres, and would be playing some serious high speed catch up. It was almost as it they were on a training course, but Martin knew that whoever was texting them was just ensuring that no one else was following. That was really the team's leader - Alpha One's - job; he would no doubt be pissed off. It certainly should make for an interesting debrief. All surveillances were debriefed and often in Martin's experience they could get a bit tasty. He was sorry that they wouldn't be there to watch it.

They were further directed to head west and join the A59 which would take them towards Liverpool. Then a further recip back towards Bamber Bridge. The radio chatter was intense and Martin could only imagine the frustration mounting in the command car. Once they were back at Junction 29, they didn't re-join the M6 as he expected, but the M65 which travels into East Lancashire. Martin reckoned they still only had half the team behind them. The armed car - Foxtrot One - announced that it would have to use its hidden blues, just to get back to Bamber Bridge; they were that far behind. Alpha One authorised them to do so - usually a big, no, no on surveillance - but to turn the equipment off before they joined the M65.

Ten minutes later, they left the motorway at one of the feeder junctions for Blackburn, a large industrial town which was the gateway to East Lancashire. They navigated a huge roundabout at Whitebirk on the eastern outskirts, and then onto a road named after Carl Fogarty, the ex-World Superbike motorcycle racing champion. A number of texts further directed them through some back streets until they were on a major urban road named Audley Range. Whoever was sending them directions clearly had a good knowledge of the area.

But as they left Carl Fogarty Way, the text arrived to stand the surveillance team down. Bill looked at Martin as he read it out, and then hit the car's radio transmit button to pass the instruction on. A second later Alpha One stood the whole team down, and Martin could hear a succession of call signs acknowledging the order. They were all directed to return to their Manchester base for debrief. Then everything went quiet.

'I guess this is the tricky bit, now we are on our own,' Martin said, to no one in particular. He suddenly felt vulnerable for the first time, and noted that the expressions on Olga and Cath's faces had taken on a sterner countenance.

'We won't be far away, now,' Bill said in a reassuring tone.

Then the final text came through with a caveat, that it, and all the previous missives be deleted. Martin read it out; it contained the address of Sierra Hotel 7.

'I know it,' Bill said, I've been there before; it's in the middle of a huge council estate called Shadsworth. We are literally only minutes away,'

Bill accelerated and left the main road as they entered the huge estate, and Martin set to deleting all the text messages as instructed. They'd made it without incident, not that they had really expected any. The identity of their location had been closely guarded, right up until the last moments. But he would still feel relief when they could all sit down with a nice cup of tea. As if reading his mind, Cath said, 'I hope there is a kettle and some tea bags in the house.'

'There will be everything we need. It's an end terrace and we also own next door, so we shouldn't be disturbed,' Bill said.

'What is it with you Brits and tea?' Olga asked, and a laugh rippled around the car as Bill navigated them deeper into the estate.

Chapter Forty-five

A little earlier.

Colonel Pavel Popov was in his office when the door suddenly opened without being knocked on first. If it was his staff officer, Boris, he would be in for a severe bollocking. But Popov closed his mouth as Artem from the SVR came striding in. He paused as he slammed the door shut before he turned back to face Popov. He didn't look happy. In fact, he looked less happy than he had sounded on the phone when Popov spoke to him the previous evening.

'This is a fuck up. We have lost a long-standing and trusted sympathiser thanks to the gung-ho tactics of Igor. Typical GRU; all brawn and no brains,' Artem said.

'Hang on, there is no need for such insults,' Popov said, as he sat upright from the slouching position in his chair.

'You think not?' Artem said, as he loomed over Popov from the other side of the desk.

'Sit down and I'll order some refreshments.'

'I don't want refreshments.'

'Well, sit and calm down, and then we can talk.'

Artem sat in an armchair set to one side of Popov's desk, and added, 'Have you any idea how hard it is, and how long it takes to recruit these sympathisers? And it's getting harder since we attacked Ukraine; all the ideological half-wits who previously believed our propaganda have all woken up and smelled the coffee.'

'Are you sure you don't want a coffee?'

Artem glared at him as if he was making light of the situation, which he was not.

Then Artem said, 'I knew we should never have given you access to our hidden assets.'

'You still have your other asset in place, with the promise of much more once Olga is fully accepted.'

RED HERRING

Artem went quiet for a moment as he looked to be chewing over what Popov had said. He'd witnessed Artem's tantrums before; he usually blew himself inside out quite quickly.

'And we don't want junior officers hearing their seniors arguing, do we?' Popov added. He could imagine Boris's ear firmly attached to the other side of the door.

In a lower voice, Artem continued, 'What will your nutter do next, and why can't you contact him?'

'You know he will have gone dark, normal escape and evasion protocol in case any signals are intercepted.'

'Okay, granted, but he hates Olga, and truly believes that she has gone over to the other side. It was her who led the Brits to him, after all.'

'Yes, and it was all part of the script. The *agreed* script, remember?'

'I know, I know, but he's escaped and is on the loose. You assured me that he was not an idiot, and that as much as he hates Olga, he wouldn't put his own safety at risk. That he would flee the UK with the assistance we had left in place for any escape eventuality.'

'This is all true.'

'But it isn't; he's killed the farmer.'

'Okay, but we don't know exactly why, I'm sure he probably thought he was just covering his tracks prior to leaving the country. You know, severing the link so as to give him a clean run of things.'

'I guess that makes some semblance of sense; albeit in a pretty heavy handed way. But that said, you are the GRU after all.'

Popov ignored the further slur. The intelligence types of the SVR were not soldiers; they were the sneaky snake types who slid from the shadows, whereas his officers were the true warriors. Often his staff would be called on by the SVR to do dirty, and wet work, while Artem's snakes sat shivering from the side-lines. Popov was more than willing to throw his understanding of their departments professional differences back at Artem, but he guessed now was not the time for such a heated debate. Then he did say, 'Look, as long as Igor remains incommunicado it can only mean that he is still observing the escape and evasion protocols. So he is no threat.'

He watched as Artem considered what he had said, which was actually true.

'And how do you know that he will stick to the letter of those protocols?'

'Because; er, no disrespect,' Popov started, and then paused to choose his words carefully, 'as my operatives are all ex-military, they are drilled senseless to obey orders no matter what.' He immediately regretted using the word senseless and half expected Artem to seize on it; if he did, then the gloves might have to come off. But thankfully he didn't.

'How long will it take him?' Artem asked.

'Twenty-four or forty-eight hours, probably the latter, depending on which route he chooses.'

Artem nodded as he got to his feet.

'And don't forget this hiccup is all the fault of the useless Brits for allowing Igor to escape in the first place.'

'Granted.'

'And once he is home safely, it means we won't have to release any of theirs in an exchange.'

'Very true,' Artem said; his voice back to normal now.'

'Any idea where they will take Olga to, because they will undoubtedly move her now Igor is free?'

'We are working on it, I'm hopeful we might find out,' Artem said.

This surprised Popov, and he asked, 'How, when?' trying to hide his growing irritation from his voice.

Artem stopped halfway to the door and looked back at Popov as he casually answered, 'The how doesn't matter. The when could be anytime.'

'And you are only sharing this with me now?' Popov asked, now unable to hide his disquiet.

'Doesn't really matter where they take her, does it? Nor that we learn where. Not really. It just matters that she is accepted.'

It was Popov's turn to calm down; he knew that Artem was correct. It was just the silly game being played which annoyed him, the 'I know something you don't' one. Childish playoffs of one-upmanship. As long as Olga was truly accepted, it didn't matter where she was.

Popov nodded a goodbye at Artem who reciprocated and then headed to the door. Once there, he stopped and turned to face Popov.

'One last thing?'

'Go on.'

'How close is Volkov to Igor?'

'Why do you ask?'

'He's on a dangerous mission, and I'd hate to think that either of us would face extra grief from the top if Igor doesn't make it back safely.'

'You've no need to worry: he will make it back, I'm sure. He's one of our best operatives, and I hear that Volkov only tolerates him as he is married to his niece.'

Artem smiled and added, 'I suspect he barely tolerates most of us.'

Popov knew that Artem was back on board fully by making such a remark, and he added, 'We will be more than tolerated once we can prove the success of our mission.'

Artem smiled wider, nodded, then left.

Chapter Forty-six

Williamson Park was easy to find, situated near the city centre of Lancaster, Lancashire's County Town. Fifty-four acres of parkland which had once been moorland and had even housed a gallows; it was constructed in the 1870s by the Williamson family. On top of a hill was the Ashton Memorial, named after James Williamson junior - Lord Ashton - who finished the park and handed it to the people in the 1880s. The memorial to his own passing was added in the twentieth century to mark his philanthropic efforts. The white stone structure at the top of the hill was where Igor was now headed, or to be more accurate, the trees which surrounded the edifice.

He had waited until the early hours to make his approach, which had allowed time to recce the area, just to be on the safe side. It was clear, as he expected it to be. This was another secret Olga didn't know, so couldn't betray. He just hoped the detour and delay would be worth the effort. Perhaps there was a secure phone he could use to contact Moscow. Notwithstanding his understanding of protocols, he knew that certain high tec phones used by the GRU were virtually untraceable and nearly impossible to intercept. They recorded a message and then sent it in a high speed burst which lasted only a millisecond. But he doubted that such kit would be in the hide. For one, it would need regular attention to keep it charged. He wasn't sure that the SVR trusted their sympathisers with such sophisticated kit. He knew he wouldn't.

Once facing the front of the monument, Igor turned to face left - it was always to the left - and then used a similar system to the British Windthrop search method. This was developed by a Royal Engineer of that name, serving in Northern Ireland during the troubled years, in order to spot subtle indications which would lead to the hide. It was now pre-dawn and there was just enough light to assist him, but he knew he would have to be quick before the first joggers of the day started arriving.

RED HERRING

Having followed the clues he quickly found the hide at the base of tree. He lifted the turf to reveal a plastic container. There was no phone inside it, but there were a thousand pounds in used notes of varying denomination, and a similar amount in euros; both would be very handy. There was also a white envelope which looked new. Igor hesitated as he examined it. There was nothing written on the outside, and the envelope wasn't sealed. He carefully opened the flap to reveal a single page of lined paper folded in two. He pulled the letter out and opened it up. On it was a note written in Russian.

Igor read the contents with incredulity. It was clearly meant for him though didn't use his name. The writer was clearly being speculative in not knowing whether he would have checked the hide. He was so glad that he did. But he had to read it several times. The narrative was short but potentially massive in its meaning. This changed everything. He quickly considered whether it was a British trap, but discarded that. If the British knew of the hide, they would have just staked it out. No need for an elaborate misdirection.

He knew that his ferry to Belfast from Heysham would be in a few hours and that the port was only a few miles away. He also knew that there were several crossings each day. If what the note said was correct, it presented him with a quandary; he should ignore it and get the hell out of Dodge as the Americans might say. But as he mused over whether to disregard it, he realised that someone had obviously visited the hide, possibly only hours previously. And that somebody knew far more than the average sympathiser should. He glanced at his watch; he'd have to step on it.

***

A little later - back to present the time.

The farther Bill drove into the Shadsworth estate, the more Martin relaxed. He guessed the same was true in the rear seat, too. They approached a T junction and turned left. The road was a mix of pre-war semi-detached houses and some older terraced ones. Bill told them that they were now on the road where Sierra Hotel Seven was situated. It was at the far end of the street on the right-hand side where the buildings stopped. Martin could see that the highway appeared to end in front of a clump of trees. They were approaching a crossroads with a similar thoroughfare to the one they were on, it had the right of way and Bill brought the car to a halt by the give way lines.

Martin heard the approaching car before he saw it. It was coming from their right and the engine note suddenly increased, as did the vehicle's speed. A boy racer no doubt. He was glad that Bill had given way. Then in an instant the oncoming saloon car veered to its left, and headed straight for them. They had no time to react, other than to brace themselves. The front of the speeding car rammed into the driver's side of their motor. It careered on forward, as they spun around in an anticlockwise direction. They came to a stop facing the way in which they had come. Air bags went off in the front and Martin heard screaming coming from both Cath and Olga.

'Are you two okay?' he asked, as he fought to deflate his air bag.

'Yes,' Cath answered.

'Look,' Olga shouted.

Martin was suddenly aware of a presence by the driver's side of the vehicle; a lessening of light. He instinctively looked and saw a silhouette facing Bill, square on. The shadow was holding a gun in an outstretched arm, and before he could react he saw fire and heard sound spit from its muzzle as the man shot Bill twice in the head.

One round passed straight through Bill and just missed Martin. The side window was smashed by the impact and Martin took in the shooter in more detail, notwithstanding the sun shining from behind him.

'Hello again, Girl Detective,' Igor said, as recognition hit Martin with the speed of the fired rounds.

'My God, you. But how?' Martin managed to say, as he continued to wrestle with his airbag.

'The how is not important,' Igor said, as he turned to face the rear seat of their vehicle. He pushed his gun arm in through the broken driver's window and pointed it at Cath and Olga.

206

'Hello my dear Olga,' Igor said.

'Igor, thank God, you've come to rescue me,' Olga said.

'Not quite,' Igor replied, as a sick grin spread across his face.

Then Martin heard three shots in quick succession before he could say, or do anything to try to stop Igor.

Then reality, as Martin knew it, turned upside down. Time slowed to a crawl as Martin watched in disbelief as Igor's head exploded into a thousand fragments of bone and gore. He immediately dropped his gun unfired which clattered to the ground, a moment before his cadaver did.

Martin spun around in his seat, his airbag fully deflated now, to check on Cath and Olga. Both were unhurt, but rooted to the spot with slack-jawed expressions of disbelief.

Martin assimilated what had just happened as time caught up, and he leapt from his seat and pulled his Glock pistol from his shoulder holster. An instinctive reaction, which could give the wrong signal, though he could not see anyone about. He quickly put his weapon away on realising what had taken place. 'Quick, you two, out now,' he shouted at Cath and Olga. 'We can cover the last hundred metres on foot, before the balloon goes up.

There was an otherworldly stillness all around the scene which Martin knew would soon transcend into one of utter chaos. They had to get moving.

As all three of them joined the pavement and quickly crossed the junction to the other side, Cath said, 'Who were they?'

'Must have been the SAS troopers from the house. They must have been covertly following us after the surveillance team pulled away. Just to watch us in.'

'Well, thank the Lord they did,' Cath said. 'But how the hell did Igor know?'

'That's a question for another time, and for someone else to work out.'

'I thought I was dead,' Olga said, as she shuffled along the pavement trying to keep up with Cath.

'"Igor, thank God, you've come to rescue me",' Martin said.

'I was just trying to stay alive, thinking on my feet,' Olga added.

Martin didn't answer, he could understand; just.

Two minutes later, as they approached the front path of the end terraced house, Martin could hear approaching sirens and risked a glance behind. A crowd had now formed at the crossroads, but thankfully no one was looking their way. They were all too preoccupied looking inwards at the gruesome scene.

As soon as they approached the front door, it was opened by a man in casual clothes, who said, 'Quick, get in.'

All three of them did, and as soon as they had the man slammed the front door shut. He was in his thirties and about 5'6" in all directions. He said his name was Ged as they all came to a halt inside a rear living room. They were immediately joined by a second man, who was taller and slimmer with longer dark hair. He introduced himself as Chris; both troopers from 22 SAS.

'You guys didn't waste any time getting back here. But thanks so much,' Martin said.

Cath yanked the handcuffs, which brought Olga into the conversation.

'Yes, thank you so much. A second later, and I for one would be dead. And if I know Igor, and I do, all three of us would probably be gone.'

'We were watching you in,' Ged said.

'And we recognised Igor Jakinsky, the fugitive from our briefing notes,' Chris added.

'But not the other two,' Ged said.

'What other two?' Martin asked.

'The shooters,' Chris answered.

'I don't understand,' Martin said who then looked at Cath and Olga, and could see that they didn't either.

'We saw Igor hit your car and pulled our weapons and were about to engage, when the other two broke cover and opened fire,' Chris said.

'We were about to go after them, but a van pulled up and they were off in an instant. This meant that the threat was over, and our primary mission in keeping you safe kicked back in. We had to watch them leave, though Chris has just updated our control room, who will speak to yours.'

'So who were they?' Cath asked.

'No idea, but they were military, that much was obvious,' Chris said.

'Not blue on blue, surely?' Martin asked.

'Just don't know; could have been; Paras perhaps; or not,' Chris answered.

'I reckon, not,' Ged threw in.

'So what now?' Cath asked, as she took a seat on a settee dragging Olga with her.

'We have to consider this place compromised,' Martin said.

'Agreed,' both Ged and Chris said in unison.

'I'll ring Colin for instructions,' Martin added.

'Well, be quick, I don't fancy hanging around should the shooters decide to have another go,' Ged said.

'I'll put the kettle on, we can always fit a quick brew in,' Chris said, and then headed into the kitchen.

Chapter Forty-seven

Colin took a deep breath before he entered Don Rogers' office. He knew Rogers would be prancing up and down, and Sue Jennings would be trying to calm him. He also expected Jeremy and the Home Sec. to be on screen, he was the junior rank and shit only ran one way. But all this aside, he couldn't help thinking about the MI6 driver Bill who had lost his life. First an MI5 escort, and now Bill. The atmosphere would be thick. And it would become even thicker once he had said what had been tormenting him ever since he'd taken Martin's call.

Until they knew exactly what they were dealing with he'd instructed Martin and Cath to take a car from their SAS security detail, and head to a hotel, any hotel, and to tell only him which one. He'd also told him to do so without their SAS minders. Not that he suspected them for one second, and it would be arguably much safer with them in tow. But until he had answers as to who the gunmen were, and how they got to the safe house, it would be safer that way.

He knocked on the heavy mahogany door and started to enter without waiting for the 'come' command from the chief. The room was as he expected with the added surprise that Jeremy was actually present. He also noticed that the monitors were switched off, so no Home Sec. They all convened on the Chesterfields.

'What a weapons-grade fuck up,' Rogers opened with.

No one responded.

'How are we managing the scene?'

'I've spoken to the ACC Crime and she is aware of the sensitivities,' Sue Jennings said.

'Where is the body of our chap?' Jeremy asked.

'Under guard in a local mortuary, along with Igor,' Sue answered.

'And where are your staff and the lovely Olga?' Rogers asked Colin.

'I've moved them to somewhere I know is safe,' Colin answered. He swallowed as he knew what was coming next.

'I didn't ask you what type of place, I asked you where?'

'With respect, sir, it's probably best I don't share that.'

'I'll decide what is best and what is not, Chief Inspector.'

'Nothing personal, sir, but we obviously have a serious breach here, so in order to protect you, and everyone else, it is best only I know where they are. Just until we figure it out.'

'We fucking know what went on; a cluster-fuck, that's what.'

'I demand that you tell us where Olga is, now,' Jeremy added.

'Why, what difference would it make? Just be thankful that she is still alive.' Colin said.

'I'll decide what difference it would make, so I'm telling you again to identify where they are,' Jeremy said.

'Not until we work out what has happened,' Colin said. He could feel the pressure in the room heading towards critical mass, and all of it on his shoulders.

'Come on chief constable, order your man here to comply,' Jeremy said to Rogers.

'Don't tell me what to do,' Rogers replied to him.

'Well, someone has to,' Jeremy said.

The chief's face was almost comical, it had become crimson and his jaw hung open. Colin needed the chief on his side, and saw his chance to change the dynamics; redirect the pressure towards Jeremy. 'Don't take this the wrong way,' he started with, while holding Jeremy in a fixed stare. 'But the leak didn't come from our side, as neither Martin nor Cath, or I, knew of the location of the safe house. You actually hinted that it was in Manchester, not Blackburn.'

'Meaning what, actually?'

'Meaning only your lot or the SAS troopers knew the location. So unless we are accusing the SAS of murder…?'

'This is preposterous, chief constable, do your duty,' Jeremy said.

Bingo. Colin sat back and waited, and it wasn't long before Rogers bit.

'What do you know of duty? And if you try to order me to do something again I'll—'

'You'll what?' Jeremy interrupted.

Colin jumped in before it went too far, 'As far as we all knew, Igor was operating under escape and evasion protocols. Then something must have changed.'

'No shit, Sherlock,' Jeremy said.

Ignoring the slight, Colin continued, 'That change can only be that he was not only made aware of the safe house's location, but the time that the escort was due to arrive. We all knew the latter, but only the security, and intelligence services knew the former.'

Jeremy turned to face Colin square on. 'Meaning what exactly?' he said again.

Colin took a breath and a moment's pause, here goes, 'Meaning, did you leak the details to the Russians in order to draw Igor out?'

It was now Jeremy's turn to go puce in the face. After a stunned pause, he answered, 'And I suppose the shooters were other SAS on my orders, too, were they?'

Colin had expected a more robust reply and was waiting for the bollocking of a lifetime from Rogers, but he was surprised when Sue Jennings jumped in with her first comment.

'It would explain why the SAS detail from the house didn't engage the shooters as they fled. Come on Jeremy, I know how your mind works.'

'My God, you too, Sue. You really think that I would set this up, just to get at Igor. Have you forgotten that one of mine lost his life in the attack, and that Olga nearly did too?'

'As nearly did, two of mine,' Rogers said.

Colin could feel the whole dynamic shifting as all eyes were now on Jeremy.

'And you are the one demanding to know where they now are,' Sue added.

'Perhaps you wanted Olga dead, too? Perhaps timings went astray?' Rogers said.

Jeremy threw his hands up in the air, Colin had never seen the man look less arrogant, and wondered what was coming next.

'Okay, yes I wanted Igor, but not at the expense of Olga.'

'I hope she turns out to be worth it,' Rogers said.

'But I've truly no idea how the identity of the safe house was leaked, or how the hell that information was passed to Igor. But I accept that your side didn't know where the safe house was.'

'So I think we can all now calm down, and agree that DCI Carstairs has every right not to disclose where Olga and his staff currently are.' Sue said.

Colin breathed a sigh of relief; he now had a powerful ally on his side.

'Chief?' Sue asked Rogers.

Rogers nodded and grunted his acquiesce.

'So let's all take a breath, and try to work out what happened. And firstly, Jeremy, I think it prudent for you to start by telling us what it is you are holding back?'

Jeremy looked at Sue long and hard in clear consideration.

'You know who the attackers were, don't you, my God,' Rogers said.' It *was* from you.'

'Oh course it wasn't from me. I may have wanted Igor, especially, after what he did when escaping, but even I have my limits. But I accept I was being protective, but with good reason.'

'I always felt that you only ever told us as much as you felt you had to,' Rogers said.

Colin knew it was now time for him to sit back and just listen.

'Go on,' Sue said to Jeremy.

'Okay; my observer at the scene—'

'What? You had someone there?' Rogers interrupted with.

'From what my observer says,' Jeremy pushed on with, 'the attack had all the hallmarks of a Russian trained hit squad. The two SAS troopers who saw it have agreed.'

'A Russian hit squad on UK soil! How the hell could they have been arranged at such short notice? And how the hell could they get such a team into the country in time?' Sue asked sounding agitated for the first time.

'That's the bit I was trying to hide. We have long worried that they had a highly trained GRU kill squad implanted as sleepers over here. But this is the first proof we have that they actually exist.'

'My God, it just gets worse,' Rogers said.

Colin was shocked too on hearing this revelation, but kept silent.

'But I truthfully have no idea how the intel was leaked to them. That is of even greater concern. I promise you that only a handful knew, and I would bet my life on each and every one of their loyalties. Though they will all have to be looked at, obviously.'

'Does the Home Sec. know all this?' Sue asked.

'That's why she's not here. She's at a Cobra meeting with the Foreign Secretary discussing the ramifications of a high level compromise, together with the proof that a GRU kill squad is imbedded here. Plus, she said that she didn't want to witness the fallout amongst us.'

'So you honestly have no idea, how the information was leaked to Igor?' Rogers asked.

'Of course not,' Jeremy answered with.

'If I discover different...' Rogers said.

'You won't, you have my word.'

'Okay, for now; so let's move this on. Do we now believe that Olga is on our side?'

'The million dollar question,' Jeremy answered, with some of his gusto back in his voice.

RED HERRING

Chapter Forty-eight

The door to Popov's office burst open again, and in strode Artem with all the fanfare of his last visit. Popov got up from behind his desk and shut the door which Artem had left opened this time. He returned to his desk as Artem slouched down in the armchair.

'You know, we really must stop meeting like this. I much preferred it when we met at a kerbside café near Red Square.'

'There will be no more café's.'

'Well, whatever it is, just get it off your chest and then perhaps I can get back to my work.'

'It's your work that has caused all the problems.'

'Tell yourself that every morning do you? Practice it in the mirror whilst shaving?'

'This is not a joke.'

'Get to the point.'

'I knew it was a bad idea trying to run a joint operation with you.'

Popov sat up straight and glared at Artem, before saying, 'You agreed everything from the start. Look, what is this?' he was becoming rattled now.

'Joint leadership never works in an autocracy.'

'So this is a coup?'

'I've had to take executive action without you.'

'You've done what?'

'Using *your* sleeper assets.'

Popov was reaching critical mass. He'd no idea that Artem even knew about his buried GRU operatives, let alone have access to them. 'You wouldn't, couldn't,' he spluttered.

'And it was just as well, and just in time. You should be thanking me.'

'What have you done?'

When Artem elaborated, Popov was astonished.

'Your maverick Igor had already killed one of our sympathisers, and was about to deal the same fate on Olga,' Artem finished off with.

'Not possible. He had no idea where the Brits were taking her.'

'You leave the intelligence bit to me.'

'Your deep asset found out.'

Artem fell silent for the first time.

'But how would the asset be able to get the info to him?'

Artem failed to answer again. Then Popov smiled as he guessed a message drop at a back-up hide. 'So it was *your* fault that Igor was given the address.'

Artem said, 'Well, yes but by a misguided judgement, which I was able to stop.'

'You mean you have just, and only just, managed to clear up your own shit, and as a result I have lost a top operator,' Popov said, as he rose to his feet and walked around to the front of his desk. He could see that Artem's expression had lost some of its conceit.

'As you once said, "the mission comes first".'

'How did you manage to activate *my* GRU sleepers?'

'I ordered your staff officer Boris to pass the message, said it was a Red Star emergency.'

Popov was taken aback by Boris's disloyalty. Red Star priority or not; he would ensure he paid a heavy price for it once the operation was over.

'It's not his fault.'

'Why didn't you speak to me?'

'You were busy on one of your little jaunts that you think no one knows about, and I didn't have time to spare. As it was, they only just managed to stop Igor at the last possible second.'

Popov was stunned anew. He returned to his seat and wondered who else knew about his dirty little secret. Perhaps Artem didn't know all the details.

'Relax, I'm the only one who knows, and your secret's safe, for now.'

'Are you blackmailing me?'

'Into taking charge, yes. We will still appear to run a joint command, but I will have the final say. You will not take action without my agreement.'

So that was the bastard's angle. Just another power hungry snake who resented the military's power. Popov sat in contemplation for a moment, Artem had him.

'Look on the bright side; the catastrophe has been averted.'

'Caused by your department,' Popov interrupted with.

'And the mission is back on track.'

'At least this much is true.'

'So, as it is all about the intelligence side of things now, surely you can see that I am better placed to run things. I mean, once we were both satisfied that Olga had been fully accepted, it was always going to remain with me long term. I could argue now that the GRU are no longer needed.'

Popov knew that long term, what Artem had said was true, though the mission was not complete yet. He would hang on as long as a GRU intervention may be needed. But he was still incensed at being overruled and blackmailed into the bargain. But what could he do. The sooner the mission was truly over the sooner he and Artem could part company; that much he found attractive. 'Okay, but if we need my staff to fix any more of your cock-ups, you do it through me.'

'Agreed,' Artem said, as he got to his feet. 'See, that wasn't too bad, was it?'

Popov didn't answer, he just watched Artem leave his office and purposely leave his door ajar again. He would have to dig deep to stifle his growing hatred of the man. Minutes ago he considered him a friend - of sorts - but certainly an ally. One thing was clear though, when the operation was over he would deal with Artem and Boris. Not just for their effrontery, but they were the only two who knew his secret. And that had to be kept hidden at all costs. Boris would be easy to sort out, Artem would be trickier, but he'd find a way. The egotistical snakes at the SVR thought they were the brains, and the GRU were just the muscle. Popov would make it his next mission to prove the head snake so wrong.

Chapter Forty-nine

Martin, Cath and Olga settled into a Premier Inn on the outskirts of Manchester. As per Colin's instructions they had taken the SAS's Range Rover. Ged, in particular had insisted that they should go with them, but eventually gave up the debate. Martin told him that he would text him the following day to let him know where he could collect the motor from. Their instructions were to keep on the move and only tell Colin where they were, until they all worked out what had gone so catastrophically wrong. Martin had the firm's credit card and was to use that for everything. They ate in the restaurant next to the hotel and retired to the room early. It had a double and a single bed in it. Cath and Olga would obviously take the double. It was the first chance they had to reflect and talk in private about what had happened. One thing Martin was certain of was that he had not seen Olga looking less together; she was seriously shaken by the attack.

'I can't get my head around how Igor knew where to find us,' Cath started the conversation with.

'Me neither,' Martin said. 'We must have a serious breach somewhere.'

Olga didn't offer a view.

'But we are safe now,' Martin said, and then patted his jacket to feel the reassuring presence of his holstered sidearm.

'How long do we stay here?' Olga asked.

'Just tonight. We just keep moving until Colin tells us different. Only he knows we are here and he will not tell anyone, no matter how high up the food chain they are,' Martin said.

'Who were they?' Cath asked.

Martin turned to face Olga, and said, 'Olga?'

'I just thought they were your lot protecting me from Igor.'

'If they were, we wouldn't be on the run and in hiding,' Martin reminded her.

'Igor is dead. The threat from him is over. So, whoever they were, no need to run,' Olga offered.

'We keep moving until we can be sure, and it's now time to be open with each other, Olga,' Martin said.

'Not sure what you mean, but you first.'

'I'd like to say that the intervention was by one of our lot,' he said.

'But your SAS men said not,' Olga said.

'But until we know for certain, we don't take a chance, which is why we left Ged and his mate behind.'

'You are suggesting that they are rogue SAS?'

'No, we are just playing it safe. But I think you know who they were.'

'What, you are suggesting that they are Russian? How could such a team be brought over here in time?'

'You tell me.'

'Oh my God,' Cath said. 'When Ged said it wasn't them, he really meant it. I just thought it was some other unit or suchlike.'

'Not according to Colin,' Martin said. 'And I will never buy the rogue suggestion.'

'Which also means they are still out there,' Cath added.

Martin turned to look directly into Olga's eyes and said, 'So why would a Russian squad not kill you and save Igor? This is the wrong way around. Care to share, Olga. Because I'm buggered if I'm putting Cath and me at further risk until you tell us what is really going on?'

'I honestly don't know who they are. But I suspect you may be correct, they probably are Russian.'

'How?'

'No point denying it, and you wanted trust, so here it is; I do know that the Russian Federation has a highly trained GRU unit imbedded in the UK. They have never been used until today. So as you Brits might say, "the cat has escaped the bag" so no point in denying it.'

'A sleeper kill squad of Russian special forces, here in the UK?' Martin said.

Olga just nodded; it looked like she was not happy at sharing the information.

'So why would Russia expose this highly prized secret?' Cath asked, looking like she had got over the shock. 'Just to keep you alive?'

'Yes, why would they do that?' Martin asked.

'Oh no, I'm sure they were there to kill Igor, and me.'

Martin thought back to the events of earlier in the day. The kill squad clearly were intent on stopping Igor, and once they had done that they were off. He'd not had chance to discuss it with Colin or Cath in any detail, as to exactly what had taken place in Blackburn. And he suspected that the Holy Trinity were working on the theory that both Igor and Olga had been in the sights. He would have a private conversation with Colin now they were settled. He'd go through the attack in every detail. But he needed to push Olga because he was getting a sickening feeling that the game was still being played. It was time to push hard. He turned to face her again, 'There is no doubt in my mind that as soon as the shooters had dropped Igor, they were off.' He glanced at Cath and saw a troubled look envelope her face.

'Meaning?' Olga asked.

'Meaning you are *not* a double agent. You have no intention of working for us, but you want us to believe so. That was your whole mission all along. Otherwise, you'd be dead now.'

'Absolutely,' Cath spat, as a look of realisation spread across her face. 'They had to stop Igor, to protect you. As to how they got the intel. Well, that's another matter altogether.'

'Okay, I can help you with both quandaries; it's time to level with you,' Olga said.

***

The meeting in Don Rogers's office was coming to a close, with more questions than answers. They had all decided to sleep on it and reconvene in the morning to start again through fresh eyes. That would also allow time for Colin to speak to Martin in detail, and Jeremy could do the same with his 'observer'. Then his phone rang. It was Martin. He took the call and listened in silence to his tale. He had to pause it to shout to the others to stop them leaving. They all turned back and were watching Colin intently as he continued to listen to Martin's briefing. When he had finished, he thanked him and told him to keep on the move as planned as they decided what to do next.

Colin then re-joined the others back at the Chesterfields. 'Things are a little clearer now,' he started with.

'Go on,' Rogers said.

'Olga has finally opened up. Her original mission was always to infiltrate us. To sell out Igor and stop the bombs, or stop the second only as it turned out, in order to penetrate us. But appearing to defect to us *for real* is a sham. Her mission was always to pretend to do so. All part of Russia's elaborate plan. In reality, she was always going to remain a loyal entrenched Russian operative within our security services. To *out* herself was always part of the mission. Like a police undercover officer who tells the criminals he is really a cop, but one gone bad, in order to really infiltrate them. A high-risk double bluff.'

'I knew it,' Sue said.

Jeremy just gasped loudly.

'So why is she telling us this now?' Rogers asked.

'Martin challenged her because he was sure that the kill squad were only there to drop Igor, in order to protect Olga. Why else would the Russians want to protect her?'

'Granted; as they believe she is still their asset. But how the hell does anyone know whose bleeding side she is on?' Jeremy asked.

No one answered.

'She says that she also knows how Igor was made aware of the safe house.'

'How?' Jeremy asked.

'They already have an asset within the security services, not as high value as Olga, but an asset, nonetheless.

'So she says,' Jeremy said.

'There you go, Jeremy, being defensive again. I think we had already worked this bit out for ourselves,' Rogers said, and then turned back to face Colin, 'Go on.'

'Her mission was to not release the details of the asset to us until she was sure that she had been fully accepted. Burning of such an asset is naturally a last resort, and only to be done once she is firmly in place and able to supersede the asset.'

'They are treacherous bastards,' Rogers said.

'The name?' Jeremy asked.

'They'd burn their own mothers if they had to,' Sue added.

'The name?' Jeremy asked, louder.

Colin first went on to explain that the asset could have placed the safe house intel in a dead drop for Igor, knowing that Olga had betrayed him, but without understanding the true mission.

'And we are to accept that she has now truly come over to our side?' Sue asked.

'Yes, because burning the asset is the signal to Moscow that she is properly in.'

'She could still be playing us, she might only be telling us this because she has to; due to the ham-fisted way the GRU kill squad went about things. They showed their own hand,' Sue said.

'The name?' Jeremy said, again.

'And you said that you trusted all those who knew about the safe house with your life,' Rogers said, pointedly at Jeremy.

'We still need to tread carefully with Olga,' Sue said.

'Agreed, until she starts to provide more intel,' Rogers said, and then he turned to Colin. 'Come on Colin, you've kept us all waiting long enough. Who is the asset who blew out the safe house to Igor?'

'I'm afraid she works at MI5,' Colin started to say. He was interrupted by Jeremy letting out a loud sigh, which sounded more like relief than disappointment. Typical of the man. Whether the mole is in Five or Six made little difference to the seriousness of the situation. Colin took a breath, and then continued, 'She is an analyst working out of the MI5 field office in Manchester. Her first name is Gill, and she's been privy to all the intelligence throughout this whole investigation. She's been working hand-in-hand with our Cath as our single point of contact. She has seen everything.

Chapter Fifty

Colin and Sue Jennings left Rogers's office with a clear strategy in place. It was obvious that Gill, if indeed she was the mole, could have been passing untold amounts of intelligence to the Russians. Neither Colin nor Sue knew for sure whether *their* intel was correct, or whether or not this was still part of Olga's games. Jeremy had pointed out that he was now leaning on the side of believing Olga, as she knew that Gill *was* an analyst at MI5's Manchester office. Colin had tasked Martin to try and find out more from Olga, but he had reported back that she simply knew of her existence.

The fact that Igor was dead was a secret not yet shared with Gill, thankfully. But they had orchestrated a ruse to be fed into Gill via Cath about the attack. But the timing of the release would be everything. Jeremy was of the opinion that she would have limited contact availability with Moscow at the moment. But Sue had said she was not convinced that this was true. All agreed that they should assume not, to be on the safe side.

That left them with Gill, who believed that Olga is a traitor and sent Igor to attack her. They could work with that. As Igor is dead and the kill squad have stood down - or so they all hoped - in the belief that Olga is still a loyal Russian agent. Colin told Martin that there was no longer a need for them to hotel-hop. He had ordered Martin and Cath to bring Olga to police headquarters where accommodation was being prepared for them within the secure confines of the training school.

Colin had wanted to move on Gill straight away, a natural response, but it was Sue who suggested that they go the following morning. This is where they were now, en route to Manchester. Sue's rational had been sound as Gill had already rang Cath's unanswered phone and left a message asking how they were settling in at the safe house; and it was only 8 a.m.

As they negotiated the rush hour traffic on the approaches to Manchester, Sue's phone rang and she put it on loudspeaker so that Colin could hear, too. It was Jeremy. As expected, but he was cutting it fine. Salutations over Jeremy got down to business. He had spoken to his equivalent at Five and made her aware of the development - a woman named Shelia Stanley who was one of the directors. Colin had never known Jeremy's rank or position, so he guessed that Jeremy was also a director. Shelia had arranged for an IT system routine maintenance sweep to keep Gill locked out for the first hour. It was a regular security scan that made sure that no bugs or suchlike had invaded their cyber infrastructure. Usually carried out at night, but today's alleged check had run a bit late. She was confident that Gill would not be suspicious of this. Then came the background update.

'Gill had been an analyst at Greater Manchester Police headquarters for five years, and whilst she was there she attended night school to learn Russian,' he said.

'Any given reason for that?' Sue asked.

'None that we can find, but when she applied for a transfer to the Security Service, the fact that she was a Russian speaker obviously stood out. She was put through the usual vetting procedures and passed with no issues.'

'When was this?'

'Three years ago; she would be due for re-vetting anytime now.'

'Any clues as to what flipped her?' Colin asked.

'None, but we have traced a bank account in an alias linked to her, with unusual payments in it.'

'Regular?' Sue asked.

'Yes, and they increased in amounts around the time she passed her Russian language course, and significantly more so the moment she joined Five.'

'So are you working on the assumption that she has been a long term infiltration?' Sue asked.

'It appears that way.'

'Someone has gone to a lot of trouble; five years at GMP and then night school, just to enhance her chances of getting a job with Five,' Colin said.

'Indeed, Chief Inspector.'

RED HERRING

Colin hated it when Jeremy dropped the prefix 'Detective' to his rank, he knew the pompous swine did it on purpose, but now was not the time to have a go back.

'So, she is a high value asset indeed, it would appear,' Sue said.

'Indeed.'

'A lot for Moscow to lose,' Sue added.

'Which is why, I think we can start trusting old Olga. Gill is a very big fish to serve up.'

'Indeed,' Colin couldn't stop himself from saying.

'Quite,' came the reply.

Another example of Jeremy's annoying parlance, he then wished them luck and ended the call. Colin had to admit, he found himself in agreement with Jeremy, a rare event; perhaps Olga was on the level. Gill *was* a lot to give up. He asked Sue what she thought, and she said it was a stumbling block to her continued distrust of Olga.

Thirty minutes later, Colin parked the car in a nondescript underground car park in central Manchester. They were met by a tall handsomely dressed woman in her fifties who introduced herself as Shelia Stanley. They followed her through a subterranean door where after signing in, both Sue - who was dressed in civvies rather than her usual uniform - and Colin were given visitor badges. Shelia led them up two floors and then into an ante office next to one of the analysts' communal open-planned syndicate rooms. Colin texted Cath to give her a five minute warning.

They were then led into the main office and introduced to Gill. Colin wasn't too sure what to expect, but he hadn't expected what he saw. Gill appeared to be a Trans woman in her thirties, smartly dressed, slim, tall and attractive. Sue dropped in a cover story as to their visit, but added that they wanted to say hello in person whilst they were in the building. Nice to put a name to a face, etcetera, etcetera. Shelia casually asked if their systems were back running and made an obligatory curse when told not. Then Gill's phone rang and she excused herself to take it. Colin guessed it was Cath, and he could soon tell that it was. She would be telling Gill that Igor actually turned up at the safe house, but had managed to escape when challenged by the SAS detail.

'Oh my God, that's awful; how are you and Martin?' Gill asked.

Colin noted that she hadn't inquired as to Olga's state of being, after such a near miss.

'So where have you moved to?'

Colin pretended to be deep in mindless chatter with Sue, as he hung onto every word he heard Gill say.

'A Premier Inn. Where?' she asked. 'That doesn't sound very safe,' she added. 'Oh, I see. Just for today. That makes sense.' Gill followed this with a pause, and then said, 'Of course not; just glad that you guys are okay.'

Gill ended her call, and Colin and Sue made their excuses. Shelia said she would show them out, but as soon as they were clear, she took them to anteroom again. The main reason that Colin and Sue had to be there in person was to arrest Gill if the ruse failed, and she tried to make a run for it. Contrary to what a lot of people think, officers from MI5 or 6 have no power of arrest. Plus, it's always thought best that they don't get over-involved in the criminal justice system where it can be avoided.

Two minutes later, Gill walked passed their room with her coat on. A quick phone call from Shelia confirmed things. Gill had suddenly remembered a dental appointment she had forgotten all about, and had left the building on foot by the main entrance. A full surveillance team were awaiting Gill's egress, and for good measure, a tiny tracking device had been slipped into her jacket lining when she'd earlier powdered her nose.

Shelia rushed Colin and Sue out through security and gave them a surveillance radio so they could monitor the commentary. Their job was not to take part in the following, but to tag themselves onto the rear of the surveillance team, to be called through as and when required.

Gill apparently then picked up a car from a nearby hire firm and then headed to the motorways. Once clear of Manchester she hit the M6 northbound. Ninety minutes after that, Gill turned off the motorway at Lancaster, and eventually parked up near a public park. As soon as Colin and Sue arrived they had to run a parallel route up a hill to stay level with the team that were stalking Gill, but not to get in the way.

Gill stopped at the top of the hill by a white-stone edifice and then headed into the woods and came to a stop by a tree. She obviously knew exactly where she was going. She was watched lifting some earth and then putting an envelope into the ground, before she replaced the sod and set off back down the hill. Sue told the team to stay with her while they checked what was obviously a dead drop.

They carefully retrieved the envelope, and opened it. Inside was a handwritten note which appeared to be in Russian.

'I'm afraid I don't speak Russian,' Colin said.

'No but a special app on my phone does,' Sue said.

Colin watched as Sue scanned the letter with her phone and then she read the display before smiling, and then turning the device to face Colin. He read it: 'Igor, it's me again. The SH was obviously difficult for you, but they have moved her to a Premier Inn in Denton, Manchester. They have no security this time and will only be there today.' The note was timed and dated. 'We've fucking got her,' Colin said.

'We fucking have,' Sue replied. She then spoke hurriedly into her radio and the reply established that Gill was back in her vehicle and about to move off. 'RTC intervention, now, please,' she said, and then turned to face, Colin, 'Come on, it's our fun time now.'

Sue set off down the hill at a pace and Colin struggled to keep up. He knew he really did have to lose some weight, but at least it was easier going downhill. He knew that RTC was a police acronym for Road Traffic Collision, and guessed what the intervention bit meant. It looked like Gill's and a surveillance team member's car would soon be needing repairs.

Sure enough, as soon as the scene came into view he could see that Gill's rental was at right angles to where it had been parked. With a huge BMW saloon crunched into its offside wing. As they neared he could hear a man stood with Gill going through the motions. Gill was gesticulating and shouting at the man and didn't notice them approach, not until the last second. She spun around and her mouth fell open when she obviously recognised Sue and Colin. That was her first shock.

Her second came when Colin arrested her on suspicion of committing offences against the Official Secrets Act, 1989.

Chapter Fifty-one

Then it was Colin and Sue's turn to be stunned as Gill turned to face them with a look of seething hatred in her eyes. It had obviously been about far more money for Gill, judging by the expression on her face. Colin quickly took hold of her arm to prevent her from trying to escape, and noticed that the 'other car driver' had positioned himself directly behind her. Sue was stood facing Gill.

'That bitch will pay an even heavier price for her betrayal of me. She will never be safe, no matter what you do with her. The Motherland will not rest until they have exacted their revenge. They never forgive or forget,' Gill said.

Colin noted what she had said but made no comment. He knew to do so prior to Gill being given her rights at a police custody suite would breach PACE as an illegal interview. However, Sue must not have received that particular memo.

'I assume you are referring to Olga?' Sue asked.

Gill literally spat her response onto the pavement.

'What if she is still a loyal agent,' Sue said, and then waved the envelope in front of Gill's face, before she added, 'And you are sending Igor to kill her.'

'Moscow would never sanction my removal. I am far too precious to them. It has taken too long to get me to where I am now.'

'Think a lot of yourself,' Sue said.

'And apart from seniority, loyalty works both ways in my world. Something you know nothing about.'

'You are deluded.'

Ignoring the slight, Gill said, 'Olga has given me up, I know it. It's the only explanation. I hadn't realised that she had been briefed of my existence, but she must have been. There is no other way that makes any sense. You thick bastards could never have found me, otherwise. She betrayed me, just as she gave up Igor.'

'Maybe, maybe not?'

'I've been under your arrogant noses for years and you never smelled me.'

Colin realised he should really stop Sue from continuing, but he found the exchange fascinating. And in any event, Sue was an assistant chief constable and head of the counter terrorism unit.

'Just answer me one last question,' Sue asked.

Colin was relieved. They did need to get Gill out of here, regardless of the enthrallment.

'What?'

'Why? What turned you against your own country?'

'I don't have the energy to tell you.'

'Well, you'd better save your energy then, because you'll need it once we hand you over to MI5 and 6; they will empty your head of all your betrayals, and more,' Sue said, before turning to face Colin, 'Come on, let's get her out of here.'

Colin nodded and tightened his grip on Gill's arm as he prepared to escort her to their parked vehicle. Then Gill suddenly resisted, and forced them both to stop.

'You think so, bitch,' Gill said, her remarks clearly aimed at Sue, who stopped and turned to face her.

'MI5 and 6 will learn nothing from me; because unlike your kind, I put my loyalties above my own self-interests.'

Colin ignored Gill's comment as simply more political rhetoric, though he felt like saying, 'Not according to your hidden bank account!' But instead, he started to tug her arm so as to move her forward once more. But Gill looked at him squarely and grinned. Then she laughed, and then she opened her mouth wide. She turned away and he saw her quickly put a finger from her free hand into her mouth. It was only in there for a second, but she clearly had done something purposeful. As soon as her finger was out of her mouth she bit down aggressively. Colin heard her teeth snap together. Then she threw her head back and swallowed.

Before Colin could even embrace what was taking place, it became evident. Gill coughed and spat, as all colour washed from her complexion. Her eyes started to bulge and then she began frothing at the mouth.

Sue shouted, 'Oh my God, ring for an ambulance.'

The MI5 surveillance driver quickly pulled his phone out and started to use it. Colin watched as Gill's legs went, and he held onto her arm as she fell to the floor. He let go as she lay on her back. He was about to put her into the recovery position when she spewed a foul smelling bile out, and then her head rolled to one side. Her body went limp. She was clearly dead.

Chapter Fifty-two

Popov was preparing to leave work early for the day. It cost him a small fortune to keep his unwilling lover in place, and he was in a serious amount of credit when it came to getting his money's worth out of the arrangement. He had considered ending the situation, permanently, once he realised that Artem was in the know. But he couldn't. He may have to replace lover boy if he ever went too far, but that would be a different matter. He was becoming aroused as he imagined the post-sex beating he would give him, when, guess who, waltzed into his office to spoil his thoughts.

'I have big news,' Artem said, as he closed the door.

'I hope it is of the good kind,' Popov replied, recovering his composure.

'Olga has finally been accepted by the Brits as a turncoat.'

'Are you sure?'

'As instructed, she has given up the deep asset.'

'And we know this without doubt?'

'I told you before to leave the intelligence side of things to me.'

Popov had to dig deep to swallow his contempt for Artem's arrogance, he took a breath and said, 'Humour me, I am just a soldier.'

Artem took up his usual disrespectful slump in the armchair in front of Popov's desk, and said, 'She missed her contact call, and in any event, the Brits couldn't wait to tell us via back-channels that they had her.'

'I never understood the logic in that.'

'They like to rub our faces in it when they discover one of ours in their midst. Letting us know that they know. To be honest, we tend to do the same.'

'But why not keep quiet and then try to turn it to their advantage?'

'Because she is dead. They only tell us when they die.'

'The bastards.'

232

'True, but she took her own life. It was always going to happen that way. A poison vial hidden beneath a fake crowned tooth. But let us not dwell on that. It means that Olga is truly in.'

'I take it, that there is no *other* way the Brits could have found out about her?'

'None. Of that we are sure.'

'How can you be 100 percent certain?'

'I'm afraid that is classified,' Artem said, and then smirked.

Popov again had to delve deep, and then said, 'We are supposed to be running a joint command.'

'On paper only; or have you forgotten our little arrangement?'

Popov held his tongue.

'Let us stay on the positives. Olga was only to betray the asset, who incidentally, is an analyst - but not Russian - once she was fully accepted.'

Popov knew this so just nodded. Though, he hadn't known that the asset would commit suicide. He was tempted to ask Artem how he could have been so sure that she would self-destruct; but it would give the man a further opportunity to show off, so Popov kept quiet.

'She was an expensive asset to lose, which is why we chose her as the final proof. Once we knew that Olga was in, she will supersede the analyst many times over. An acceptable trade-off.'

Popov knew this, too; Artem was grandstanding, so he just let him carry on.

Artem concluded by saying, 'Our "Trojan Horse" is in, and hidden in plain sight. You know what this means?'

'Of course I do,' Popov snapped.

'It not only means that we can finally say that the mission is a complete success, but your work is over. And irrespective of any misunderstandings, it is a joint success for both our units,' Artem said, and then extended his hand.

Popov hesitated as he would have loved to strangle Artem with it, but then took the proffered hand and shook it. He had to play nice; for now. 'What about the old hag?' he asked.

'We can't keep Olga's mother "on holiday" forever.'

'And I could do with my men back.'

'She can return to her apartment and her pitiful existence, now that Olga has fulfilled her infiltration. We can get a message to Olga. She will realise that we can get at her mother at any time we wish. It will be a continuing threat.'

'An open-ended deterrent.'

'Exactly.'

'What will be Olga's first mission?' Popov asked, immediately regretting the question. He knew that Artem wouldn't tell him, and he had just given the supercilious man the opportunity to disrespect him further.

'Classified, as you are fully aware, but you can trust me, it will have all been worthwhile.'

Popov grunted.

'So, I believe here ends our joint mission. Thank you for all your assistance, you can now leave the ongoing intelligence work to us.'

Popov ignored the comment, and instead asked, 'And what of my kill squad which you so recklessly exposed?'

Artem sighed, and said, 'Stood down and back in the shadows, as you know.'

But before Popov could have a further dig, Artem stood and left. As soon as the door closed, Popov stood and grabbed his coat. He'd already thought of a new act of violence to try on his lover. He'd feel much better after that. But before he left - now that the mission was over - he had one last administrative task to complete. He opened his draw and pulled out a prepared written order. He signed it. Sergeant Boris Ivanov - son of Ivan - was to be transferred to an outpost in Siberia with immediate effect. He'd leave it on his desk, just in case the nosy disloyal toad decided to do some snooping. He would officially give him the good news in the morning. Popov was feeling better already; maybe he wouldn't have to punish his lover quite so much after all.

RED HERRING

Chapter Fifty-three

Martin drove through the guarded entrance to Lancashire police headquarters at Hutton, on the outskirts of Preston. Cath and Olga were chatting like old mates in the back seat. Olga had dropped her dislike of Cath. But she was such a good actress, who knows which persona is the real Olga. Though, Martin thought she seemed more natural now, and she had given up a huge asset in Gill. He'd had the call from Colin about events in Lancaster and would wait until they were settled before he shared what happened with Olga.

Instead of driving straight on to the main headquarters building, Martin turned left into an inner road which led to the force's large training complex. The road between the two compounds was edged on the left with a number of houses, which had originally been police houses when the complex was built in the early '70s. Long since turned into offices. Except the one at number seven. Martin knew that this had been refurbished back into a house, and it was where protected witnesses, vulnerable informants and the like could be housed securely as a temporary measure.

It had armed officers in plain clothes stationed at the front and rear aspects, and once inside, they all started to relax. They would all be here 24/7 until Olga was handed over to the security services properly. Cath showed Olga her room which was complete with fresh clothes for her to use until she could be properly kitted out. Martin made a brew and took the three mugs of coffee into the through-lounge just as Olga and Cath walked in. They all took a seat and Martin enjoyed taking a sip of a beverage that wasn't nuclear as was the case with most police vending machines.

'How long will I be here?' Olga asked.

'Not sure, but I don't think it will be long,' Martin answered.

'Why, are you going to miss us?' Cath asked with a smile.

'You have sort of grown on me, and I'm starting to feel that you believe me now.'

'Gill was a huge asset to give up,' Cath said.

'A huge loss to Moscow without the expected benefit. They must never suspect the truth. You have to protect me.'

'Don't worry, we will. I take it that Gill must have informed Moscow that she had left a message for Igor, after doing do so?' Martin asked.

'Yes, and they wouldn't have chastised her, as to do so would have given the game away. But it gave them time to launch their counter measures,' Olga answered.

Martin took a further sip of his brew; it was a sobering thought that without Gill leaving Igor a message, the nutter would still be on the loose.

'But look on the bright side as you Brits say, you now know about the kill squad. They wouldn't have been deployed had Gill not acted on learning that Igor was free, and that I had defected. So apart from the obvious danger we'd have been in from Igor, the kill squad would have remained a secret.'

'True,' Martin said.

'I still can hardly believe that of Gill, she seemed so nice,' Cath said.

'Happy enough to see us all dead,' Martin said.

'What will happen to her now? Will another Martin and Cath be talking to her?' Olga asked.

Martin thought he saw a flash of concern on Olga's face; it would make the next bit bite even more. 'I'm afraid, she's dead.'

'What?' Olga screeched, and jumped to her feet, with a look of real shock on her face.

Martin stood up and told Olga to sit down, and added, 'It's not what you think; it wasn't us.'

Olga was next to Cath on a three-seat settee and he saw Cath move across and put her hand on Olga's shoulders.

'I just thought she would be interviewed and then used in an exchange,' Olga said.

'She was British, not Russian,' Martin said.

'But her blood was red. Moscow would have looked after her.'

Martin shook his head.

236

'So what did happen, if not you? You're not telling me that the kill squad did it?'

'She did it,' Martin answered, and then went on to explain what Colin had told him. They all sat in silence for a couple of minutes and Martin could see the genuine look of surprise on Olga's face. She had a visage which looked like disappointment etched with sorrow.

Then she said, 'She must have been prepared to do this. It must have been part of her instructions.'

'Some instruction,' Cath said, and then added, 'I'm surprised that she went through with it.'

'You'd be amazed how fanatically loyal to Moscow some of them are. They are more Russian than most Russians.'

Martin shuddered at the plural used and said, 'On that, we will need to know about the entire network of sleepers; names and positions.'

'What, so that they can all kill themselves?'

'I suspect that Gill was an extreme example. And in any event, we will be ready next time, we can ensure that they don't get the chance to do what Gill did,' he said.

'I want to believe you on that. It's important; you probably think I'm a robotic heartless bitch, but I'm not. I'm an intelligence officer, that's all. The stone-hearted ones are those of the GRU, such as Igor.'

'I must admit, I wasn't aware of the difference,' Cath said.

'GRU are military, SVR is not, but both are involved in intelligence matters, though SVR are more external, like your MI6,' Olga said.

'Well, according to those photos we showed you, you and Igor seemed to get along okay,' Martin said.

'I'll now tell you something about that, shall I.'

Cath glared at Martin, so he took the hint and stayed quiet. He didn't want to wind Olga up, too much.

'Go on,' Cath said.

'The bastard raped me, made a joke about us pretending to be married so we should act so in all ways. Claimed that his boss Colonel Popov had told him to.'

Martin hadn't seen that coming and was genuinely sorry for his comment now. But he noted the boss's name, nonetheless. He could also see by the expression on Olga's face that she was telling the truth. He apologised. Olga nodded her acceptance. Then his phone rang, it was Colin, he was grateful of the timing and walked into the kitchen to take the call and left Olga and Cath chatting on the sofa.

Colin was keen to know how everything had gone and Martin quickly explained. Colin was surprised, and then shocked at the news that Igor had raped Olga, and said, 'It might have given those photos that MI5 took far more weight than we realised. Proof of not just his infidelity, but of rape should Olga have ever complained to her bosses once the operation was over.'

'I hadn't thought of that, but it makes sound sense. Thank God that the MI5 surveillance team, who were having no more than a casual look at a Russian strawberry picker, managed to do so well. Without that, who knows how things could have panned out differently.'

'If she is to be believed,' Colin added.

'You're not still having doubts are you?'

'I wasn't, but there has been a development; one which is worrying the Holy Trinity a bit. Are you totally alone?'

'Hang on, I'll just step outside,' Martin said, and then headed through the back door into the secure parking area. 'Back with you, go on, boss.'

Chapter Fifty-four

Martin made his excuses and told Cath that he would explain when he could, but he was needed in the Chief's office. He made it an administrative excuse for the benefit of Olga's ears and walked the short distance to the main building. He was met in the anteroom to Rogers's office and followed Colin in. Rogers was sat at his desk, with Sue Jennings and Jeremy sat opposite each other at the top of the long conference table. Colin and Martin quickly tagged on at the end.

'It's been quite a day for everyone, so let me start by thanking you all, and in particular, Sue and Colin. It must have been tough for you with what happened with Gill,' Rogers said.

Both Sue and Colin nodded, as did Martin. Then, Rogers turned to face Jeremy. 'I don't suppose you had any inkling that this could happen?'

Jeremy threw his hands up in the air theatrically, and answered, 'Why do you always think I act lower than a snake's bollocks?'

'Because we know you,' Sue threw in.

'Off my Christmas card list,' Jeremy answered.

'No one sends them nowadays,' Sue retorted with.

'Well?' Rogers said. 'I'm waiting.'

'Oh course not. We wanted her alive. She could have proved a rich vein of gold.'

'Well, you'll no doubt get that and more from Olga,' Rogers said.

'Is she or isn't she. It's still a dilemma,' Jeremy said.

'I can't see anyway she would have given up Gill, and told us the real reason for doing so, if she wasn't,' Colin said.

'Agreed,' said Martin, 'and when I told her what happened to Gill she was genuinely shocked. That was never part of *her* script, that's for sure.'

'Well, as you all know there has been a development,' Sue started with, and then reached into a large bag by her side and pulled out an A4 sized document case. She unzipped it and pulled out two photographs. 'Our technical staff have managed to unlock the phone from the second dead drop. And only hours earlier theses photos were sent together with a message. We've all seen them,' Sue said, and then pushed the prints across the table to Martin. Each looked to be of the same scene. They depicted a low light picture of a woman sleeping in a bed with a masked man pointing a silenced handgun at her head.

'Who is she?' Colin asked.

'According to the note, it's Olga's mother,' she answered.

'How do we know, for sure?' Colin asked.

'We don't, but Olga will,' Jeremy said.

'What does the note say?' Martin asked.

'"This is what we can do should you forget your mission, Olga. No harm will come as long as you remember that. Your mother will not see you for a long time as you know, but if you want to be reunited one day when your mission is over..." written in Russian,' Sue said.

'They really are the worst of the worst,' Martin said.

'They are,' Jeremy said, 'But it has made us all jumpy.'

'Especially when you consider other than the obvious meaning in the text,' Sue said.

They'd all had more time to consider it than Martin, so he asked what Sue meant.

'Meaning that the mission is far from over. What if giving up Gill was part of her script, not just as a final declaration that Olga had been accepted by us,' Sue said. 'But what if her *telling us* that, is Moscow's aim? Not just to prove that she has been accepted, but appearing to blow out Moscow by *telling us* could also part of her mission.'

'So we would now accept her without doubt,' Jeremy said.

'Absolutely,' Sue said.

Martin thought about how this could all be true, how Olga might still be playing them, after all. But he also recalled how shocked Olga was to learn of Gill's death, and reiterated that to them all.

'That's good,' Jeremy said. 'Maybe a crack in the door. These photos may pry it open a bit wider.'

'Or slam it shut,' Sue said. 'Keep her in line, as intended.'

'Even if it does, we now know, or certainly suspect,' Rogers added.

'I've told her that we need the list of all the sleepers like Gill. That would be the final test. Moscow may be happy to blow out one Gill, to cement Olga's infiltration, but surely not all the Gills.'

'Agreed, but what if she claims not to know the details of the other Gills?' Sue asked.

'Then we'll know that the lying bitch is still a loyal Russian agent. I need to take over, no disrespect; I need to speak to her. It's time we took her off your hands.'

'I agree,' Rogers said.

'So do I,' Sue said, and then added, 'But because of the rapport Cath and Martin have built up, perhaps they should show Olga the photos and the note first?'

Ten minutes later, Martin was back at the house with a large envelope under his arm. He'd no chance to pre-warn Cath, but muttered under his breath that they had been played, but that he had a hand grenade in the envelope. Cath called Olga who was upstairs watching TV in her room. As she joined them at the settee and armchairs their faces must have been telling.

'What is it?' she asked.

'We know,' Martin said.

'Know what?' she replied.

'You are very good.'

'Ah, we are back to games: what has happened?'

'When it comes to games; you are the expert. Along with your double and triple bluffs.'

Olga pulled a quizzical expression in reply.

'I have one last task to perform before we hand you over to the director from MI6.'

Olga didn't answer, so Martin pulled out the photographs and placed them on the coffee table in front of her.

A second later Olga shrieked as she stared at the prints, and then picked them both up and scrutinised them for what seemed like ages. She then put them back on the table and turned to face Martin, a savage glare replaced her shocked expression.

'What the hell is going on?'

'I take it that the lady in the photos is in fact your mother?' Martin asked.

Cath said, 'Oh my God, no,' with genuine fear and surprise on her face, which was the reaction he was hoping for. He needed Olga to believe what she was seeing, and to know that it had nothing to do with them.

'You know it is,' she answered.

'We didn't; but the note said that it is.'

'What note?'

Martin passed over a third photo, the one of the message as it appeared on the phone's screen. He told her where it was from, then sat back and scrutinised Olga as she read it, and then read it again.

'You know what it says?' Olga asked.

'Yes,' Martin said, and then pulled out a piece of paper from his pocket and read the translation out, mainly for Cath's benefit. 'I take it that the translation is correct?'

'It is.'

'Now, it's time for the real truth, and nothing but the truth.'

'It is. Until two minutes ago I was still a loyal Russian operative. Gill - as you know her - was all part of the plan - even if she was unaware of it. Though her death was a genuine shock to me.'

'Congratulations,' Martin said.

'For what?'

'You had me fooled - eventually.'

'And me,' Cath threw in.

'Thank you. I am the best at what I do. And my *telling you* that Moscow wanted me to out her as proof of my infiltration, was also intended to convince you that I had defected. When I had not. I always thought it was an unnecessary extra layer of deceit, but I had my orders. Blow Gill out to prove my fake loyalty, and then compound it by telling you that it was Moscow's plan that I do so.

'But they have gone too far. This evil insurance, as it clearly is, is a threat I can never get away from, I can never be free of it.

They have perversely left me no choice. This is all on those bastards. I will make them pay for this.'

'So what happens now?' Cath asked.

'Now, I am truly your asset.'

'No offence, but we will need some convincing of that. Or to be precise, the director of MI6 will. He is dying to meet you.'

'I know you will, but what I can give you will be mind-blowing, proof a thousand times over.'

'Your intel is that good?' Cath asked.

'It is, and there is more.'

Martin had no idea what the 'more' bit meant, but, instead asked, 'Okay, where do we start?'

'I want my mother to be safely removed from Russia. Moscow must not realise. And once she is safely with me I will tell you everything. Can you do that?'

'I can't I'm just a detective sergeant caught up in all this, but I know a man who can.'

Chapter Fifty-five

The next forty-eight hours were manic, but no so much for Martin, Cath and Colin. Martin and Cath took turns babysitting Olga, whilst the other grabbed some down time and a change of clothes. Colin stepped in to help. Jeremy had to put off his introduction to Olga as he arranged things though the Foreign Secretary - ultimately his boss - and the Home Secretary. Apparently, Six had their own team of SAS troopers, who were all Russian speakers, stationed in Finland. They slipped across the vast border and made their way to Moscow. They swept up Olga's mum, Oksana Sokolov, at an appropriate time with the help of a video call they had arranged with Olga to facilitate her smooth exfiltration. According to Jeremy, at one of the many Holy Trinity briefings, she had made a strange remark to the undercover troopers asking if she was going on another holiday.

Regardless, they soon had her out of the country and then flown to the British Aerospace company's Warton aerodrome on the outskirts of Preston. All done within 24 hours, start to finish. She was then brought to police headquarters where an emotional reunion took place with Olga. There was a lot for Oksana to take in. Number 5 Hutton Hall Avenue was quickly turned back into a house, of sorts, and Olga's mum was made comfortable with easy access to her daughter next door at number 7.

True to her word, thereafter, Olga sat down with a pen and paper and wrote down all she knew about the embedded sleepers and sympathisers situated across the UK. Martin gave the list to Jeremy and the following morning, he and Colin joined the Holy Trinity in Rogers's office once more. Once the supplementary stuff was talked through, they all turned to Jeremy for his update on Olga's list.

'Well, everyone, this is quite a goldmine. She has named two tiers of spies. The first is a list - with either names or places, or enough so that we've been able to identify them.'

'How many?' Sue asked.

'Thirty.'

244

'Jesus,' Rogers said.

'Well, actually 29 after Igor's intervention in Ormskirk. But they all live and work among us. One of them is a mechanic for Greater Manchester Police, and works on the counter terrorism unit's vehicles.'

Martin gasped.

'We have had all our fleet electronically swept and found that five of the surveillance vehicles had sophisticated wired-in trackers that aren't ours,' Sue said.

'Have you ripped them out?' Rogers asked.

'No, on Jeremy's advice we have left them in play, but moved the vehicles to none sensitive jobs in order to keep the illusion of non-compromise ongoing.'

'All sympathisers will be closely monitored for now,' Jeremy said.

'Understood, but what of the sleepers?' Rogers asked.

'The sleepers are on a different level. The "Gills" as we have started calling them, are all British nationals with ultra-left tendencies. All are suspected of having received proper field agent training, including weapons drills with some of them.'

'How many of these rats do we have?' Rogers asked.

'Fifteen, er, I mean fourteen, now. They are strategically placed across industry and public service.'

'Which one is at the highest level?' Colin asked.

'Internally, we think Gill was the highest. They would have only been willing to sacrifice her once Olga superseded her. She's told us that this was Moscow's aim, and intended to help further her entrenchment into us. But in the wider British infrastructure, we believe the highest one is a P.A. to a SEO of a company which makes laser-guided weaponry for the MOD.'

'Jesus,' Rogers said, again.

'It will take some time to assess all the damage which might have been caused, but the last one is obviously the most worrying,' Jeremy started to say, before pausing to look at his watch, before continuing, 'as of an hour ago, she became the unfortunate victim of a hit and run accident, and having suffered a broken leg, will be off sick for some time.'

'When are you planning to have them all locked up?' Colin asked. 'Because our units across the country can assist with that, if you wish?'

'A kind offer which Sue will no doubt take you up on, in support of counter terrorism when the time comes,' Jeremy said.

Sue smiled and nodded her acquiesce.

'When will that time come?' Rogers asked.

'Not for quite a while. If we act too quickly, the Russians will know there is a compromise. We need them to believe that Olga is still in-play as theirs. So we plan to monitor and remotely control all of them for as long as we can.'

'Makes sense,' Rogers said.

'Think of all the fun we can have, feeding in disinformation to the Russians via their most trusted sources. We can even remove the odd one or two along the way, if they become dangerous. Our use of them will only be limited by our own lack of imagination.'

'Sounds like a top wheeze, this. I'm jealous,' Martin couldn't stop himself from saying.

'Quite,' Jeremy said. 'Anyway, we are hoping to run this for 12 months if we can stretch it that long. In which time we can empty Olga's head completely and maximise the outcomes many times over. And when the day comes to act, we will take them all out at once; completely smashing Moscow's entire network of hidden assets in the UK. But first, we want to work with Olga to identify the kill squad. We can act quickly on that as they already know that we are aware of its existence, after their clumsy use of it near the safe house.'

Everyone nodded.

'What will eventually happen to Olga and her mum Oksana?' Martin asked.

'When the bubble is burst and even the thickest Russian can't help but realise that they have been shafted par excellence, we will give them clean passports in any nationality they choose and house them in whichever country - within reason - that they want to settle in. They will be paid a lifetime allowance that will keep them comfortable.'

'What about security?' Colin asked.

'It will be given. It will be a lifelong commitment as it is important to keep rubbing the Russians noses in it. Their ongoing failure in getting at them. Plus, who knows how many more spies - our effective treatment of Olga and Oksana - may be encouraged to flip sides and join the righteous.'

Martin was glad to see the political element to the strategy, if nothing else it would make Jeremy honour his commitments in keeping them safe. 'I guess it will be a constant reminder to Moscow of one of their darkest hours,' he said.

'An open sore we intend to never allow to heal.'

'I can't wait to hear what Olga comes up with next,' Sue added.

'Yes, the "and there is more" remark she made, is enticing,' Rogers said.

'Quite. But unfortunately, as you all know, whatever comes next will be classified,' Jeremy said in his smuggest of voices.

'That aside, I'll be glad to get back to normal police work. This stuff that Jeremy and Sue do all the time would burn me out,' Martin said.

'Ditto that,' Colin added.

'Your team Colin have done a first class job,' Rogers said.

Jeremy and Sue came straight in with similar comments, and then Jeremy added, 'Well, in order to facilitate your exit, all that remains for you to do, is to finally introduce me to the lovely Olga.'

'Be my pleasure,' Martin said, and then suggested that they go straight across to number 7. If Jeremy waited in the kitchen, Martin would explain what was happening and then call Jeremy through.

'Agreed, but let me explain the end game to her. That way I can start off with presents to sweeten the start of our relationship.'

'Good idea,' Martin said, and they all rose to their feet. Jeremy said he would follow them over in a couple of minutes. As Martin and Colin walked back to the house, he turned to face Colin and said, 'This should be interesting.'

'I was just thinking that, but Jeremy will need to dial it down a bit.'

'If he doesn't, the rapport won't be there.'

'If that happens, I can see you and Cath on a recall.'

'For God's sake don't say that, not even in jest.'

'Who's kidding?'

Martin couldn't tell whether this was another example of the new Colin's attempt at humour, or the old Colin warning him of what might happen. Regardless, they'd soon find out.

Chapter Fifty-six

Martin had a quick word with Cath to bring her up to speed, and Colin said he would leave them to do the handover as it would get too crowded otherwise. Olga was upstairs watching TV. He asked Cath how Olga was.

'She seems like a different person now she has truly flipped. It's like she is now able to drop her fake persona and be herself. It must feel liberating,' Cath said.

'Yet, she played us all along and right up to the very end.'

'It was the threat to her mother that brought about her epiphany moment. A realisation that the evil insurance policy was not just in place for the here and now, but forever. They had shown that they could get at Oksana anytime they chose.'

'Any news on how Oksana is?'

'I'm told she is settling in okay; it was obviously a shock to learn what her daughter actually did for a living. The only stumbling block was that Oksana would not believe the threat against herself. Like a lot of Russians of her generation she is blindly loyal to the state having been forced-fed bullshit for decades.'

'What are we doing to convince her?'

'Already taken care of; Olga showed her the photographs.'

Martin nodded and then said that they should crack on. Cath agreed and called Olga down. As soon as they were all sat in the comfortable chairs, Olga asked how her list had been received. Martin chose his words carefully so as not to give away any of the agreed tactics going forward. He said enough to show that they accepted all the details as genuine.

'I'm relieved to hear that. I know I have to earn your trust in order to get the best outcome for my mother and me.'

'It's all good, trust me,' Martin said.

'Strangely, I actually do.'

Martin grinned and then said, 'You are no doubt keen to know what happens next.'

'Of course.'

'Shortly, I will introduce you to the director of the Secret Intelligence Service who takes over from us. They will want to debrief you further and run you for as long as is feasible.'

'I understand that, but what will happen to us in the end?'

'I'll let Jeremy explain all that but trust me, you will be looked after.'

'Jeremy?' Olga said, with a startled look. 'That director?'

Martin didn't know how many directors there were at Six, nor did he understand Olga's comment. He then heard the back door click shut, so said, 'Yes, erm, he's waiting in the kitchen to meet you.'

Martin saw Olga's stunned face shoot up to look toward the kitchen door, which opened seconds later. In walked Jeremy with all his usual grandiose demonstrative style.

'Yes, I'm Jeremy, and I have to say, it's a thrill to finally meet you, Olga, old girl,' he said, with his thickest Etonian accent. He stuck out his hand. Olga reached up and tentatively took it, before Jeremy sat down in the vacant armchair directly opposite. 'So it seems you have heard of me?'

'They said it would be you, I didn't know how they could know that. But they assured me that it would be you,' Olga said.

Martin exchanged a confused look with Cath, and then both sat back in their respective chairs to let the conversation flow.

'I'm getting the feeling that this is part of your original brief?' Jeremy asked.

'You could say that. It's time I gave you "the more" bit.'

'We are all ears.'

Martin for some reason then instinctively looked at Jeremy's ears and nearly smiled. He hadn't noticed before just how big they were. Must be a plus when you are a professional eavesdropper.

'Once accepted by MI6, my main mission was not just to spy and feedback as much sensitive intelligence as I could.'

'Go on,' Jeremy said.

'They told me that I would be handled by you personally, but if for some reason I was not, I was to ensure that I did get access to you. I was told that in the event of the latter, nothing else mattered, and I was to take as long as I needed to achieve this. I would be given really sensitive information with which to pass to you in order to achieve my main objective. And that it would be serious stuff. Serious enough to keep you convinced that I had indeed turned.'

'Why was I so important?'

'Because you were always the primary objective of the entire operation.'

Jeremy sat back in his chair and looked stunned. He took a moment before he continued, 'And to what aim?'

'I was to turn you.'

Jeremy then roared with forced laughter and said, 'And how the hell would you have achieved that monstrous task?'

'By any means necessary. Sleep with you. Find out your weaknesses and blackmail you. Trick you by saying my Russians masters would expect some decent intel, to prove you had accepted me as one of yours. And ways yet to be devised.'

'I would never betray my country; surely your Russian profilers will have told your stupid bosses that?'

'My Russian masters think that anyone, even you, with the right incentive, be that money, fear or whatever, can be turned. And that once turned, you may one day reach the heights of Director General.'

'It's one hell of an assumption to have, especially, given the lengths Moscow has gone to. But I do like their thinking on the latter bit; I can see myself as the new C.'

Martin rolled his eyes at Cath.

'They do not think like you Brits: to them everything is possible at the right price. My boss at the SVR is Artem—'

'Yes, yes we know all about Artem,' Jeremy snapped. He was starting to sound annoyed.

'The head of the GRU Special Unit, Colonel Popov is worse.'

'I know of him too. But worse in which way?'

'He sees the world through his own twisted prism of a mind.'

There was a long pause, and then Jeremy said, 'Thank you, Olga. I really appreciate your candour.'

Olga looked a little confused, and Cath threw in, 'Truthfulness.'

'Yes, thank you,' Jeremy said, as he glared at Cath, before returning his attention to Olga. 'We will work well together, I'm sure.'

'This was to be Moscow's greatest intelligence achievement of all time,' she said.

'This will now become one of our greatest, thanks to you.'

Olga then asked what would happen to her mother and her, and seemed very pleased once Jeremy had outlined the end game.

'I'll have to speak to mum, but America might be nice,' she said.

'That would be the simplest of options,' Jeremy answered, and then asked his own question, 'But for the threat to your mum, would you have remained loyal to Moscow?'

It was Olga's turn to rock back in her chair and take a moment before she answered, 'I'm not sure if I'm being entirely honest; perhaps you would have made me an offer I couldn't refuse. Maybe we all do have our price.'

'Well, I don't, your mission would have failed.'

'Maybe that's when I would have come clean.'

'I guess we'll never know.'

'They went too far, or Popov did. Irrespective of what he allowed Igor to do to me, I'm sure that the threat to my mother was his idea.'

'Why do you think that?'

'It's his style. He's horrible. Let me give you an example—'

But before Olga could elucidate, Jeremy raised his hand to stop her. Martin took the hint; whatever Olga would say hereon after was not for their smaller ears. They didn't need to know. Their part was thankfully over. Martin nodded his understanding, and he and Cath stood and formally said their goodbyes. In one way he was genuinely sad to be saying farewell to Olga. Maybe not so in Jeremy's case, but in every other way it was a huge weight off his shoulders. As soon as they were outside, Cath voiced the same thoughts.

'Come on, let's find Colin, he'll be in the canteen eating something unhealthy no doubt,' Martin said. 'He's not going to believe what we have to tell him.'

Chapter Fifty-seven

Twenty four hours later, Colonel Popov was at his desk looking through a list of potential replacements for Boris. He needed to make sure that his new staff officer was totally loyal, and that he would be more open-minded than Boris. He always seemed to be tolerant, but Popov often wondered if his agreement was obsequious. He would need to choose with care this time. And then he would plot a political sanction for the high and mighty Artem. He had already taken measures to protect himself by moving his lover to a different apartment. This one was on the ground floor - albeit with steel bars on the windows. It came with a basement which he hoped to turn into a dungeon of sorts.

He was riding high on the crest of their operation's initial success. He was relieved in some ways that his role was over; any further mistakes in the second phase would be on Artem's shoulders alone. Perhaps he should allow time for this to happen before he moved against Artem; it would make his retribution a much easier fix. He would mull this over. But he did miss being in command - even jointly - of what would become Russia's greatest ever intelligence coup in the UK. And if it didn't work, that would not be his fault. His success would never be affected. He was expecting to be called in front on one of the generals at some stage, and was slightly surprised that this had not happened straight away. Perhaps, they were considering a promotion for him. Major General Popov had a wonderful ring to it. He wasn't sure which thought was currently exciting him the most, that or the basement in his new apartment.

Then his musings were interrupted by - whom else - Artem, barging into his office. At least this time he closed the door behind him. 'I thought your little visits here were over, unless you've come to gloat; Olga can't have got to Jeremy at MI6 already?'

'Give her time, even Olga's not that good.'

'Well, what is it; I'm busy choosing my new staff officer?'

'A problem.'

'What kind of problem?' Popov said, barely able to contain his excitement. Had Artem cocked-up already? He could only hope so.

'A big problem,' Artem answered.

'Your problems are no longer my concern.'

'It's not my problem.'

Hearing this made Popov sit up. 'What do you mean?'

'I mean that your little secret is out.'

'What! You absolute bastard, you promised if I agreed—'

'And I kept it,' Artem interrupted with.

Popov fell silent, his first thought was Boris, but he didn't know the specifics and Popov was sure that he only suspected, and in any event, Boris thought that his lover was a woman. Not that that should matter, but it still did in Russia. But it was the extracurricular stuff that really bothered him. He was sure that Boris knew nothing of this. 'I don't understand.'

'Nor do I, but I have my orders. I just wanted to give you the courtesy of a minute's warning before the guards outside arrest you.'

'Arrest me?'

'Yes; apparently your lover has been released from the basement of your new apartment and taken to hospital. He has already told them everything.'

'Where's the proof?'

'The fact that they found him chained up like a dog, and his injuries, for starters.'

Popov didn't respond to that, but asked, 'Okay, but if not you, then, from where has all this come?'

'They won't tell me, but they acted on the intel quickly so that they could bury it and therefore "disprove" it, and deny it. You know what they are like when it comes to saving face.'

Popov slumped back in his chair. His finest hour had inexplicably just turned into his worst. 'What will happen to me?' he asked. He knew the answer, but asked anyway in the vain hope that what Artem said would be somehow different to the answer in his head.

'You will not be seen or heard of again. I'm really sorry. I know we had our differences, but I wouldn't wish this on even you. But the chance of this getting out is too great. The embarrassment would too much. I'm told to tell you that your wife will be told that you were killed on a secret mission. And that you should be grateful that you will be made a hero of the Motherland.'

On realising his true fate, Popov vomited over his desk and Artem jumped back.

'Sergeant,' Artem shouted.

Then in a final insult, a grinning Boris Ivanov walked in with two officers from the VP - Russia's military police.

The larger one of the two VP officers told Popov to stand. He reluctantly did, but his legs were barely strong enough to take his weight.

***

Martin's head was a little heavy when he first arrived back in their Preston office. Rogers had taken them all for several drinks the night before, and he, Cath and Colin had stayed over at the training school. They had arrived for work late, and would leave early today, and not much else would take place in between. Apart from lunch, which they were preparing to go on; it was to be Colin's treat. But just as they were organizing themselves to leave, the mail arrived and a grubby envelope caught Martin's eye. Handwritten on the front were the words, 'Detective Martin Draker.' He opened it to find a single sheet of lined paper, on which written in biro were the following words: 'Dear Mr Draker, I got a bender thanks to your advice, so I rang Fisher and Fishers to thank you, but they said they had no briefs by your name. So I rang round the other firms, same answer. Then it twigged; I should have realised. I rang the cop shop and they said they had a detective called Martin Draker but you were busy or sommat. So that's why I wrote this letter. I'm still clean and sorting myself out thanks to your help. But I want to thank you proper, so please bell me at the number at the bottom. I've got some good info for you, not that I'm a grass, I'm not, but I reckon I owe you. Oh, and please bin this when you've read it.'

Martin glanced at the number at the bottom and wrote it on his blotting paper pad, before he scrunched up the note in his hand.

'What's that?' Cath asked.

'Proper police work by the sound of it, and I can't wait. I'll tell you over lunch.'

The End.

Printed in Great Britain
by Amazon